CO-AYH-290

# Threshold
# of
# Eternity

———— ∞ ————

## JOHN BRUNNER
## &
## DAMIEN BRODERICK

*an imprint of*

**MANOR**
Rockville, Maryland

ISBN: 978-1-61242-369-2

**www.PhoenixPick.com**
**Great Science Fiction & Fantasy**
**Free Ebook Every Month**

Published by Phoenix Pick
*an imprint of Arc Manor*
P. O. Box 10339
Rockville, MD 20849-0339
www.ArcManor.com

**To the memory of John Brunner, star dreamer**

*When the first star shivers and the last wave pales:*
*O evening dreams!*
*...to seas colder than the Hebrides I must go*
*Where the fleet of stars is anchored,*
*and the young star-captains glow.*

—James Elroy Flecker

# CONTENTS

# INTRODUCTION

## by Damien Broderick

In 1957, when a shorter version of this novel was serialized in three issues of *New Worlds* magazine, the prodigious 23 year old John Kilian Houston Brunner wrote:

"Basically, what I've tried to do in *Threshold of Eternity* is to write an adventure story that reflects in its development a few unprovable but, to my mind, stimulating speculations about the nature of the universe—particularly time—and the place of human thought in the whole scheme. (I suppose one would have good grounds for saying that this makes it not a science fiction novel at all, but a super-science fantasy.)

"This undertaking," he went on, "is not a new idea. The grand master of the form used to be A.E. van Vogt, before he stopped writing for the magazines. I'm not trying to invite comparison between my story and anything of van Vogt's; however I feel that he tapped a worthwhile vein with his tremendously fertile crop of imaginative assertions about the cosmos. He mingled philosophy and metaphysics with his science, and this seems to be a commendable practice, within limits, for to declare that science is nothing but the truth and the key to the whole truth smacks unpleasantly of dogma.

"So what I've tried to do is write on two levels: and I hope the result can likewise be read on two levels—superficially for entertainment, and also to provoke the flow of some new ideas. The nature of science fiction is speculation, after all, and it doesn't matter if some of our fantasies appear rather wild. Who in the nineteenth century imagined anything as improbable as our modern world?"

I was a 14 year old schoolboy in Australia when I first read this astonishing serial, loaned to me by a neighbor who also passed along copies of *Astounding Science Fiction* and *Galaxy*. These were magazines almost unavailable in my nation at the time. It was a genuinely thrilling experience to follow John Brunner into the technological future but also into deeper domains: the nature of conflict with unknowable foes, of time and being and destiny.

My imagination was supercharged by the adventures and ordeals of Red and Chantal and the others in this complex narrative, but at the same time I felt a frustrating sense that there must be more going on beneath or behind the surface. Decades later, as a professional science fiction writer myself, I yearned to answer some of those questions, to revisit this realm at the threshold of eternity and bring back some more of those treasures.

By then I already had been permitted to expand the story of characters from Grand Master Robert Silverberg's most famous novella, "Born with the Dead." My extension, "Quicken," was published in 2013, together with Silverberg's slightly updated original, as a joint novel: *Beyond the Doors of Death*. Now, with permission from the late John Brunner's British agent, Jane Judd, I've followed Brunner's footsteps into a complex cosmos of branching universes and timelines, peeking into some of the crannies to learn what was hiding there. As one does when reading any science fiction, I stumbled quite often over evidence of its own epoch, the late 1950s, some 60 years ago. This is always what we find, walking into the visionary sf worlds from earlier decades: these are yesterday's tomorrows, not today's.

So it was exhilarating to work out ways to update the physics and cosmology from that now-antique era—and, even more, to see how the social changes we've since experienced, from the 1960s into the twenty-first century, might suggest to a writer today how to modify and expand the range of the tale. Brunner was always ahead of the social curve, so I've tried to capture this edginess as he might have framed some of the relationships if he were writing nowadays. Of course I'm wryly conscious that in another half century, or sooner, my additions will be just as clearly the insignia of the second decade of this century.

How I wish John Brunner were still with us, to read my version of his novel and, of course, to keep adding new marvels, if he wished, to his extensive bibliography. For any readers who are not yet familiar with his considerable range, I can only urge you to find his books and launch your imaginations into pleasures that remain fresh: *Times Without Number*, *Telepathist*, *Total Eclipse*, *The Traveler in Black*, the mordant social extrapolations that built his fame, *Stand on Zanzibar*, *The Sheep Look Up*, *The Jagged Orbit*, many others, not least wonderful shorter pieces like "Earth is But a Star" and "No Other Gods But Me." More than twenty years after his premature death in 1995, these remain doorways not only beyond the threshold of eternity, but also into speculations on infinity—and the human and impending post-human condition.

*San Antonio, Texas, March 2017*

# CHAPTER I

## 4029: Artesha

On low orbit around the fifth planet of a star identified in her weapons systems only by its binary code, Artesha Wong lay cocooned in a nest of probes and telefactor interfaces, directing a tactical squadron of one thousand and twenty-four almost autonomous attack drones. Weightless, she felt phantom tugs and shoves as the squad flung itself at an Enemy raider.

Dark energy beams wove chaotic vortices in the contested volume at the edge of space. Antigravs in her command system vehicle fought the gravitic turbulence, maintaining her geodesic curve around the blackened world. In the boiling ruin below, human colonists in the millions were dying.

She was twenty-five years old, with a body full of seething youthful juices, and if she had not been drugged from cortex to thalamus, Artesha would have wept in her grief. But she was a critical part of the engine of local planetary defense, and those who perished on the surface and in the air were sacrificing their lives to protect distant Earth.

Few of them knew that. Perhaps even fewer would have embraced their martyrdom.

Far to the east, in shadow, an Enemy vessel precipitated out of transluminal space, blazing briefly with Cerenkov emissions as it shed transform energy. Instantly, Artesha's squad oriented on it, flung their brutal thousand-fold net to encompass the craft and hammer it with directed energy, railgun kinetic matter, nuclear charges. Gouts of light spat in the darkness. And then there was another, unfolding, and another.

Artesha knew hatred as a distant, mobilizing pressure, under formal control, as monstrously dangerous to the emerging Enemy as her weapons systems. This time, too, as in every deadly encounter, she wanted above all to capture one of those accursed craft, peel it open, suck out for retrieval one or more of the unknown foe. A second Enemy ship disintegrated, taking fifty-four of her squad with it. A second wing swung, wrapped about the third Enemy attacker.

Hold back! she ordered the drones. Wait. We must imprison at least one of these creatures.

Too late. The third vessel vomited a mass of hyperkinetic death at the dying planet, and for that fraction of an instant left itself vulnerable but still hideously dangerous. It had located her own orbiter, and dark energy twisted spacetime in her path. Her accelerated mind saw the trap, computed the response, and ruefully destroyed the Enemy down to the level of quarks and leptons.

Its death was very beautiful, against the silent, distant stars and the blackness between.

It was also infuriating and frustrating to lose one more opportunity to isolate and capture a member of humanity's genocidal rivals.

What madness or greed drives them? she asked herself, as always. At a level of reflex, she brought back her remaining drones, arrayed them optimally around the orbiter. Is it hatred for the Other, simple mindless xenophobia, imprinted in their genes and never removed by culture or medicine? Is it fear of extermination at the hands of those it imagines are mirrors of itself? Is it a deluded hunger to capture every resource in the reachable heavens? Absurd, absurd.

She dreamed of Earthhome, so far untouched by the foe. Sky and sand, cloud masses and rain and snow, vast deep oceans swarming with their pelagic inhabitants, hills and mountains and green valleys, cities brilliant with light in the night, the very air washed by a million tangs and scents of soil and machines and people.

She would do anything to preserve Earth. Of course she would die, if it came to that, but she would strive with all her wits and heart to live, to hold the pass and the gate, to obliterate the faceless foe forever and utterly if it came to that.

She would do that for herself, and for the future lineage of humankind, and above all for her beloved Burma.

—— ∞ ——

## CHAPTER II

# 1951: Red in Korea

*Advancing...under mortar and shell fire the soldiers had to walk over the bodies of...soldiers who had been blown apart by shells and were strewn with rubble in the bottom of the trench... the bones and the flesh of those slain rolled under foot...on the sorry carpet of their remains.*

—Korean War Veteran's Letter

In near-freezing mud to the ankles of his boots, Corporal Lawrence Hawkins trips, skids, falls, holding his weapon high as he goes down. Noise everywhere as he lies half on his face in the slush. Cursing as quietly as he can manage, he squirms up on the other hand, hoists himself to his feet. Before he arrived in Korea he thought well of himself as a recent college athlete—fast and resilient on the field, running with the ball, passing it, slamming and being slammed by other large powerful young men in padded clothing and metal-masked polymer helmets.

Here that counts for nothing.

Skinny cold-eyed kids from the Bronx, auto mechanics with extra senses, fat men with gristle under the lard, these are the naturals for this pointless war. Like the peasants they are fighting. Except that the peasants know this place as if they'd been born here and lived in it all their lives, which is not very surprising because they have. It has grown in him that their foe is defending his own turf, fighting with the bitter relentless energy Americans will easily summon if Koreans or Russians ever invade California.

Well, too bad, the bastards are trying to waste him, hang him out in the cold. Red has to do unto them first. Simple survival of the—

There is a tremendous cracking crash, like a gun going off next to his ear, and when his hearing returns the screams of wounded men. Red stays still, estimating his situation. By no means frozen,

15

he reassures himself. No, just analyzing the way the land falls away. That *is* it, right? Yes, he is frightened, his stomach is cramping but he is not actually paralyzed with fear. Is he? C'mon. His heart convulses. He can hear its drumming, feel it in his throat. Mortars slam at them. If he stays where he is, he'll actually freeze, or more likely be slaughtered by weapon fire.

I can't do this, he thinks in despair. I can't move.

Get up, you stupid bastard. If you don't move, you'll lie here until you're dead.

I have to move.

I can't move.

In the bone-aching cold he remembers himself at nine years of age, pestering his fourteen year old brother Dave into taking him on a camping trip with the older boys. They must have gone six miles through difficult terrain that almost brought him to tears. When he woke up in the morning, under the branches and protective leaves of a large oak, cool mist was falling. Every muscle in his body ached. He knew he was not going to be able to get up and walk back out of the woods. A rescue team would have to come and get him. He sank hopelessly down into his sleeping bag, then thought of what his brother and the other boys would say. Somewhere he found the strength to push himself up on his elbows and slither out of the sleeping bag, get to his feet, put one foot in front of the other. Dave was lighting a fire, and sent him a grin.

No fire here, just the sucking cold, and through that the stink of dead men and the acrid bite of gunpowder.

Are they North Koreans ahead, or Chinese troops? It makes little difference. I have to go on, he tells himself. One of the guys is yelling nearby. All right, all right. Somehow he forces himself forward, lurches and then runs with three other men down a trail of slushy dirt, firing almost at random. His head swims, his body rocking with shock waves from the incoming mortars. One of the boys falls directly in front of him, shoulder and arm blown away, blood gushing. Red skids to a stop and bends to him, but Chirpy Granger is dead already. He had been carrying a light machine gun. Red snatches it up, finds it undamaged, moves ahead in a sudden zone of muted sound, as if his head is being held underwater.

He fires the machine gun. Perhaps his rounds strike a Chinese or a Korean, or the trunk of a tree. Far below, Charlie Company's tracked vehicles are withdrawing. Red staggers after them, firing almost blindly until the magazine is exhausted.

Something kicks him hard in the calf of his right leg. Oh, shit. He is on the ground. He tries to get up, and his left leg scrabbles for purchase but he cannot stand. He cannot crawl.

Mortar fire is moving away. His hearing is coming back.

A South Korean Corpsman leans over him. Trousers cut away. Injection. Morphine? Must be. Drifting. He is lifted, dropped onto a canvas litter. Thudding of the medevac chopper rotors. Lurch into the sky. Hammer of machine gun from open doorway.

"Sorry, son, we're going to take this off," says a gruff voice. A mask covers his face, the unpleasant odor of ether. Someone is screaming.

He wakes, vomits, lies wretchedly, agony in his right leg. But his leg is not there, not all of it. It's missing in action. Red Hawkins, corporal, twenty-one years old, wounded, maimed, out of the war, utters a ghastly laugh.

— ∞ —

## CHAPTER III

## 2037: Chantal in Paris, France

Once again, Paris was burning.

Twenty-six year old medical resident Chantal Vareze pulled a paper mask over her face and ran for the hospital stairs. The Groupe hospitalier Pitié-Salpêtrière had been born in strife, seen horror in the Revolution, supported Jean-Martin Charcot in his redemption of psychiatry from superstition, and, a century later, Jacques Lacan in his own tortuous disquisitions on the mind. Now it reeked again of the stench of weapon fire and doused flames. Shouting and screams, fire trucks and ambulances hooting, media drones skittering like bats, police whistles, howls of rage, men and woman running, clawing at windows and locked doors, detonations, skidding in retardant foam—

Chantal reached the cardiac wards, moving briskly. Gurneys passed her, patients trussed to intravenous drips, nursing staff grim, sliding past each other with practiced skill a centimeter from the walls. The wards were emptying as patients and staff were taken out to safer locales.

"Over here, Dr. Vareze."

The nurse, a gruff Algerian named Mohamed, thrust a MedPad into her hands. Mohamed told her, "This one's been waiting for surgery. Her heart—"

"Yes, I see, thank you. What's her name?"

"Paquin. Dominique."

She flicked through charts, test results, diagnosis, cardioversion meds ordered and administered. Much was still incomplete. Understandable, in this nightmare panic. A monitor sounded from the gurney's diagnostics: ventricular fibrillation was worsening.

The young woman on the gurney looked three-parts dead already, a ghastly pallor beneath her dark skin. Somebody had hastily removed her clothing and got her into a blue hospital gown, administered basic treatment.

Chantal bent, opened the gown. A circle of charred skin on the woman's chest was coated with a slick emulsion. Someone lurching past banged hard into her hip, muttered a curse or an apology.

One of the demented ideologues in the street had hit this poor young woman with a massively high frequency *pulsion.* If she survived that assault, she'd be lucky to find her hearing unimpaired.

A moan, and beneath the closed lids eyes flickered. Chantal reached again for the MedPad. Mohamed held it, presented it to her.

Leaning close to the patient's right ear, Chantal said clearly, "Dominique. Can you hear me? Are you awake?"

A groan, the slightest movement of the head. Chantal took her cold hand, squeezed. Despite the drugs, erratic weak pulse as advertised. The diagnostics showed her status deteriorating. Eyes opened, a gasp of pain and fright. "You're in the hospital, Dominique, but we'll take good care of you. Nurse, in my opinion she needs a temporary transvenous pacemaker." Tumult outside the heavy stone walls of the hospital was increasing. Chantal's own heart accelerated. *Ne paniquez pas*, she instructed herself severely in her grandmother's stern, remembered voice. Stay calm. Do your duty. Those filthy bastards.

She flicked the MedPad. Icons for all the surgeons showed active blue. They must be up to their elbows in ruined flesh, she thought. A surgical icon went to yellow; she clicked it, and gave her code. "Christ, what a nightmare. I was on leave and saw the reports."

They rolled quickly but without haste to catheter lab C3.

"Paquin," Mohamed said. "That's Norman, I think. Her father, I guess."

"Her mother must be beautiful," said Chantal, and transferred her patient to the waiting surgical nurse.

—— ∞ ——

## CHAPTER IV

## 1952: Red in Northern California, United States

Red Hawkins, war hero, hated the wheelchair, but it was the only way he could get his scrap metal from the yard to the workshop, and from one part of the workshop to another. He had limited storage space, because he could no longer scramble up ladders or hang tools out of the way above his head. For several months after moving to this old farm house, he had tried with his brother Dave's help to construct suitable storage shelving and containers that he could ratchet up and down to conserve working space at ground level. It worked, within limits, but all too often the unstable raw materials tumbled off as he hauled on the chains, clouting him as they fell, getting lost or jumbled. He was obliged to haul himself out of the clumsy wheeled thing and stump about in pain on his damned aluminum peg leg.

But the joy of *making!* Watching from behind his welding mask, hands in leather gloves against the sparks and flame, as the creatures of imagination and dream came together on the bench. He had started small, with random assemblages of steel that looked curiously unbalanced at first glance but were not. The steel was cut from old car bodies his brother trucked in every couple of weeks. Turning ruin into design, into aspiration. Dave was endlessly patient. With a kind of native wisdom the damned cautious doctors never seemed to possess, he did only the heavy grunt work of chopping into chunks chassis and rusted engine and bent wheels. Red could cope with those, in his detestable wheelchair, on his stilted fake limb.

And within a year of his return from the hospital in Japan, Red had progressed to Dadaist confections—a toppling Humpty Dumpty with enormous bared pointed teeth displayed in a silent shout, a bent Eifel Tower leaning against an upright Tower of Pisa, a wire-frame ambulance mounted on four steering wheels, with a skinny metal driver crouched over an actual rubber-tired wheel welded to a steering column. Rich women came up from the city, after the word got around, attended by bored lovers and stuffy accountants, and paid Red enough for his jejune inventions to keep the wolf from the door. He never attended any of the exhibitions where his work was shown.

After another year, and a wretched affair with one of those tanned connoisseurs, he grew more seriously playful in his work. His skill burgeoned, and his sculptures shrank in dimension but increased in detail and nuance. He built a ferocious bristling tom-cat that alarmed Ruth, his German Shepherd companion. Between outbursts of fury at his limitations, he kept himself in shape heaving larger pieces of metal from the staging areas where Dave had piled them, spot-welding them into wide-winged hawks stooping with gleaming claws extended, and dragons snorting out curling gusts of brazen flame, and chess pieces at battle. They slowly filled his yard at front and back, and occasional motorists paused to marvel at the mad displays of this surly cripple in his chair or hobbling on his prosthetic leg, shamelessly revealed in the hacked off Levis he wore during summer.

For a time he drank heavily, until Dave refused to bring him whiskey and he was forced to bribe the local bike-riding kid who fetched him his weekly supplies. He stopped only after he set part of the workshop on fire, maybe accidentally. Luckily he had a fire extinguisher handy, and he sat with his face blackened laughing in a kind of hysteria at the dollops of dry chemical foam.

In the third year he met Joanna, a widow some fifteen years older than Red who ran a small farm a dozen miles to the west. A couple of times a week she drove over in her pickup truck and they went inside, or sometimes lay in the grass at the back where they were shielded from the empty road, and made a kind of desultory love. If you could call it love.

"You know I love you," she said one afternoon, under a sky glazed like a Chinese plate. "Ever thought of getting married?"

In the pit of his stomach, something convulsed. Memories of pain and anger.

"Once," he said. "Before the war. We were in college together."

Joanna waited, gazing at him, then said, "And?"

"She dumped me. 'Dear John' letter when I was in hospital."

"Christ, that's ugly." She reached into one pocket of his dungarees, where they hung from a machine dragon, found his Luckies, took one between her lips and offered him the pack. Automatically, he took one, then handed it back. Shrugging, she lit hers with his Zippo and flattened herself on the grass.

"I'm the ugly one," he said.

She stared at him. "Red, that's crazy talk. You're a fine looking man, especially with your clothes off. You looked younger, know what I mean? And strong." Lightly, she punched his bunched left biceps. She carefully avoided looking at the twisted healed wound on the end of his stump, at the wasting muscles of that thigh.

"Younger than what, Jo?"

"Well, I mean—" Flustered, she turned away her face. "The war left its mark on plenty of men, Red. I know, I know, you guys don't like to talk about it. But I'm in a serious mood just now." She sat up, put out the red glowing stub in the loamy soil, took his hand. "We get along okay, right? Red, look, I guess this isn't what you're expecting, but how about we get hitched and get that farm going proper again. It could be a comfortable life. You know?"

Red's skin crawled, and he didn't quite know why. He wanted to snarl his anger at her, anger from the ruin done to his body and his future, but he blocked the impulse. Instead, he looked at her silently for a moment and then sent her a slow smile.

"Cradle snatcher."

That hurt her. Red blinked. He hadn't meant to hurt her, he was trying to deflect her absurd suggestion.

"You can't be that much younger than me, buddy," she said tightly.

"Christ, Jo, how old do you think I am? I was in Korea, not the Pacific."

He saw the shiver go through her. She did not draw away, but she covered her face with one hand, and when she lowered it he saw tears leaking down her face.

"I'm sorry, honey. Somehow I always thought—"

"What, that I'm thirty-five?"

"When you get to my age, babe, you stop thinking in those terms. It's the...." She twisted up her face, reaching for exactness. He thought: I know that look. That's me, holding a broken piece of metal, turning it, understanding it. "You have sorrow, Red," she said, then. "Grief. But you also have strength and perseverance. That's what I feel in you. We wouldn't need no wedding vows, you know. Just—"

The kindness of women, he thought, face buried then in Joanna's dry hair, his teeth gritted, and silently raged at himself for his ingratitude, lack of love, the distance he maintained from everyone, even or especially his brother.

Janna got to her feet, brushed away from grass stuck to her moist skin, and looked down at him.

"What you need, Red, is a dog."

Finally the only thing that kept him from blowing his brains out when the mad wind blew across the plains was shaping the metal, rebuilding the tiny universe of his two acres and populating it with strange creatures from his ailing soul. The clarified creations of his pain.

—— ∞ ——

## CHAPTER V

## 2037: Chantal in Paris, France

"*B*onjour, Dominique."

"*Adieu tristesse*," her not-quite-patient said with a moue. She was positioned at an angle, neither sitting up nor supine.

"*Tristesse, non. Bonjour jouissance*," Chantal cried with a grin. The scar tissue from the burn was almost gone, she was happy to see, replaced at an accelerated rate by programmed stem cells. Pity medicine was not yet sufficiently advanced that the same treatment could repair Dominique's damaged heart tissues. Eventually, no doubt, if these barbarians of every stripe would settle down and let history—life!—pick up its trajectory again. "You have no pain?"

"Not from my wounded heart." She let the fingers of her left hand move lightly over the dressing. "But from my heart, yes, always."

"Your parents," Chantal said, remembering. "I'm so sorry. But that, too, will heal."

"It was meant to be a holiday," the young woman said through a catch in her throat. "The Silver anniversary of their wedding. At last, a family trip to Paris! Nobody told us there was a war about to erupt."

"It's not a war," Chantal said, anger roughening her tone. "It is an outrage of stupidity and superstition and strutting male belligerence."

"The one who shot me was a woman," Dominique said in a small voice. "A woman…."

"Do you have anywhere to stay in Paris? It says here you're a student."

"We know only an aged aunt in this city, and she is in a hospice."

Startling herself, Chantal took her hand and said, "You can stay with me. I don't have much room, but I can make up an inflatable."

"Doctor, I couldn't possibly impose—"

"There is no problem." She made a note. "There, they'll let me know when you're due for discharge. I'll pick you up."

Her face felt hot. This was undoubtedly inadvisable. But then, after all, Dominique was not really her patient, since her case had been in the hands of a qualified cardiac specialist.

"Thank you, Dr. Vareze. You are very kind."

"Please, call me Chantal." Happiness rushed through her. *Jouissance* indeed.

A year and a half later, immediately after Dominique graduated with her engineering doctorate from the École centrale de Lyon, they married.

Five years after that, they were divorced.

Early in 2044, Chantal took a post in London's St. Peter's Hospital, and one evening, in the mist, vanished without a trace.

—— ∞ ——

## CHAPTER VI

## 1957: Red in Northern California, United States

Extract from an address to the opening session of the British Science Society, September 27, 2031: "*When the sum total of knowledge about the universe is finally collated into one grandiose all-embracing Encyclopaedia—and incidentally when the human race has thereby lost its reason for continuing to exist (loud applause)—then the history of scientific endeavor will probably be divided into three sections....*

"*The first, naturally, will cover the period in which humans—having learned they were capable of formulating ideals—attempted to construct idealized schemas for the cosmos. We might instance the Ptolemaic version of the Solar System.... The second would deal with the growth of such disciples as relativity and quantum theory, and humanity's attempt to comprehend the actual workings of the universe....*

"*The third would be the period whose opening date may well be some time in this tercentennial year of 2031! It would be the*

24

*period in which humans admitted that the universe's rules obey laws which to us must inevitably appear as capricious as the untrammeled whim of a human mind."*

"There's a new star in the heavens tonight, and it was put there not by American scientists but by the Soviet Union," the announcer said in a tone halfway beyond excitement and alarm. "It's called 'Sputnik,' which is Russian for 'fellow-traveler.' This first artificial satellite should be visible as a small bright dot in the skies above Northern California. Experts say that it is too small to carry an atomic—"

Red Hawkins switched off the radio. The German Shepherd female, Ruth, looked at him and then at the door. "All right, sweetie," he said. "Time for your constitutional. We can look for this Sputnik while we're out there."

Red opened the security screen door with its welded steel gryphon poised to leap, the heraldic "sejant guardant." Ruth stepped out ahead of him, waited politely on the path. Tonight the sky was velvet black, and a waxing gibbous white moon hung low over the hill. Red hesitated a moment in the doorway, and then limped toward the gate, glancing with relaxed satisfaction at the fragrant peppermint lawn he had populated with those fantastic birds and hunting cats in junk metal and stone.

With him went that noise he could never get away from—that tiny, almost imperceptible click of the joints in his aluminum leg.

It stopped when he halted at the gate, and he listened to the silence. The road, which ran from Orris Peak on his right to Three Waters on his left, lay still and cold in the pale moonlight, a single street light a hundred yards away atop a slightly leaning old wooden pole. There was no sign of any movement as far as he could see—a perfect night for Sputnik watching. He stood in the cool of the early night, one hand on the gate, gazing above him, from zenith to horizon, but saw no tiny glint of light moving across the sky. Well, maybe the uncanny device was hidden on the far side of the planet by now.

Just as he was turning to go back, a sudden dazzling flash of light hit him like a blow. Instinctively he flung up his hands, but it was over

25

before he could cover his eyes. Stumbling blindly back, he lost his footing and sprawled on the soft grass.

The afterimage burned painfully blue and red on his retinas. It was somehow localized, as if a tiny sun had winked into existence on the road, but it was long seconds before he could bear to look around.

When he did, he saw that the yellow tongue of light from the open kitchen door to the sculpture garden had disappeared, as had the dimmer illumination from the curtained window. Power failure? The street light was out. Other than the moon and a scatter of the brighter stars, darkness was almost complete.

He started to get up, more annoyed than alarmed, but something made him halt in bewilderment and disbelief. From no more than a few yards away, he heard a young woman's voice speak loudly and with a hint of anger.

*"Merde! De quoi s'agit-il, alors?"*

But that was impossible. Barely seconds ago he had seen no one on the road for half a mile either way.

Cursing the afterimage patch that had now shaded to green behind his eyes, he got upright and called out uncertainly: "Hello! Who's there?"

"Hello," the voice came back tremulously. "What happened to the lights?" She had a marked French accent.

Lights be damned, thought Red; where did *you* spring from? Without asking her, he went to the gate and made out her shape moving dimly on the roadway.

"Power failure, I guess," he said after a long pause. Now that he paid attention, he could no longer hear the hum from the small generator behind the house.

"Oh no! This heavy mist is bad enough without—" Her foot touched something lying in the moon-shadow cast by a tree, and she broke off to bend over it.

Mist? Red repeated under his breath. Where does she think she is?

Then her voice came again, stressed. "There's a woman lying here! She's hurt. Do you know who she is?"

Red pushed the gate open and swiftly covered the ten paces separating them. As he came up, the French woman spoke in a crisp tone.

"A light, quick. She must have been run over."

He touched her arm lightly; the fabric of her clothing was indeed slightly damp, on this clear evening. Feeling trapped in a nightmare, Red cupped his hand around the small flame of his lighter. Run over? No car has been past in four hours.

But sure enough, there was a second woman here: her right arm twisted, a thin line of blood creeping over her brown, somewhat Oriental face.

The French woman took the stranger's wrist with competent fingers and went on without looking up. "Go alert the hospital, will you? She needs immediate attention."

"There isn't a hospital nearer than Walton," said Red sharply. "That's twenty-five miles away."

The young woman turned her face to him. Even in the modest illumination from his lighter he could see that she was quite pretty, in a regular girl-next-door way, and yet somehow strange, as if made up for some beatnik Halloween party almost a month away; she had light brown hair layered short on one side, with a streak of electric blue-green running through it, dark shining eyes and an up-tilted nose. His artist's eye took in garments that seemed suitable only for a model in some science fiction movie—sleek, tightly fitted, decorated across her chest, absurdly, with a version of the Coca Cola sign bearing a black slash through it. A bag hung over one shoulder, swinging free as she crouched. With forced patience she was saying, "The hospital is just 'round the corner—I should know. I work there."

"God damn it, woman." Red spoke more bluntly than he had intended, unsettled as much by her indefinable oddness as by the inexplicable injured woman on the road. "There isn't even a doctor nearer than Three Waters."

As if she were taking stock of her surroundings for the first time, the girl slowly looked around. Her eyes widened, her shoulders tensed, and her mouth opened to shape a shout or a scream. Red made to catch her, thinking she might faint, but she shook her head.

"I'm all right," she said with an effort. "I....I—Where is this place?"

"You're about six miles from Three Waters," Red told her. She still looked blank. "Pulman County, Northwest California."

27

"But I can't be," she burst out. "I'm in London! I—Oh, *seigneur Dieu!*"

Red waited as she struggled to get a grip on herself. "All right," she said after a pause. "If you say so, it must be right. Is that your house over there? We ought to get this woman off the road."

"We can do that. Listen, call me Red. What's your name?"

"Chantal."

Silently, Red watched her feel the stranger's injured arm and lay it carefully on her chest. Between them, they carried her awkwardly up the path, through the front doorway and into the front room. Ruth trotted along quietly at their side, and plopped herself down on the front porch as they entered the house.

When they had settled the woman on a couch, Red crossed to the light switch and flicked it, knowing it was useless. He found candles and lit two with the last flame of his lighter.

Chantal eased the unconscious woman's arm from the sleeve. The garments were peculiar and distinctly unfeminine: a coverall of unusual design, with nothing under it but a pair of shorts and a kind of halter. The cloth of which all three garments were woven was very fine and, unlike Chantal's, completely dry.

Red brought bandages, hot water, a clean towel and some disinfectant, together with a piece of board to serve as a splint for the woman's arm. Seeing that Chantal appeared competent to handle things, he went out to the shed behind the house to see if he could find the trouble in the generator.

The air was foul with scorched rubber. A single glance informed him that it would take a mechanic to repair the set—it was as if lighting had struck it. Something impelled him to look at the engine of the old truck parked alongside. He had to pinch out smoldering insulation there, too. The thing was fried.

Swearing, he returned to the house, pausing on his way to drape a wet cloth around the clay sculpture he had been working on before he paused to eat and listen to the news. He would get no further design work done tonight—the flow of inspiration was broken.

He found Chantal dabbing away blood from the wound on the stranger's scalp. The trickle had run across her brown face. While the French girl struck him as attractive, in her odd way, this dark-haired woman with her closed, tilted eyes, despite her unconsciousness and injury, was entirely startling, the living, breathing model for a Leonardo figurine, if that renaissance genius had been given the chance to render a powerful Asian queen into bronze. Suddenly he ached to sculpt her himself. "Shallow cut," Chantal muttered as he entered. "Probably no brain injury. Have you called an ambulance?"

"No phone, and my truck's been hit by a lightning bolt," said Red shortly. He didn't want to seem as displeased as he felt, so he added with an effort, "Doesn't look as if she needs any more help than she's getting. Are you a nurse?"

The French woman gave him a sharp look, shrugged, and applied a bandage to the scalp cut. "I'm a physician. What do you mean, no phone?" She touched her left ear, looked startled. "You're right, no service."

Absently, Red picked up the coverall. He found something weighing down a small pocket on its chest, and took it out. It was a cylinder of dull metal, some five or six inches long, and astonishingly heavy for its size—too heavy even to be lead.

He hefted it a second and put it back.

Wiping her hands, Chantal turned to him. "That's all I can do for her," she said. "Have you a glass of wine, please?"

He took a bottle from the ice box, opened it and poured a glass for each of them. "Just local domestic stuff," he said, handing her the glass of Napa Valley white. "We don't exactly run to fine French wines out here in the sticks." Red shrugged. "I don't drink much anymore."

The woman's hand trembled so much that she could hardly hold the glass, as though she were fighting to control herself.

After a second sip, she dropped her drink as a look of panic crossed her face, the glass smashing on the flagstone floor. Her fingers beat against her ear, as if trying to clear it of water. "Dominique! Her pacemaker! Was it an EMP? Oh my god, how is this happening. What's wrong with me? No phone, no Google. Are we under attack?"

Pacemaker? Google? "Is Dominique your daughter?"

"What? No, no, she is my ex-wife."

Red stared at her in the shadowy light.

"Your ex...*wife*? Forgive me, but I thought you were a girl."

She turned on him in fury. "A *girl*? Do I find myself in some damnable backwoods enclave of American sexists? I am a grown woman, not a *girl,* and yes, Dominique and I were married for five years. What is *wrong* with you?"

Embarrassed and utterly confused, Red bent to pick up the pieces of shattered glass, watched sidelong and helplessly as the demented woman ran to the door, flung it open, stared wildly at the dark sky. Ruth let herself in, skirting her, sniffed curiously once or twice at the injured woman, and retreated to her cushion under the kitchen window. "Good dog," Red murmured. "Stay quiet, Ruth." Then he spoke more loudly. "What's an EMP?" he asked the woman's shaking back. Some sort of bomb, he supposed. For an instant he was back in Korea, huddled, mortar shells battering the earth around him. The blazing pain of his shattered leg.... He shuddered.

"Electromagnetic pulse. That would explain why everything is so dark outside, why your power is off. But why should I—" She found a chair, sat down beside the unconscious woman. "I'm sorry for my outburst," she said wanly. "You have been hospitable, despite your sexism. It's just—I think I must have *amnesie*—lost the memory. Until I found I was talking to you outside, I thought I was in London, where I have been working this year. How...how long have I been that way?"

"It's the fourth of October," said Red slowly. Sexism? Were the French now advocating that lesbians be permitted to wed? Impossible!

"Oh no! Nearly eight *months?*" the woman whispered. "Poor Dominique, she will assume—"

"It's still 1957, but you're wrong about—"

"*Mais—c'est ridicule, ça!*" She sat up sharply and began to feel in the sling bag she carried on her shoulder. "Look! Look at these."

She pulled out a small laminated card, apparently of some hard yet slightly pliant plastic, with embossed printing identifying her as Chantal H. Vareze, next to a small colored photograph of her face *that moved slightly when he turned the card.* She ignored his grunt of shock, brought out a flimsy white sheet of paper addressed to Dr. Chantal Vareze, St. Peter's Hospital, London W 1. With shaking fingers she indicated the date at the top: February 17, 2044.

"The seventeenth of February—that was *yesterday!* October is months away," she insisted. "And why isn't my cursed phone working?" She tugged a small almond of plastic from her ear, stared at it balefully, pushed it back in.

Twenty forty-four? The 21ˢᵗ century? What kind of stupid gag was this? But that impossible card—

Red glowered. Her mad hair, her slinky clothing—some sort of theatrical prank? Yet she looked so genuinely upset. And why would anyone pick him to pull a complicated practical joke like this?

"What do you remember before you found yourself here, doc?" he asked after a silence.

"Call me Chantal, please."

"Sure, thank you." He reached out his iron-roughened hand; she touched it lightly. "I'm Lawrence Hawkins. Red's a nickname, but it's what I go by."

"For *les cheveux roux*, yes." Her eyes shifted to the right and up, reaching for something forgotten, misplaced. "I was coming off a very long emergency surgery, Red. It was about—oh, a bit past six in the morning. It was bitterly cold." She unconsciously hugged herself. "No wonder I'm so tired. There was a lot of mist—not quite thick enough to call smog. The streets were very quiet."

Red could not take anything she said literally. And yet he had seen for himself that she appeared as if from thin air on a bare, cold road.... Ignore the ridiculous year on the letter. "That would be Greenwich time. Here in Pacific Standard time, it's now," he glanced at his watch, "about 10.20. And you and this other poor woman have been here less than half an hour."

She looked at him with horrified eyes.

"In fact," he finished deliberately, "it looks as if you have just covered about six thousand miles in literally *less than no time*. That's faster than the new star circling the globe overhead, that Sputnik. If we ignore the little matter of it actually being October the fourth. And yes, in 1957."

—— ∞ ——

# CHAPTER VII

# 4041/4061: Magwareet

"**A**nswer quickly, Paulo. Clearly and cogently," the Academy instructor told him. She seemed pleasant but implacable, the first human teacher he'd had since beginning the course. It made a change from throttled AIs. "I see you have completed spin-vectors, tensors, spinors, and twistors."

"Yes," said Magwareet.

"Challenge: I am an identical or monozygotic twin. My twin is four times as old as I am."

Young Magwareet thought swiftly. Cryonic suspension was an obvious and cogent answer, but *too* obvious. Was the instructor a clone? But probably she was in her eighties, and even with today's powerful life-extension remedies and rejuvenators it seemed hardly credible that her twin was deep into her third century. He was aware of an inner clock advancing relentlessly, urging him to blurt out anything that made even minimal sense, just to get through this ordeal. Suppose her twin sister had been born in the last minutes of some year, 3040, say, and she was born in the first hours of 3041. Absurd, how could that possibly make a sufficient difference in later years?

He was sweating. His intuition had led him astray.

Or perhaps not. Wait—

"Reframe. Your sister was born late on the evening of February 28th, back then," he said, as if he'd known it all along. "You were born in the very early morning of February 29th."

"I knew you were keeping up, young Magwareet," the instructor said.

"So yes, in the year I had my first February 29th birthday, my sister was already four years old. When I turned two, my sister was eight."

"We are talking notional sisters, I think," Magwareet hazarded. It would be rude to be more explicit. "After all, those calendrics are nearly two millennia out of date."

"Naturally, silly boy. I appreciate the compliment, but I am not *that* old. Now let us turn to the classics of Japanese literature. *The Tale of Genji is*—"

On his son Joaquin's 16th birthday, in 4059, Paulo Magwareet met the young man in the best restaurant adjacent to the Academy. They dined well if austerely on constituted shellfish and a single glass each of an excellent tart white wine. When they rose from the table, Magwareet handed him a gift-wrapped printed copy of *Genji* and watched with some anticipation as he opened it.

"This looks very old. Paper?" Joaquin carefully turned a page or two, showing no enthusiasm for the bizarre gift.

"Family heirloom, kid."

"I thought you came from a deep space birthery, Father. Or do you mean that Mother had a family that kept—"

"This is the very launching moment of the tradition, my boy. I studied this noble volume when I was a student at the Academy, and I've carried it with me ever since. It's the first novel ever written, and the mores of the ancient culture it records are almost incomprehensible."

The youth gave him a wise look. "All the better to grapple with the societies of the Enemy, eh? If we ever meet them."

"Just so." Magwareet grinned his broad, quite ugly grin, and the smile was echoed in the gleaming oversized teeth of his son. "Heirloom, Year One. Let's hope the Enemy don't turn out to be as ferocious as the old Heians." He ruffled the kid's shaggy locks. "High time for you to get your hair streaked."

"Yes, sir."

"What's your specialty?"

"I'm hoping command will accept me for anchor team training."

Magwareet felt pressure in his chest, and diagnosed it as a blend of pride and terror. My son! Oh my dear boy.

"You'll do fine," he said. "Just keep your wits about you, and try not to get into too many fistfights. Otherwise you'll end up with a nose like mine."

The young man's eyes were bright with unshed tears. "You know you could have that fixed in ten minutes."

"Ah, yes, but this is a battle scar from my own time in the Academy." Magwareet put his arm companionably around the lad's broad shoulders. "I'm bound to end up looking a lot worse if we ever get our hands on an Enemy vessel." He gritted his teeth. "Those bastards will be tough opponents, whatever shape they turn out to be."

Two years later, the complexities of Madam Murasaki's ancient Heian culture were almost entirely displaced from Magwareet's memory, replaced by frantic practical war work against the Enemy. He gazed into the simulation: unpeeling edges of ruptured spacetime.

"Bi-glomohedric prisms constitute the phase space of 4-dimensional rotations," Burma Brahmasutra reminded the action team leaders gathered for her briefing. "These will be the fundamental mappings for the anchor teams."

"Yes ma'am," said Alexander Ramirez, the high-ranking officer from the Centauri system. "But these temporal surges we've detected, they operate in higher spaces, folded dimensions."

"So we need to find ways to pack them back inside their broken shells." Burma smiled at him, almost gleefully. "Or at least deal with their consequences. I have three research teams preparing a portable device we're calling a 'time map'." She opened a case, withdrew a large ceramic rhombus.

"Rather hefty," muttered somebody Magwareet did not know.

"We'll miniaturize and encapsulate this so it's portable and not so likely to poke the user's eye out."

Burma ran a finger down one edge of the lozenge, and two adjacent surfaces sprang apart. The interior was entirely solid state, of course, emitting a green glow. "This little machine tracks the local entropic field, and locks onto its exact spatial and temporal configuration. If your crews are caught in a temporal eddy and dragged away into the past, they will be able to return to their point of departure—unless the internal power source is drained by the disaster, or the crew are hurt and unable to activate their units, or any number of other variables."

"Remarkable. I see a problem, Burma." Magwareet frowned, reached out, withdrew his questing fingers instantly. "These observed fluxes appear to be associated with massive energy events—weapon detonations and the like. Not the kind of locus one would wish to return to."

"We hope to allow some measure of control over the return destination. Understand, this device is not yet ready to be implemented beyond the laboratory. Any other problems?"

A tough little commando from the Tau Ceti brigade said, "We don't yet know what causes a time surge. It seemed most likely at first to my research advisors to be a weapon used against us by the Enemy, but then they are also suffering from its impact." She hesitated. "If I might say so, Coordinator, it's rumored your wife has suggested that some, uh, extratemporal entity might be at the root of the problem." Her mouth tightened, and she held Burma's gaze.

"Yes. Artesha can be whimsical. She's dubbed it 'the Being,' Not, say, 'the Force' or 'the Field.' She might be right, but I suspect that attributing intelligence or even sensitivity to such an immensely powerful agency is seriously premature." Burma carefully closed the device and returned it to its secure case.

"Understood, ma'am," said the commando. Branigan, that was her name. "Even so, if there is sentience involved, the proposed anchor teams will have to tread carefully."

"Always. Any more questions? Other points? No? Very well, dismissed."


Magwareet struck up a conversation with an exo-ethnologist named Catriona. Her profession offered the nearest approximation to expertise in the Enemy they possessed, given the drawback that nobody had yet laid eyes on one, and he found her opinions fascinating. The restaurant gave him the uncanny impression that he'd been there before. Admittedly, architecture in military emplacements tended to be stereotyped. The wine was tart on his tongue. Ah yes, this same constituted vintage. Joaquin's 16th birthday.

"Paulo, you suddenly look grim. Or sad. Cheer up. More wine?"

"Forgive me, Catriona. Not sad, but unforgivably distracted for a moment." Magwareet shook his head, forced a smile. "This war, you know. I found myself thinking of my son."

She held his gaze. Sympathy, and something more. "Is he—Has something—"

"Oh, no, no, Joaquin is fine. Almost finished at the Academy, following in his Dad's footsteps, actually. It's just—"

"I know," said Catriona, and stood, drew him to his feet. "Let's dance, feller, and then there's a non-competitive contact sport we might play that should take your mind off the war. At least for a little while."

He laughed aloud at that, and went into her embrace as the music pulsed.

—— ∞ ——

## CHAPTER VIII

## 1957: Red and Chantal in Northern California, United States

Red waited for the moment of calmness to pass. It lasted only seconds. After that, reason insisted that this whole affair was stupid and he became resentful that a wild vision should break into his life and disrupt it. And yet—he could not convince himself.

"I've heard about things like this," said Chantal slowly. "But you never believe them. You class them with ghosts, and you never expect to find yourself involved—"

"Damned right you don't," said Red, with sudden force. "I'm not going to accept this till I have to. Must be *some* explanation. And her—the woman with the broken arm. What do you make of that?"

"That she was hit by a car, I told you."

"She wasn't. No cars go past here. There's a truck that goes up to the logging camp at Firhill Point with supplies and mail, but no one else lives this way at all. And I was watching when you—arrived. Both of you."

And I don't give a damn how, his mind ran on. I just wish you hadn't.

He felt suddenly certain that his careful defenses were going to crumble. If his isolation could be disturbed by this fantastic intrusion, he could never feel safe again.

He moved, and the joints of his artificial leg gave their inescapable tiny scraping sound.

"Oh, hell," he burst out, and Chantal's eyes widened. "It's all right—it's not your fault."

She turned to face him. "*What's* not my fault? I didn't ask to be thrown halfway 'round the world. I don't know how I got here, but I do know this, sir—I'd give anything to be back where I came from."

They faced each other, meaningless tension mounting between them. A sound between a sob and a shout from the other room punctured it.

After an instant's hesitation, Chantal got up and ran through the door. Red limped after her, to find the woman with the broken arm writhing on the couch where they had laid her.

"Have you a thermometer?" Chantal asked, her anger vanishing. Red nodded, and went and got one from the bathroom.

"Fever?" Red inquired in a low tone.

She nodded. "I don't know why. She seemed perfectly fine when I left her."

Suddenly the woman in distress uttered a short sing-song phrase, full of strange off-key arpeggio intervals. Her voice appeared to cover the range from treble to contralto.

Red picked up the coverall again, hoping for some clue to the woman's nature from it, but all he found was the same impossibly heavy cylinder of metal.

After a while, the writhing was replaced by an even more frightening stillness. It was as if the woman were visibly gathering strength, disciplining her body into rest. Eyes closed, she licked her lips and said something musical and interrogative.

"What can she mean?" Chantal asked helplessly, and at the words the woman's eyelids flickered open.

She looked at them without expression, barely turning her head. Then she shifted her gaze to the Indian matting hung against the wall, and shut her eyes again.

"*Hablas español?*" she said in a flat tone.

"We speak English," said Red slowly, and the bronze-faced woman used a four-letter word that startled him and made Chantal turn her face to hide a smile.

"Never so far before." She struggled to sit up, and found the injury to her arm. The sight of it seemed to dishearten her still further. She stared up, pleading. "It is broken? And you have used splinters to mend it?"

That's an odd mistake, Red realized suddenly. A simple foreigner would probably not know the word this woman was trying to find—but equally likely, she would not know the one that had been substituted.

Chantal nodded, trying to soothe her into lying back calmly, but she continued with intense determination, "Tell me! Tell me when I am!"

"Lie still," said Chantal comfortingly. "You'll be all right. You've been hurt, and—"

It was then that the exact meaning of the question struck home.

Not "Where am I?" Instead—"*When* am I?"

Red felt the last of his protective barriers go down. His isolation was forever at an end. He was naked against the world, and his aluminum leg creaked.

"You're in nineteen fifty-seven," he said, and his body began suddenly to tremble with terror.

"Further than ever," said the woman. "I—I feel ill. I am not immune to your diseases, sir and madam. Please, have you an illness? I have asked my system, but it seems to be somewhat damaged."

Staring, Chantal shook her head. "No. We are quite well, I think."

The woman put her hand up to her heart, then between her breasts. "My coverall, where is it?" Again she struggled frantically to sit up. "Have I lost it? Did I not have anything with me?"

Chantal reached for the garment and held it as the woman rummaged with her unbroken arm in the pockets. Sinking back, she shook her head. "So it is lost. So they will not know."

"You want this?" said Red sourly, holding up the heavy metal cylinder, and the woman seemed to go limp with relief.

"Yes, that is it. Please, hold it up above me with your hands on the ends, and turn them oppositely. It is important."

Red hesitated, but Chantal appealed to him with her eyes. Feeling foolish, he extended his arms and did as the woman had said. The hard metal felt as if it were running like water, and it suddenly began to *grow*, pushing his hands apart. With an oath, he let go in amazement, but the thing did not fall. It remained in position, stretching until it was three feet long, and the moment it stopped growing it began to glow.

After a second, the whole room was alight with the luminescence of brilliant green bands apparently within the substance of the cylinder.

Chantal drew back. "*Que se passe-t-il?*" Her voice held a sob.

Seeming suddenly lighthearted, the woman answered as she studied the shifting patterns of greenness. "It floats because it is not all here, so to say. It exists, after a fashion, for thousands of years both ways." Her voice was more certain and her English better now. "You could not understand how," she added.

"What made it so big?" Red demanded.

"It was compressed." The woman seemed to hunt for words. "Solid is not really solid. It is mostly empty space. The map is pushed together—"

"You mean the atoms are packed closer," said Red sharply.

He resented the stranger's assumption that he knew nothing.

Startled, the woman glanced from the glowing cylinder to the candles burning around the room. "But you—" she began, "you know more than I had remembered at this time."

"What we want to know is who you are and where you come from," said Red harshly. "And why."

The woman closed her eyes wearily. "You could not pronounce my name correctly. Your language has no tonal values. I am Burma Brahmasutra. You may call me Burma, for that is where I was born, on Earth."

Chantal said, "We call your nation Myanmar now. I mean in my time."

"Names and boundaries come and go." Burma glanced up. "And who are you two?"

"Red Hawkins," he said sullenly. Born, on Earth?

Chantal spoke her name in answer to a piercing stare.

"Please, then, Red," Burma went on, "place your hands on the map, at the brightest of the green places."

"I've had enough of this lunacy," Red muttered, and began to turn away with finality.

Burma's broken arm reached with dazzling speed to intercept him even before his movement began, but the pain and her fevered weakness overcame her.

"My god. How did you do that?"

"My people have a wider perception of *now* than yours. I can shift attention *within* a single instant of now—backwards and forwards." Slumping back, setting her white, perfect teeth in quite apparent agony, she said, "You could not know, poor man," And added in a queer, rhythmic manner. "Red Hawkins! Do what I tell you."

Astonished, Red found himself turning and lifting his hands towards a patch of green on the cylinder that shone like a cold sun. Angrily, he fought back, and when his arms fell to his sides, his own not-so-perfect teeth were chattering.

"Nearly," said Burma with detachment, and repeated, "Do what I tell you."

This time, Red could not stop himself.

There was chaos.

But there was form in the chaos: a sense of slow ages unrolling as they existed in total silence and total darkness, and through and beyond it there was an awareness of Being.

Then ground suddenly slammed Red under the soles of his feet, knocking him instantly *upwards* half an inch, and pitiless yellow sunlight was blazing out of a blue sky. They were on a bare hillside, between bare brown rocks. A few paces from him lay Burma, as if she had been twisted in falling and landed awkwardly, and behind him Chantal moved with a sound of shoes crunching against a gray sand. When he turned his head, he saw that she had fallen forward, trying to crush the solidity and reality of stone into her hands. She whimpered a little.

Red whirled on Burma. "God damn you! What is this insanity? Are you satisfied with what you've done? Look at this poor woman."

Burma had her eyes shut against the glare. Her good hand clutched the cylinder in its original closed form. She looked very ill.

"You must not waste time," she whispered. "A few kilom—miles from here you will find men working. I have tried to contact them but my system is dysfunctioning. Go and bring them here."

Red opened his fist and bent so that he was able to slap Burma in the face with it. "Stop your babbling! Where are we? How did we come here?"

"You're in my time," said Burma, more faintly still. "You have come two thousand years. Go quickly, Red. I have no resistance to the diseases of your era, and I need help."

"Get us back where we came from," said Red passionately. "You're no concern of mine. Attend to your damned business yourself."

Chantal came down the slope from behind him, very pale, and walking as if in pain. A little blood fell from a cut on her temple, and her hands were filthy with sharp sand. She spoke quietly.

"Burma is very sick, Red. She needs help, and we can't give it to her."

"Be damned to that! Why didn't she *ask* before? I don't know how she made me do what she wanted, but she forced me, I know, and I won't be ordered around. I didn't ask to come here, and I don't want to stay another minute." He stared at her, then said with finality, "If you're so eager to help her, go yourself."

"I—don't think I could." Chantal swayed. "But I'll try, if she says so." She put her hands to her head and brought them away blood-stained; she looked at the wet color wonderingly.

"Red," said Burma very softly, "I could make you go—I don't like to, but I can. And I am important to the human species, very important."

"And I'm not, I suppose."

"Oh, *Red*," said Chantal pleadingly, and turned to Burma. "How far is it to where your friends are?"

"About three…uh, two miles," said Burma in a weak voice. "It is not far. Red, I think Chantal is hurt, and cannot go."

"Hurt! My God," said Red with bitterness. "Two miles is not far? Look! Look at this."

He made a violent gesture, and pulled up the leg of his trousers. The Sun glinted blindingly on a shaft of polished metal.

Chantal fell silent. Burma, screwing up her eyes against the light, stared at the prosthetic leg for a long while.

"I'm very sorry, Red," she said at length. "I did not know. But I am too ill to undo what has been done. I promise that—if you still so wish—you will be returned to your time the moment I am safe and well." She opened her dark eyes fully and gazed at Red. "You cannot

41

appreciate the importance of what is happening, but I give you my word that I must reach help if a terrible disaster is to be avoided. I throw myself on your mercy. I will not command you to go."

As Red stood hesitant, his anger fading, a flash of incredible light made the sunshine turn to shadow, and after a moment it was followed by a sound like a hundred claps of thunder rolled into one.

"What—what is happening?" Red asked. Burma looked at him steadily.

"We are losing a war," she said. "The human species is losing a war."

—— ∞ ——

## CHAPTER IX

## 4070: Enemy Attack

Everywhere now was the stench of the strange god. From whence had it arisen? What was its ambition? Even deep in the pool, rolling limb over limb toward the churn of the bright lights, Yeptverki suffered that abiding presence. In every spatial direction, and perhaps outward and inward along the temporal dimensions, the Beast spread a foul heathen taint.

Yeptverki made the gesture of obeisance. Liquid flowed away from its five limbs, and its hundred trillion cells sang with intent. The True God and the True Way are all-powerful! The vermin of the Beast had been permitted for a time as a test of faith to spread outward from star and world, more and more and yet more, like a willed contagion, a congealed blasphemy. In the great war to rid the universe of their filth, the vermin's starcraft were now on the run, contracting at last toward a knot of stars midway between the darkness of the intergalactic void and the blazing turmoil of the galaxy's center. It was joy to kill them. Finally, when all were cleansed, the vermin god would surely depart and the heavens again be purified.

An alert sounded, driving a pulse of furious excitement through its body. *All cleaner crew assemble at the debarkation port. We approach the vermin star city. Policy Research Exploration is in force. No nuclear or dark energy weapons will be employed in this instance until mapping is complete. Our mission is rated Maximal Urgency: To locate and destroy the primary planetary system of these creatures, inflicting correlative damage upon the Beast.*

With swift, heavy strokes of its body, Yeptverki reached the egress ramp, pulled itself with a heave into gravity. Machines and parasites scurried, wrapping its golden surface with evaporative sheeting. Robust enhancements cloaked its symmetrical torso, instantly powering up and hoisting Yeptverki into its customary martial posture. It brushed the support team aside, strode with determination to the ship's nearest internal translocator. With a flick of a tongue, it stepped through the gateway into the debarkation hall.

Overhead and on every side, immense screens showed raw space, stars deformed in the usual way by their vessel's transluminal velocity. Both warcraft had matched velocities with target. Shielded, they could not yet be detected. To port, the companion Cleaner craft was opening its weapon turrets. Directly ahead, fleeing at the same transluminal velocity, the vermin city appeared to hang equally motionless against the backdrop of eternal night.

*Greetings, Master Cleaner*, a lieutenant uttered, lowering its coelom cavity. *What is your plan of entry?*

*Guile replaces force. Infiltrate a squadron of molecular data swarmers as I prepare for superluminal space. Build me a generalized map of the city's interior. Find an unattended point of entry in the shell and melt me a portal. Take care to set off no proximity alarms nor allow the escape of the vermin's atmosphere. The vermin will not expect a single attacker.* It turned its attention elsewhere. *Armorer!*

Clad in heavy shielding that hugged and supported its flesh, Yeptverki exited the attack craft on a maintenance sled that flung it through cascades of twisted spacetime to the diamond-hard shell of the vermin habitat. Optical displays revealed no sign of the twin warcraft at its rear, and neither was there any indication ahead of the sealed opening created through the shell by its swarm. The sled braked, stopped fractionally before the encapsulated opening. Master Cleaner made a final virtual inspection of the route traced by the swarmers to what must be the control center. It peeled open the temporary blister cover, entered, found a compacted wall of dark soil threaded with roots.

It began to dig.

A convulsive shock went through its body. In its visual feeds, blazing light vomited at its rear. The cloaking shields of both raiding vessels of the True God collapsed. Master Cleaner Yeptverki snarled, thrusting its heavy body deep into the matted soil. The Beast was shaking spacetime in great waves as dark energy weapons from vermin attack vessels tore the ships of the True God into shreds. The isolated Cleaner shrieked with rage, hurled itself free of its tunnel in the soil, stood in the city. Vermin stopped and stared at it with their soft wet optical apparatus, and ran in terror.

There would be no hiding now, no subtle infiltration. Guided by the swarmers' maps, it tore through the city toward the tower in its center that was the structure's obvious place of control. Here it would take command, have its revenge, find the key vermin planet's location at last and—

Thunder rang though the devices of its armored suit. It was jolted. It fell, heavily, then found itself weightless and floating as the antigravs went down.

The curved surface of an internal road rose to strike it. Centrifugal pseudo-force!

The city had begun to spin up, against all reason, vibrating and splintering the delicate structures, rotating now ever faster upon its axis.

An immense twistor field had been activated. Impossible to predict such suicidal madness. What was the vermins' goal?

Another disrupting convulsion in the time dimension. The Beast, the strange god.

Yeptverki screamed in fury, and ran powerfully on all limbs toward the central tower as the spin accelerated.

Panicking vermin fled on every side, or lay supine, or clambered desperately to higher ground where the spin "gravity" was less intense. Even so, as spin picked up speed, many bodies were flung helplessly from the spired structures. Those nearby that stood their ground Yept-verki swatted away, did not pause for more than an instant to see skulls cracked open, spines fractured, limbs smashed. It found an empty shaft in the middle of the tall building marked by its swarm, keyed its suit's propulsion unit and rushed upward to the control center.

Doors were locked or jammed shut. The Cleaner hammered down a wall, too infuriated by this absurd resistance to bother with weapons. More walls cracked and broke apart.

It burst into a modest space of machinery and vermin belted into seating equipment. Even here, nearer to the empty central regions of the spherical city, its weight was becoming oppressive. Its lifting unit was not designed for nuance, and in error Yeptverki crashed its stiff suit against a bank of computers, damaging one limb and inactivating the lifter. Vermin began clambering atop it, tugging at its four effective limbs. Yeptverki slapped them away, crushed bodies under the weight of its limbs and core.

At the alien information devices, the swarm was a pale cloud coating and burrowing into the machinery, seeking some intelligible coded structure of meaning. With a vast hissing burst and an electrical stench, safeguards of some sort went critical inside the machines and they died. On every side, vermin lay dead as well. Yeptverki wailed and left the wreckage, plunging down again through ring after ring of increasing spin gravity. Its suit stiffened and auxiliary motors took up part of the load.

The Cleaner could almost feel the vast network of intercommunicating cells that comprised its essence being packed down into uselessness. Consciousness wavered. The ship had gone, and the ship's raider companion, it recalled through a haze of misery and resentment. It felt its mind coming apart, sinking into millions of unintegrated babbling urges and maddened voices.

There was a tunnel in the soil at the rim of the city, the faintest chance it might escape, flung from the whirling city into deformed spacetime, perhaps call for aid. Its thoughts grew ragged and scattered.

Into the gaping hole. Down, down.

It cowered finally, mindless as an animal.

—— ∞ ——

## CHAPTER X

## 4070: Magwareet

Defense fleet (coordinates 408513924)—speaking: *Two enemy raiders detected and destroyed during attack on 129 Lyrae star city. Defense subject to 41 percent losses. Request reinforcements.*

Anchor team (baseline AD 4070)—speaking, triple red emergency: *We were shifted four years by this one and there's more to come.*

Center to all units, triple red emergency: *Prepare for violent temporal surge.*

Paulo Magwareet was in space, less than fifty kilometers from the milling lights that indicated his anchor team's position, when the temporal surge hit.

It was spectacularly powerful, and yet there was almost *nothing* to see. In fact, there was literally nothing to see. The lights of the anchor team were suddenly not there. That was all.

But it threw Magwareet into instant action. He slapped open his time map to make sure that the anchor team, and not himself, had been struck; keyed the code controlling his defensive screen, and reversed his progress with a shuddering blast on the drive unit.

After that, he had time to be afraid.

There was long-embedded protocol for this, a methodical series of steps that acknowledged his terror, the frightful emptiness of interstellar space, all that would be lost, wasted, if he permitted his dread to allow his death. I will live, one small sheltered part of his self told the rest of him. I will not succumb. For myself and for humankind, I shall survive. For a moment now, yes, in the absence of immediate threat, I will lower my shields against terror and let this rush of emotion shake me, and then pass away, flow from me like water from an opened faucet. And then, when I am cleansed of fear, I shall close the faucet and accept reality, my purpose, and move forward. Not quite yet. But soon. Soon.

Now.

Coming to himself again a few minutes after the passing of the time storm front, he found he was mouthing curses, damning the sheer waste involved. There had been sixty brilliant, highly trained specialists in that anchor team. Now—if one could rationally apply the word— they were scattered across history, to recover, perhaps, and fight their way back to bring news of yet another peak of the temporal surge.

He clamped a firm control on his mind. It was no good railing against the universe.

Finding his voice, he spoke in communication mode, asking for Artesha Wong. In a moment, her hard, familiar voice was in his ears.

"Have you tracked that one?" he asked, and received a counter-question: "Have they really gone?"

Burma had been with that team, and rage threatened to boil up in him again. Poor Artesha—it was shameful that two people who meant so much to each other should be torn apart by insensate violence. He replied as calmly as he could.

"Yes, I'm afraid I saw them go. I'm sorry, Artesha, but out of them all, at least, Burma is the most likely to find her way back. She'll make it if she has to train the Being to bridle and saddle."

"You can't train a creature maddened with pain," said Artesha. "I'll have a ship out to pick you up in just a moment."

Switching off communicator mode, Magwareet sighed and closed his eyes with a twinge of guilt. It was beneficial to relax on the ultimate softness of space. Mostly, there was not enough time to relax.

*Not enough:* the words burned into his brain. It was always *not enough*—not enough time to rest, or space to move around in. Most ironical of all, there was not enough of *anything* to make maximum use of the potential of the human species.

He was turning slowly relative to the stars. He stared at them in his display field, wondering which—if any—of those in sight had shined on the implacable enemy.

"Do you realize you're beating us?" he whispered into nowhere. "Do you know that you're wearing us down? And yet it's not you alone, damn it! If it was only you we had to face, we'd wipe the sky with you, and I'd lay bets on our chances. But we're trying to carry a ton of weight and fight at the same time. We're doing our best, and it's not good enough."

Where had Burma been tossed to? he wondered. Had she found herself alone, perhaps injured, in the vastness of space beyond Pluto? She was driftwood on a surge of movement that reached clear across the Solar System and a thousand, or a million, years through time.

"Did they bring you?" he whispered to the Being. "Are you a weapon of the Enemy's?" He was inside its field here. Throughout the Solar System he was inside it. And yet to it he was no more than the film on one of his blood corpuscles. He and his world were broad in three dimensions and very short in time.

But the Being was enormous in time. Literally and precisely, it moved in four dimensions, perhaps more. And it could suffer pain. Whenever the defending fleet released its huge gouts of energy to destroy an invader, the Being suffered. Sometimes the anchor teams trying desperately to repair its injuries, and return it whence it came, failed to control its writhing—and then the problem was doubled.

Magwareet felt that he had been hunting a solution to it all his life, and he was infinitely tired. But he knew he could not rest—that no one dared to rest, or the human species was finished.


He opened his communicator again as he noticed mass approaching on his proximity detectors. "Were those raiders just destroyed the ones that intercepted the city from 129 Lyrae? I didn't hear what happened."

"Yes, they were the same," Artesha informed him as if sparing him only a little attention. "They'd lost the city though—a long way out. Apparently whoever was piloting simply outflew them. I don't know who the pilot is, but it was brilliant work—sounds like a candidate for coordination."

"Is that the city coming in now?" Magwareet reeled off coordinates swiftly to identify what he was talking about.

"That's it," agreed Artesha. "Your ride is on its way, Magwareet. I'll see you back here at Center."

Magwareet turned and saw the lights of an unpressurized vessel heaving up towards him from the direction of Spica. The pilot, fastened into his control frame by magnets on his spacesuit, threw out a line and before Magwareet had done more than catch hold started back the way he had come.

There remained a few minutes until he must fall again into his role of Coordinator—one of the chosen few who formed a multiple brain for the concerted efforts of the entire species. He tried to use the time to continue his brief rest, but it was no good. It was equally useless to feel angry that he should be a Coordinator; he was qualified for the job the only way he could be—by doing it well.

He looked down at his proximity detector again, and began to frown. "Artesha," he said. "That city from 129 Lyrae—there's something wrong with its mass."

A moment of checking; he waited. Then Artesha answered, alarm showing only in the speed of her words. "It's carrying spin! Vantchuk—get in touch with them."

Straining his attention, Magwareet listened. At this distance, it was useless trying to make out details of the flying city, but he could distinctly see it: yellow, where no star or planet ought to be visible. It was not one of the complex web of spacecraft ringing Sol; he knew their pattern by heart. Vantchuk's voice interrupted his thoughts; he knew that, too.

"There's no reply, Artesha. Something's wrong."

"Vector towards it," Magwareet directed his pilot, and the stars swirled giddily. Anxious voices continued in his communicator.

"They're spinning like a top. No answer from them. The rim of the city must be under about ten gravities, and it's out of control."

"Magwareet," said Artesha levelly, and his trained mind took over.

"Impose a tensor field to kill that spin," he directed. "Their population is about four million, if I remember. We'll need two hundred hospital craft—"

Mechanically, he detailed the supplies they would require, the probable order in which they would use them, and the time it would take. At Center, his orders were interpreted into concrete terms; equipment was loaded, staff detailed to report, a computer programmed to double-check Magwareet's proposals—but that was probably not necessary.

The dizzying whirl of the city was already visibly slowing when Magwareet told his pilot to match velocities. A possibility was irritating him as he watched the rescue ships line up nearby, and he called Artesha again.

"Didn't you say that the pilot outflew those enemy raiders? Yet there was no report of an accident or damage, was there? A pilot that good doesn't just let things get out of control."

Artesha spoke soberly. "What are you getting at, Magwareet?"

"I think we'd better hold off the rescue ships for a while. I want a team of trouble-shooters—about fifty—to come in with me ahead of the rescue party."

They did not question his decision. When he clawed at and caught the personnel ropes floating stiffly out from the nearest polar airlock in the globe enclosing the city, crew were waiting.

The commander of the detachment at this lock identified himself. "Inassul, sir."

"All right, Inassul. Let's take a look."

Passing the upper axis lock, Magwareet came out on a small platform and steadied himself against the remaining coriolus force, looking about him. He caught his breath at the sight.

This city from another star was fantastic. It sprouted inward from the shell, like a forest of beautiful ferns, into light bridges of synthetics and tall impossible buildings having nothing in common with planetary architecture. Of course, its people had never been shackled by gravity; they built from the start with antigrav.

And they had torn this city up by the roots; they had closed it in with a diamandoid sheath and mounted it on an interstellar drive. They had loaded it with four million people, of whom one perhaps might be indispensable. They had sunk thousands of hours and desperate energy into bringing it where its resources could be utilized in battle—and at the moment of success, disaster awaited.

Here and there the symmetrical beauty was marred by ugly gashes, showing where generators driven to the limit had failed to withstand the force of the equatorial spin. Arches and walls had tumbled, not downwards towards what had been their local footings, but toward the spinning circumference.

What had caused this disaster? The trouble-shooting team moved forward apprehensively. Staggering a little, Inassul made his way down the broad helical road from the lock. Weapon ready for anything he might meet, he pushed at the door-switch of the nearest house and went inside.

Moments later, he reappeared. There was a tremor in his voice when he spoke to Magwareet.

"They're—crushed against the walls and floors," he said. Looking at him, Magwareet saw that his right gauntlet, with which he must have steadied himself, was wet and red.

"Shall I call the rescue party in?" Inassul asked. Magwareet cut him short.

"No! We can't risk more personnel until we know what the trouble was. Follow me."

His order was relayed to the parties at the other locks of the city. As they moved together towards the control center, in the middle of the city, he gave directions.


Inside the control room—a hall a hundred feet long—men and women lay broken and dead: some at their places opposite panels of signal diodes that still flickered, and others dashed against the walls and roof. A gap loomed in the outer wall on the side opposite the entrance Magwareet had used.

"Why are these people dead?" he said explosively. "We're near the center of the city! The acceleration should have been negligible here."

"An enemy shot—" began Inassul.

"Use your head. How did it get through without breaking the diamandoid sheath and losing the city's air? And look at *that!*"

He threw up an arm and pointed to the gap torn in the wall facing them. Someone called out.

"I saw some pavement torn up while we were coming in—and not far from here! There are several walls broken like that, too."

"That's it," said Magwareet. "Something enormous deliberately killed these people—smashed them, threw them around."

He felt his words drop into a sudden chilly silence. "And even now it might be loose in the city."

—— ∞ ——

## CHAPTER XI

## 4070: Enemy Attack

Pain was gone. Yeptverki unwrapped its limbs, aware of the numbness in the damaged limb. Gravity was gone, and pressure. Somehow the rotation induced by the twistor field had been reversed. In a blur of recovering logic, the Cleaner understood that some intentional agency had produced this change. Others devoted to the True God and the True Way? Perhaps. It felt the jolt of molecules surge through its tissues, confidence replacing the torpor of grief. Another jolt: the insight that this was more likely to be the work of new vermin. The city, after all, was still on course to the home worlds of the vermin, perhaps guided by the Beast. Well, then, let them face it! Yeptverki would—would—

After a further time without awareness, it reached out with its suit's sensors. The rasping clutter and noise of the small creatures was undeniable. It felt weak. Hunger! For too long it had been denied sustenance; the supplies in the suit had been exhausted, and its liquid surround was growing rancid. Time to leave this squalid hiding place. Yeptverki lurched forward in the darkness, found purchase, moved in the weightless burrow toward the inner spaces of the wrecked city.

Weight returned, abruptly, pressed it against the foul soil. Surely the vermins' doing—they had reactivated the damaged gravity-antigravity system, at least in part. Forward, light glimmered.

Yeptverki gathered itself, still dangerously confused and knowing it, driven by the urge to wreak vengeance and complete its task.

It could not recall its task. To survive. To learn—what? To punish—

— ∞ —

## CHAPTER XII

## 4070: Magwareet

Magwareet looked at the suddenly drawn faces of the engineers with him. Apprehensively, they half-turned to keep the surrounding area in view.

"What could it be?" said Inassul. "A battle machine—or an Enemy itself?"

"I don't know. Is our transluminal communication equipment in order, somebody?"

A tall man gave a swift glance at the displays on a portable unit and flicked through a bank of icons. The sound of Center's never-ceasing random scramble broadcast filled the air for a moment. "It's working," he said.

Magwareet shouldered his way over and pressed the call icon to bring in Artesha. "Have we an expert on the indigenous biology of 129 Lyrae?" he demanded.

"I'll find out. What do you want one for?"

He explained briefly. "We'll have to get rid of—whatever it was—before we dare risk the rescue crews coming in."

"Magwareet," she said sharply. "You aren't thinking of going after it yourself?"

"Artesha, of course I am. Since we lack any accurate data, there will have to be a Coordinator directing the search." He tried to deny to himself that his real reason was a desire for action in which he personally would partake, and of which, if he survived, he might see the result.

Artesha went on arguing against it, but there was a sigh from the circle of engineers, and in the silence when she stopped speaking for a moment, a heavy scratching sound came to them. They grew even more alert, waited, poised for action. Inassul moved to the gap torn in the wall, sent a camera through it, studied the display. Excitedly, he beckoned.

"We won't have to go in search of it, Artesha," countered Magwareet softly. "It's coming to look for us...."

They drew back, weapons in their hands. The tension grew intolerable, and then the scratching sound changed—was *here!*

Something gigantic and powerful, as terrifying as an enraged Tyrannosaurus rex, smashed down the wall at a different point, bringing the panels of the roof falling in a welter of plastic and a tangle of wiring. A man screamed, and sprawled with his scalp cut across. They had a glimpse of a five-limbed creature slate-blue and glistening. Then a human weapon hissed, and a bolt of energy seared the edge of the gap.

As they flinched from the brilliance, a stench filled the air like something rotting. The alien animal tossed in agony. It turned, and crashed away through a nearby building.

"I got it," yelled the man who had fired. Magwareet snapped into action.

"Got it be damned! Now it's hurt, and gone wild! We must go after it before it does more damage. Inassul, tell Center what's happened, and the rest of you follow me."

They went after it at a dead run.

What kind of beast is this? Magwareet asked himself. It was gigantic, and incredibly strong. Had it been picked up when the builders rooted out the city's foundations, lain dormant until driven crazy by the strain of the interstellar drive?

"It's probably heading for home," he shouted to encourage his companions. "It won't be far now."

"We passed a park where the ground had been torn up," panted someone alongside him. "We assumed something had been installed there. I think it might have come from underground."

"They wouldn't have brought a thing like that in the zoo," Magwareet yelled in answer. "Far from here?"

"Another half-kilometer," the man told him.

And in minutes they found themselves on the outskirts of an open space, where stacks of supplies that might be useful here in the Solar System had been piled. The track of the beast through them was twenty feet wide.

There, in a patch of broken trees, they found a burrow that slanted downwards steeply, toward the outer shell; the soil around it was freshly turned. From its mouth the stench of putrefaction poured like steam.

"Find out if the park is walled off below the surface," Magwareet rapped, and a woman broke away to check. The chances were good that the park was a miniature ecological unit, set in a basin of reinforced shell material, but there was no telling whether the beast might not be strong enough to break through.

Shortly, the woman returned and reported that though there was a subsoil barrier, it extended only as far as the heavy bed of clay a couple of hundred feet under them. Fortunately, she had passed a stack of subsonic detectors on her way, and had brought back one of the instruments.

Handling it with skill, she turned around to let the stream of pulses from its generator filter into the ground. In an astonished tone, she said, "The ground's riddled with tunnels! Look here—you can see them showing up when the sound bounces off the walls. This hole leads into a maze."

Magwareet weighed the chances of finding the beast in its warren against the risk of having it recover and break out to wreak fresh havoc. There was only one possible decision.

"Disperse throughout the park," he told his crew, hoping that the beast would not burrow up and come out somewhere else—but it was stupid to think of guarding the whole city with the few men and women he had. "But I want a volunteer to come down with me and see if we can find the thing."

There were shouts, and several people stepped forward grimly, but Magwareet chose the woman who'd had the intelligence to realize a subsonic detector would be of use. He asked her name.

"Engineer generalist Tifara Cassiopeia," she told him.

"Well, Tifara, this is a damn fool thing to do—but it has to be done. If we flush the beast," he added, looking around, "and it breaks out again, kill it. Immediately! And let me know as quickly as possible. All right, Tifara—let's go."

They stepped over the edge of the huge burrow and began to make their way gingerly down.

The going was difficult, and the stench overpowering. After a little way, Magwareet closed the helmet of his spacesuit and breathed his canned air to escape it.

"I think the beast must be bleeding," said Tifara after a while. "Look—the ground is smeared with something slimy. That's why it's slippery."

Magwareet nodded. "That'll weaken it. I hope it hasn't gone too far.... This must be its only burrow to the surface. I expect it was driven by fear when the interstellar drive started up."

They were twenty-odd meters below the surface when they came to the first fork in the passage. Signs of the slimy ichor the creature was losing were limited to one of the two tunnels.

"It's bleeding less heavily," said Magwareet, as they followed the trail. "I only hope it doesn't stop altogether."

But the trail thinned and grew more scattered, until sometimes they had to go five or ten meters before coming across another drop. When the way forked again, they had seen no ichor for some distance.

Flashing his light down each passage in turn, Magwareet could make out no obvious hint of which to choose. "Go a few meters along that one," he told Tifara. "If you find any spoor, come back at once. I'll try this way."

She nodded, and went out of sight. Magwareet stepped boldly forward, and discovered that after ten yards his branch of the tunnel bent sharply. The roof got lower, too, and then dropped abruptly to meet the floor.

Puzzled, he flashed his light up and down, wondering at the dead end.

Stones and earth rattled about his ears. He flinched and turned to run, fearing a cave-in.

For an instant he knew pure, paralyzing fear. There was no longer a tunnel before him. Instead, a flat slate-blue surface glistened wetly in the light of his lamp.

Like it or not, he had found the beast.

But it did not move again, and when he swung his lamp over it, he saw a gash in one of its thick, flexible limbs where the earlier shot had struck home. It had simply fallen in the tunnel, and writhed with its last strength to cut off his exit.

There was a simple way out, at least. He felt for the weapon at his side and turned the power control over to maximum, preparatory to cutting a hole through its body. If its locomotion resembled the gait of most Terrestrial surface creatures, he was facing its belly. Soil was smeared thickly over most of its skin, explaining why Magwareet had not noticed at once what it was.

A cry came from the far side of the motionless animal. "Magwareet! Are you there?"

"I'm here," Magwareet shouted back. "Stand clear, Tifara—I may have to burn a way through."

"Is it dead?"

"It soon will be if it isn't," Magwareet was grim. It was not until the words were uttered that he realized the voice he'd heard was not Tifara's. Faint, excited words filtered through to him.

Then someone cried in a passionate tone, "Don't shoot, Magwareet! Don't shoot."

"What?"

"Don't shoot," the speaker insisted. "This isn't an animal from 129 Lyrae."

"Who are you?"

"Qepthin! I'm a biologist. Somebody sent for me. This isn't from 129 Lyrae, don't you understand?"

"What's that got to do with it? Am I to stay here forever?"

"We'll get you out in a moment, coordinator," came the faint reply. Then there was buzzing in which he could hear no meaning. Fuming, Magwareet paced the little area he had, wondering what was going on. After half an hour, his patience could hold out no longer.

He walked rapidly to the beast's body and was filling his lungs to yell at the people he could still hear moving beyond, when he noticed something that changed his entire evaluation.

What he had taken for a chitinous carapace on the animal was torn around the great wound in its limb, and in the lamplight he could see the shiny gleam of metal.

Astonished, he rapped tentatively on the slate-blue surface, It sounded hollow at several places. A fantastic suspicion filled his mind.

Rasping and scraping broke in on his thoughts, and over the prone body of the beast a power shovel tore away the roof of the tunnel. As soon as the gap was wide enough for Magwareet to pass, the operator withdrew to let him scramble through.

On the far side he found Inassul, Tifara, and a small man with excited eyes who he knew must be Qepthin, with a group of other people, all violently agitated.

"Glad you're safe," said Tifara. "Magwareet, you've no idea what's happened! This is incredible."

Qepthin broke in. "As soon as I realized this animal wasn't Lyran, I had all work stopped. But I didn't suspect what we would discover. It's alive, too, as far as we can tell—at least, it has a circulatory system of some kind and that's still active. But we never suspected—"

"That this damned thing is wearing a spacesuit?" said Magwareet in a deflating tone, an extreme contrast to Qepthin's enthusiasm. "And therefore is probably the first living specimen of the Enemy to enter the Solar System?"

"Well—yes," said Qepthin, disappointed. "But isn't it wonderful?"

"No. It's terrifying. If one could get in this way, why not others? Are our defenses no good? Are we going to find millions of these things suddenly among us?" Magwareet felt sweat break out all over him.

Then his communicator came on, and he heard Artesha's voice. "Magwareet! They've found Burma—she made it back."

"I'm so glad," said Magwareet sincerely. Poor Artesha, he thought, she must have suffered hell for a while.

— ∞ —

58

## CHAPTER XIII

# 4070: Red and Chantal

*In the middle of the eighteenth century the foundations of Lisbon fell apart, and with them the foundations of absolutist religion.*

*In April 1906 the same thing happened to the city of San Francisco. Some people said it was just that a badman called Stackolee pulled all the waterpipes loose; more logically, it seemed that a lump of the world had vanished from below. Nobody could say where it went.*

*In 1908 something gigantic fell in Tunguska, Siberia, flattening some 800 square miles of forest. Long, long before, something vastly larger had fallen in what would be known, 66 million years later, as Mexico's Yucatán Peninsula, slaying most of the living creatures on Earth and opening the way for intelligence.*

*Of course, there was no reason to connect these things....*

Center to all units, triple red emergency: *New peaks developing (twenty-one dates further back in history than ever before).*

After the first few minutes, the journey took on the air of a sort of challenge to Red. He had not attempted such a walk since he lost his leg. At that time, he had counted it a triumph to be able to walk on a level street and appear only to have a sprained ankle. But this was different.

The heat made sweat crawl in rivulets out of his hair, and the coarse dry sand found its way into his shoes until his good foot felt as if the sole was being scraped with hot needles. The glare blinded him, the dust choked him, the irregular rocky surface made him lose his footing. But he got up again, cursing, and carried on.

Then the socket of his prosthetic limb started to chafe, and grew unbearable. After nearly a mile, he stopped to take it off and line it with his handkerchief, but the relief that it gave lasted only a short distance, and he set his jaw against the agony.

It felt like an eternity before he stood up on a rocky outcrop and looked down across a valley alive with workers.

There was a—building? Not quite. It had a naked appearance, as though it were all functional and purposive, without decorative cover. About it, huge shining machines went very quietly about their business, and men and women in coveralls like Burma's, seeming not to mind the heat and light, attended to them. Perhaps the coveralls were, somehow, air-conditioned.

Staggering, he started to descend the slope, shouting.

His call attracted attention at once. Two workers not far away broke off and answered in the same incomprehensible language Burma had used in delirium.

"Help!" Red called. "Here. Come here!"

After momentary hesitation, one of them did. Approaching, he studied Red's clothes with astonishment, waiting.

"Do you speak English?" Red demanded. The man nodded.

"Little," he said. "You—from somewhere else?"

"I'm from 1957," said Red, feeling suddenly worn out.

"You un'erstan' time move?" the man said in astonishment. "You know how?"

"Two miles back that way there's a person called Burma. She says she's one of your people. She brought me here. She's ill. She wants help."

The other shook his head in dismay. By this time, they had attracted more notice, and to the accompaniment of a faint hum an aircraft nothing like a military helicopter, hovering above the valley, turned towards where they stood. Its pilot, though, seemed to see something while dropping, and hesitated fifty feet up before bringing the craft swiftly to earth.

A door slid back and a stout woman got out. She sang two short sentences at Red's guide, received an answer, and then looked at Red.

"You know you're not in your own time," she said in English that was fluent but badly accented. "How?"

Red sat down on a rock at hand and waved back the way he had come. "Ask a woman called Burma. She knows all the answers. You'll find her two miles back there. As far as I can make out, her radio isn't working or she'd be nattering to you herself."

The woman nodded, spoke again in her own language, and without more ado took her aircraft away in the direction Red indicated. As it rose, Red grew suddenly aware that the man remaining behind had drawn a snub-nosed weapon and was leveling it at him.

"What—" he began, but a spray mist from the muzzle enveloped him, stinging his eyes and nose. He cried out. Before he had time to act on his fury, he saw that the man had turned it on himself also.

"Is to make clean," the man explained haltingly. "You from other time, have other—"

As the man hunted for the word, Red felt the stinging die down, and with it a dozen unnoticed aches and pains, and a mild catarrh that had bothered him for several days. He nodded to show he understood, and wondered what incredible brew of medicaments could be in that fine spray.

"Got any water?" he asked, and pantomimed drinking. The man nodded, and gave him a flask from a pocket in his coverall; the movement stretched the fabric and revealed the outline of a short cylinder lumping the man's side.

Red drank deeply and returned the flask with a word of thanks. After that, he just sat silently, watching the business of the valley go ahead.

The aircraft returned, buzzing quietly and with amazing swiftness overhead, coming to rest on the opposite slope. Red could just make out that two people disembarked—presumably Burma and Chantal—before it came to where he sat.

The stout woman got to the ground and looked Red over with interest. "Burma told me what happened," she said. "We thank you much. Brings important information. Wish you please to come with me."

Tiredly, Red got up. Burma made a promise, he thought. I hope to hell she does something about it soon.

He noticed the woman's eyes on him curiously as he got stiffly through the door into the cabin of the aircraft. It was no larger than that of twentieth-century planes, though he could see no controls except a glowing plate set below the forward windscreen. The woman followed him in.

Without noise or vibration, they rose smoothly and flew across the valley, landed, got out, and crossed a patch of scraped ground to enter a metal building shaped like an enormous coin—a hundred feet across but barely eight high. Inside the entrance, the woman spoke sharply to a waiting man, and the door shut behind them.

A few yards along a softly lit corridor, they came into a room where Chantal sat with a calm-faced young woman beside her. She looked pale and apprehensive, but someone had already dressed the cut on her temple and her hands were covered with some flexible transparent material, protecting the scrapes.

"I am Maelor," said the stout woman, suddenly relaxing. She pronounced it with a drop of a quarter tone on the second syllable. "I know you are called Red because Burma said to me. Please sit, Red, and be comfortable. You limp. Are you hurt?"

Red nodded a little, and the young woman took a box of what must be medical equipment and knelt before him as he sat down in a plump chair. She made to remove the shoe on his metal foot.

Red half-stopped her, and then leant back with a grim expression. What the hell was the use of trying to hide it here and now? This was no concern of his; in a little while they would be away from here, and able to forget it.

The girl's face changed startlingly when she found the prosthetic limb, but she recovered at once and carefully rolled up his trouser leg to remove it. Something soothing went on the stump and quieted the fiery pain.

Red looked across at Chantal. "Are you all right?" he said.

She nodded, and stirred a little. "They have some wonderful things here, Red," she said. "I know that medicine in our time could never have done this for us. It's hard to believe that we've really come two thousand years, but that convinces me."

Red felt startled. He had not seriously questioned the fact himself. He had merely accepted it as something to resent.

He turned to Maelor, still standing nearby. "How soon are you going to send us home?" he said harshly.

Maelor hesitated oddly. "It will take a little effort," she said reluctantly. "Is your leg all right now?"

"Yes thank you. Burma told us that as soon as possible we would be sent home. How soon is that?"

"Perhaps longer than Burma hoped," admitted Maelor reluctantly. Red scented the dullness of obstinacy in her singsong voice, and reached for his prosthesis.

"All right," he said, strapping it on. "I think Chantal and I might like to look around for a bit and enjoy the sun while we're waiting. After all," he continued with bitter irony, "we don't often get a summer holiday in early winter. Coming, Chantal?"

Nodding, she got to her feet and together they started for the door, only to find Maelor in front of it.

"I sorry," said the stout woman. "It impossible at the moment." Then, reading rebellion in Red's eyes, she put her hand on a switch set in the wall. "You wish proof, then. Prepare for a shock, please."

Part of the wall seemed to vanish.

It took Red's eyes a long time to adjust to what he saw. At first he could make out only blackness; then a flash of sunlike brilliance took his point of focus out beyond the window—for that was what it was—and he was abruptly staring into an infinity of stars.

He gasped, and clutched at Chantal, who opened her mouth, said nothing, and turned away.

Red rounded on Maelor standing impassively by. "Where are you taking us?"

"To Center. That is in space. We are not on Earth. I do not know what you know of the universe from your time—"

"Enough," Red told her harshly. "What's all this about?"

"Earth is—not very safe. We are at war, against species from another star. They have often attacked humankind, so we—I think I know how to say it—Earth has been evacuated."

The memory of that gigantic thunderclap and the flash that had drowned the sunlight leapt to Red's mind, and he felt a sudden terrifying awe at the picture of so much power. The fear disgusted him, but he could not lose it; he had to mask it with rage.

"I want to see Burma," he said. The size of the job! Evacuating—how many? Thousands of millions of people? "Bring her here! We want a few explanations. You have no right to drag us away like this—"

Into the middle of a conflict that might crush us....

"Burma is busy," began Maelor, and Red cut her short, raising his voice.

"*Get her here.*"

Maelor gave a little sigh. She pressed the switch that shut out the stars, and Red and Chantal relaxed a little. Then she went out.

"Don't worry," said Red grimly. "I'll soon fix this Burma when she shows up."

He wondered as the minutes passed whether the woman was going to appear after all, but after interminable waiting the door opened again, and Burma stood expressionlessly in the entrance. Red strode forward.

"I dare not spare you more than a few minutes," she told him flatly. "You'll get more benefit out of it if you let me speak."

Red stopped short, his mouth still open as if to speak; Burma continued in the hiatus. "I'm afraid I hadn't realized how big a job it would be to return you to your own period. Listen: when I was hurled back to 1957 I went a thousand years further into the past than anyone has ever been before, to our knowledge. We do not possess the equipment—we do not have the sheer power—to repeat it." She hesitated, as if making a calculation, and finished, "It would take the whole output of the Sun for over a year to achieve it."

Shaken, Red said slowly, "Then—how was it you went back so far?"

"It was not our doing. Maelor will spare the time to make it clear to you."

"Where are we going?" demanded Chantal, and Red tightened his lips.

"It would mean very little to you if I explained. We are going to Center, but Center is all over the Solar System, its monads connected by directed resonance. You will be taken to Artesha."

She turned to Maelor and uttered a brief command in her own language before starting towards the door. "I'm sorry," she said with a hint of a sad smile as she left. "But we are desperately short of time."

"Who is that woman?" said Chantal as soon as she had gone. Maelor frowned.

"It is hard to tell you," she began, and Red cut her short.

"We aren't complete savages."

"I know. Well then, she is expert in putting together knowledge about the thing that moved her far in time. She is chief of anchor teams, trying to stop temporal surges."

64

"And what are they?"

Haltingly, Maelor tried to explain.

Gradually the picture of the age to which they had come built up in their minds, bringing with it a sense of reality and immediacy that frightened them. The immensity of the job!

But afterwards Maelor started to question them in turn, and Red was startled.

"You speak English—it seems common among you," he pointed out. "Don't you have the history of our time?"

"I'm afraid not entirely," said Maelor soberly. "You see, there were wars. Terrible wars."

They thought that over in silence.

"Our language is based on English, though," Maelor went on. "It is compressed, and more complex, but by slowing down and thinking all the time about what to say, most of us can make ourselves understood to you."

"After two thousand years?" said Chantal.

"There has been world-wide communication since only a century after your time. When everyone could hear everyone else speak—even people of the past, recorded—the core language stabilized, aside from fleeting vernacular changes and new words for new technologies. You would have trouble with those."

Chantal pressed. "These wars—"

Maelor shook her head. "How much I can tell you I do not know. I cannot let you know something you could use on your return."

Somehow the prospect of return didn't excite Red quite so much this time. My god, thought. I'm not just in the future, I'm in a *spaceship*. He remembered what Maelor had said, something his mind had refused to accept at face value, but that he now knew in the fibers of his flesh was true: *We are at war, against a species from another star.*

Muscles in his chest tightened. He found it hard to breathe. One thought struck through his adrenalin shock: What possible place was there for him or Chantal in a world like this?

— ∞ —

## CHAPTER XIV

# 4070: Magwareet

Center—speaking to all units: *Emergency. Enemy found to have penetrated defense.*

Tired, dirty and hungry, Magwareet hauled himself out of the lock at the entrance to the city. The rescue teams drew aside to let him pass, without wasting their attention on him—and that was as it should be.

*Now what kind of a mess is the human species in?* he asked himself.

The oxygen salvage vessels suckled up like gigantic leeches and sucked the air out of the diamandoid sheath as soon as the survivors were safe; before Magwareet had finished his report to Artesha they had begun to break the city up for invaluable scrap.

Hanging in space, he watched the job, wondering what Burma would have to say when she got in.

At length they brought up a gigantic bundle of girders from the heart of the city, strapped a drive unit on the tail end and launched it into space. Magwareet thumbed the forward stud on his suit and swung down to face the man making up the package.

"Where's it for?" he said.

The man told him, and Magwareet clamped himself on. "Okay, I'll take it," he said, and without another word his gauntlet jammed the drive control over to full.

Acceleration forcing him against the back of his suit, Magwareet watched the skeleton of the city vanish. He had never flown one of these bundles before, but he had to make the trip and he dared not waste the time it involved.

He cast off from the bundle of girders and left it to circle for days, months, or years, and made the last few kilometers to the nearest part of Center on his suit power.

Exactly where he was, he didn't know. It mattered not at all. Directed resonance mechanics meant every part of Center—distributed across millions of kilometers in thousands of sections—was exactly the same distance from all the others in what was important: time. He stepped through the lock, stripped his vacuum suit off and hung it up, and walked through a door without pausing to wash up.

It led, as it did everywhere, into Artesha's virtual presence. He gave his report. For a few moments, then, he stood under her calm gaze. Then he inquired, "How about this captured Enemy, Artesha?"

"I'll know when Qepthin has his team together. I've had to pull off half a dozen of the top remaining crews on the anchor teams—the chance of finding a weakness in the Enemy is worth risking losing more personnel to a temporal surge. *Just* worth it." Swiftly, Artesha briefed him on the surge that had taken Burma, and the woman and man from the past who had brought her back.

There was a click from the door, and he turned to look at the visitors from the past.

Red did not know what he expected to see when Burma nodded at him to pass through the doorway. A larger room than this, certainly; it was only fifteen feet by twenty, lit with softly glowing panels like the one he had seen in the aircraft back on Earth.

Back on Earth? God!

He thrust that thought out of his mind and watched Burma. Chantal likewise waited, although he could see she had begun to ask something. Burma's attitude had changed subtly, and she walked forward with the air of a lover towards her loved one. There was no one in sight except a tall man in blue whose nose had clearly been fractured at some time and not repaired.

When Burma spoke, though, she was answered not by the man in blue, but by a voice from all around them. Red guessed at a communication link. Radio? Something far superior and more... *futuristic?*

After a moment Burma turned towards them, smiling. "Chantal, Red, I want you to meet friends of mine," she said. "This is Paulo Magwareet, who is a Coordinator—a director of work. He knows as much about you two as I do—we have no time for politesse, I'm afraid. He will be supervising the control of the new temporal project, so you will have much to do together."

The man in sweat-stained blue nodded stiffly, and Red fancied he saw superiority over these barbarians from the past mirrored in the guy's eyes. He said sharply, "Tell him we'd be glad if you'd hurry up."

Magwareet asked a question of Burma in their language. The answer came as an interruption in the same unlocalized voice. Burma nodded, and went on, "And this—is Artesha...."

"What—where?" Red looked around him, but Chantal nodded her understanding.

"Here," said Artesha. "All around you."

"An AI," Chantal said.

"No, not a machine," said Magwareet suddenly in his resonant voice. "Artificial Intelligence devices were strictly forbidden after the Singularity war. Artesha is an installed person, and we have few of those. She was devastatingly injured in an Enemy attack—so badly, that we could not rebuild her body. But because she was very important, we made a record of her mind."

"Ah. An upload. That was not yet possible in my time, but we knew it could be done, in principle."

"We can do that now," Magwareet told her, looking surprised and perhaps impressed at the barbarian's understanding. "But it remains both difficult and morally dubious. Still, Artesha was a key figure in the war effort, and she made her home in Center's web. Now she runs it. *Is* it, in fact."

The possessive pride that was evident in Burma's strong features struck Red forcibly. "And—you, Burma?" he asked with difficulty.

"I'm her wife," said Burma, without a flicker. Red had a shock from that, glancing, without meaning to, at Chantal, but the sexual mores of this society's and Chantal's counted for little compared with the appalling loss Artesha had suffered.

To have lost not a leg, but a body! The thought terrified Red; it had figured in nightmares since he returned from Korea—imagination and nightmare had painted the picture of him losing the rest of his leg, his other leg, his arms: being cased forever in metal, voiceless, unable to die.

"Now," said Artesha levelly, and Burma leaned forward.

"Red, we need more knowledge of your time, at a fine grain of detail that only you can give us."

"Knowledge? What can I possibly tell you that could have any significance now?"

"That remains to be seen, Mr. Hawkins," Artesha said patiently. The impassivity was infuriating.

"All right, here's a little nugget. When Burma and Chantal dropped out of the sky in front of my property, I was watching for something that had never been seen before in the sky."

Burma uttered a single sound, and learned forward even further.

"What was the exact date, sir?"

"October 4, 1957. And what could that mean to you, after two millennia?"

"Sputnik," said the synthesized voice. "The orbiting of humanity's first artificial space device. Burma, could that have been a semiotic trigger for the surge that caught you?"

Red was genuinely rocked. He set his teeth in a grimace. "Yes, Sputnik. The Russians. I didn't see it, though. I was too busy trying to help your...spouse."

"You would not have been able to see it in any case."

"What? Check your memory banks, lady. Hundreds of people were calling the radio to report what they saw."

"That is something we do have on record. It was immensely consequential, humanity's first step into space. But the Sputnik satellite was less than 60 centimeters in diameter—that is, two feet—and could not have been witnessed by naked eyesight. What was seen was not that tiny object but rather the tumbling R-7 core stage which was 26 meters long, and is what was visible as a first magnitude star—"

"All right, all right, you've made your point. You know everything."

"Not everything, Red. That is why we need your help."

"It's no business of mine," Red answered savagely. "I should be two thousand years dead, with my poor dog Ruth—not here, in this crazy world."

"So you won't help us?"

"No." Red felt sweat crawl on his forehead.

*"Not even if we give you back your leg?"*

There was a moment of almost complete silence.

"You—can do—that?" said Red in a strangled voice.

"I do assure you—we can do that," said Burma. "And will, if you wish it."

In a timeless, radiant instant, the agonizing conflict in Red's mind resolved. Blind chance had taken away his leg, but these people, these fellow humans, were going to give it back. As if he saw into Magwareet's mind, he perceived how he was assessed, and justly, by that warrior who had looked for understanding on Red's face and found only bitter suspicion. *This senseless antagonism from the barbarian has to be overcome,* he imagined the warrior thinking. *The woman doctor from the past, Chantal, is shocked and shaken, disoriented, but she is not permanently warped. Red Hawkins' mind plainly bears a deformation as real as his artificial leg.* A sob broke in Red's chest, and he leaned forward, pressing his hands against his belly. Tears covered his cheeks. The six year thorny barrier he had flung up and sustained against humankind smashed apart, and in that dazing moment he was conscious of his oneness with these inhabitants of a future age.

"Yes," he said, leaving the tears to dry on his cheeks. "All right. I'll do whatever I can to help. Thank you."


When Red and Chantal had been taken away, Magwareet remained silent for a time, to let Burma and Artesha talk privately. After they had finished speaking together, he raised his head.

"Artesha, why are these two ancient people so important?"

"I don't really know," said Artesha frankly. "But—I don't think I could explain it even to you, Magwareet. I've been part of Center for years, and I'm so absorbed in it now that I'm able to integrate information on a totally unconscious level. You might say I get hunches, that's all."

Magwareet accepted that. "Burma, I've only heard sketchily from Artesha what happened to your team."

Burma gave a quick summary, ending, "But from back there, Magwareet, the time map looked as if it were on fire! The surge that threw me into 1957 wasn't the furthest back by at least several hundred years. I suspect that there are surges running possibly as far back as the Big Bang."

"What caused the sudden violence of your surge, though?"

"I can't tell you. The only one who might would be Wymarin. Is there any news of him?"

"No," said Artesha after a fractional pause to search her gigantic memory. "What was he doing?"

"I believe it was some of his work that stimulated the Being. Not the destruction of the Enemy raiders. You see what that means?"

"If he can stimulate the Being deliberately, he's half way to controlling it," said Magwareet flatly.

"Exactly. And so we shall have to find him or one of his aides. We haven't a hope of tracing the computer memory he was using to record his data—the temporal surge will have wiped it clean with overlaid energy."

"But how could we find him, if he's been thrown anything like as far back as you were? If he was in a position to operate his time map, he'd be back already. Surely his map is anchored to the same temporal locus as yours?"

"I've been thinking about that," Burma answered. "Beloved, have we any data on co-existence within a temporal surge?"

"No one has ever tried it."

"You mean—could you use the same temporal surge again?" Magwareet suggested and Burma nodded.

Artesha answered slowly, "You could go back with no difficulty to the moment when it struck. Short-range displacement is simple. It would be risky—"

"That's *my* job, Burma," said Magwareet, "and not yours. You're needed here and now with an anchor team. You're a specialist. Agreed, Artesha?"

Artesha did not reply for a second. Then she said with relief, "Agreed. Magwareet, it won't be so risky after all. That surge has four secondary peaks—two at each end. One of them is due to come up in empty space in about sixty hours from now.

Red hardly dared to believe what he had been promised, but he went eagerly with a silent guide through corridors and into a clean, lighted place that could only be a hospital. Here a smiling young woman in blue came to meet them.

"Welcome," she said. "I hear you want absent leg replaced."

That was enough to make it seem real.

"My name is Teula," she told them, "and I must apologize that very few people have been paying attention to both you, despite uniqueness. Nowadays, almost literally no person has spare time at all—the human species has been obliged to organized efforts so thorough."

She expanded the apology with a flashing smile to include Chantal, who seemed to have been brought along merely because everyone associated Red and her in their minds.

"Teula, how long has this war been going on?" she asked.

"Well, first contacts with the Enemy came about seventy years ago, way out on the edges of explored galaxy space, but not develop into a life-and-death struggle until several decades. Back from now, I mean. I can't give you eyewitness details of the earliest years, though—it was before I was born."

"Naturally," Red started to say, and then caught himself. "How old are you, then?"

"Sixty-four." Teula seemed no older than thirty, hardly younger than Chantal. She caught their glances at each other, and said, "Oh, you're surprised by our longevity. That's a by-product of the war. We had to keep our valuable people alive as long as possible, and then we found it was quite as easy to keep everybody alive…. We used to think a life of a hundred and twenty years was enough. I think we're going to get used to living over a millennium, eventually."

All this talking had not prevented her from getting on with her job. She handed Red a pair of shorts, rather than the gown he had expected, and showed him to a changing room with a toilet attached. Minutes after he returned and found a comfortable resting position on the surgical bed, she removed Red's prosthetic leg—with an approving remark about its workmanship—deftly cut away the end of the inflamed stump with a beam of light that did not hurt and apparently froze the blood before it could run free. She fitted a sealed box over the new wound. Into the box ran tubes carrying suspensions of organic material.

Then she slipped his good leg into a long cylinder from which depended many cables.

"You're going to be highly symmetrical," she said. "A computer program will scanalyze your undamaged hoofer and ensure that the replacement is a near mirror image. Take away any scars, however."

"You're cloning his limb?" Chantal ventured. "In my time we were starting to reactivate the genomic code by dedifferentiating tissues at the budding end of the truncated limb and allowing them to regenerate much as they did in the uterus. But that would take years to—"

Teula had shot her a startled glance. "No, we don't abuse that procedure anymore. As you say, it would take far too many. This device—" She broke off and hummed for a moment. "You could call it a compiler. It does draw on the genomic and epigenomic instruction set, but we recast an organ damaged or limb severed in a number of concentric layers."

"Nanotechnology." Chantal said, nodding. "We had the beginnings of that, too."

"Not nano either. We're taught that it proved to be monster too dangerous, so it was extinguished everywhere. But, please now, I must make some lasting adjustments."

"I don't have the faintest idea what you two are talking about," Red said with an edge in his voice.

"Lie still, sire," Teula told him sternly.

"And that is all," she stated, in less than half an hour. "But there is one further thing. You won't get very go unless you catch up on our language. English is all right—"

"You speak it excellently," said Red.

"But I talk too fast, and make the slips—notice? I'm trying to talk at the speed I'm accustomed to. You'll see what I mean when you learn Speech. That's what we generally use." She uttered three fluctuating phrases and added, "That was the whole of what I've just been saying in quarter of time."

A quick step across the room, and she was bringing unrecognizable items from a cabinet. "If you expect the teacher, by a way, or recorded language course, you aren't getting either. We waste no time like that nowadays. Chantal, would you lie down to please?" She indicated a flat soft surface built out from the wall.

Chantal did so. Humming, Teula arranged her gadgets. "Leg should take about eight hours, Red, and this course in Speech about six. I'll wake you up together, though."

"Wake us up? What—" began Red, but with a smile full of mischief. Teula shook her head.

"Go sleep," she said in the odd sing-song way that had enabled Burma to command Red earlier. And they did.

—— ∞ ——

# CHAPTER XV

## 4056: Artesha Enhanced

Floating naked in zero gravity but peppered with communication transducers, and pierced or entubed for nutrition and evacuation, Artesha Wong was fifty-two years old and despite the rejuvenation treatments felt every minute of it. Coordinator General of the Defense of Humanity, enhanced with upgrades both genomic and electronic, she felt as much cyborg as woman, despite her love for Burma and the pleasure they still took in each other's bodies. When they could. On those occasions when they shared the same space. They had no children to concern them and hold them from total dedication to their task, and that was a dull sorrow in her heart.

She yearned for sleep, for dream. Well, there was dreaming of a kind, if never true sleep. Brain modules were switched in and out of service and when possible their tasks were handled by her cyber accoutrements. That was barely tolerable, but did the job of keeping her healthy, alert and functioning in her crucial command role.

Oh, she thought but did not murmur aloud, if only we had a handy AGI to do this for humanity, with all our weaknesses.

She knew better than most, though, the reasons why Artificial Generalized Intelligence was strictly and absolutely forbidden. Humankind had barely escaped the fate of so many alien cultures that recklessly developed supernormal machine intelligence and then stared aghast as it transcended their animal morality and vanished forever after looting the local planetary system. They prudently destroyed their designers' records along with the designers themselves, and anybody else with enough brains to repeat the experiments. Obviously this fate had not doomed the Enemy, which suggested something terrifyingly strange drove those aliens. Some quirk of the mind that deflected them from the path to AGI—unless, indeed, they *were* AGIs, of a self-limiting kind that no human computer analysts could imagine.

Frustrations or not, Artesha blazed at the heart of her electronic and transluminal network like a hot sun. Messages from a dozen or a hundred war fronts slid before her multiplex, machine-boosted attention, and were dealt with almost instantly. From childhood on, Artesha Wong had been recognized for her memory and analytic gifts, nurtured, encouraged, rewarded with love but taught to master, by confronting them, irritations, disappointments, annoying disruptions. When as a young woman she met her beloved Burma Brahmasutra, and introduced her to *Sensei* Lee, she knew her destiny and the way to reach it.

Yet it was hard, and every day and year it grew more onerous, on the edge of the impossible. At some point, she predicted, the pressure would become too great and she would make a slip, miss some critical item of information, forget the chain of argument leading to a correct choice.

And if that happened—or when—the fate of humankind would be fatally compromised.


"You really need to take a break, my dear one."

The command chamber was heavy with the scent of velvety roses, and with the blooms themselves, abundant if only in utterly convincing simulation. Burma had organized this manifestation of her abiding love for Artesha and in gratitude for her immense service to humankind. Lighted message icons in sharp crimson, brilliant blue, the green of a young leaf cast their muted hues, or seemed to, across the banked red and yellow roses, supported on their thorny stems. Cupped by the display like four-armed Saraswati, gold-bedecked goddess of knowledge, her beloved wife was at once triumphant and heartbreaking. Instead of a golden bejeweled crown, she wore a head-set encrusted with resonant data feeds. Beneath the crown, her scalp was shaved to the skin. Tiny monitor lights flickered about her drawn face. Like Burma, she had not slept in years, and despite the best that medical science could contrive she showed an implacable weariness. Burma's eyes were filled with tears. She blinked them away.

"I wish I could hug you, darling," she said. But that was impossible—might as well wrap yourself around a tangle of electric eels, or the inner core of a quantum computer.

"Oh, darling, yes." Artesha's mouth twisted into the ghost of a smile, while most of her remained absent, coordinating the hundred million operations of Center. "Thank you for the flowers. Their fragrance elevates my spirit. And let me tell you it needs some elevating."

"Well, I could recite you a poem."

"Can you devise one on the spot?"

"A simple one, love. A clerihew, maybe? Or better yet, what about a limerick?"

Artesha snorted, and the lights surrounding her head flashed like the insects never permitted in the hygiene of solar space. "It had better be a silly one."

"Always. You know me so well. But I'll have to ask you for a theme. Give me a couple of incongruous words, or you'll be sure I made it up on the way here."

"You would not dare deceive me. Or would you? Oh well, let's see. I'd like to hear a limerick poem about…a horse. A poor old broken down mare. Something I can relate to."

That was simple black humor, but Burma felt her heart squeeze hard. Oh, damnable Enemy!

"What else?"

"Put the brute on the market, she must still be worth something to someone."

"You're being maudlin, my heroine. Very well. Let me think." Burma did just that, and a moment later recited in a sepulchral tone,

> *"I met an old man from Marseilles*
> *Whose horse had a frightening sway.*
> *She was spavined and lame,*

*But the vendor was game,*
*Though his nag couldn't cope with a dray."*

Artesha snorted. "That's cruel. I want something more elevated to offer me comfort. Here, I want a flying horse. Do you think the genetic engineers might make me one, just a little winged mare to fly about in here and keep me company?"

Crushed with guilt and a resurgence of misery, Burma told her, "I'm so sorry, sweetheart. I can try to come here more often, but the logistics—"

"No no no. Please believe me, sweet one, I was not reproaching you. People are dying. I will not hold you from the work you do so well. Except for this one last lingering moment, when you must give me a limerick about a flying horse."

Burma smiled, paused, let her mind cavort with foolishness. Almost immediately, she said,

*"A palomino with fetlocks athwart*
*Was a pal o' mine, whom I once taught*
*To fandango all night*
*And even take flight*
*From the palace's palisades court."*

Artesha roared with laughter.

"Ah, Burma my brilliant one, you are a tonic. Getting all that into a functional language like Speech is a true miracle. I send you kisses."

"And I send you this flying horse."

Burma's own mental links to the display programs built a tiny pure white winged equine and set it free in virtual space to swoop about Artesha's head and shoulders. It settled in a moment into a bouquet of red roses, and began licking its fetlocks like a cat grooming. Again Artesha laughed, richly, and Burma felt some pained hardness in her breast ease and melt away.

The moment of disaster, months later, was no single error, but a frayed thread of time that split and blurred, casting Artesha's sublime mind adrift for just too long.

Causality shuddered, and ruptured. Almost instantly, Artesha understood what was happening, but it was too late to intervene. Quantum effects at the smallest microlevel of reality were multiplying up into the macro-world, events superposed and proliferating so that no single choice could satisfy prediction. It came like a wave, thrusting tranquil water into churning turbulence. Only her magnificently augmented mind knew what was occurring, comprehended the danger. But her capacity to divert the torrent was too meager. If she had caught the rupture at its very creation—

The roilings in spacetime intensified, and abruptly alarms were squalling and shrieking, and her enhanced brain was rapping out replies and advice to the defensive weapons emplacement.

An Enemy raider came through into real space, flung there by the tide of fractured time, and by no plan or strategic design she could have mapped in advance. Nuclear detonations flowered in the darkness beyond her defended redoubt, and dark energy beams smashed against the layers of matter and field forces keeping her protected from the void. From weightlessness to swerving gravity she was flung against the walls. Fire exploded. Messages still poured into her connected brain. The Enemy was gone, blasted into nothingness, but her own station was burning, cracking open. A gale of escaping air. She gasped, tried to find purchase. The pain was excruciating, intolerable. Her flesh was liquefying. Only the machines implanted through her dying flesh remained alert. A medical machine program reserved for last moment desperate measures activated, smothered her body with foam, severed her head, and locked her away into darkness.


"Darling Artesha! Do you hear me?"

It was nothing like awakening from a deep sleep. Her mind had shut down; now it was fully conscious.

"Yes, Burma. Turn the lights on, please."

She heard a choking catch in Burma's voice, and a sort of frightened chill passed through her, and yet it was nothing like a chill, not really. She was relaxed, comfortable, as if sweet breezes blew against her naked back and face. A fragrance of freesia. The lights remained off. Where were the many voices of the defense teams? Ah, there, remote, and her own voice was responding to them, it seemed. Yet it was not her own voice. Or it was, yet she was not speaking. Like a recorded or simulated voice, although it was not that; it was reacting to problems in real time almost exactly as she would herself, she could tell that much.

Oh.

"Am I dead, Burma?"

This portion of her mind—her *recovered* mind? she wondered—detected the lag, the further catch in Burma's chest. "Not dead, my love. But you have suffered a very serious injury."

She knew then, of course. No point in euphemisms.

"I've been uploaded into what remains of the system, haven't I?"

Pause. "Yes."

"So I *am* dead."

"No. The least important parts of you are gone, but your essence remains intact. Never doubt that I love you, Artesha, and always will."

"I know, darling. And where's *Sensei* Lee when you need spiritual comforting and guidance, that's what I want to know."

They both laughed. It was reassuring, to know that you could laugh even when you were dead.

"Burma, am I linked to all my old extensions and augments? The relevant ones, I mean. I seem to hear myself dealing with business as usual."

"A pale shadow of your brilliant self is doing that, Artesha. We hope you will learn to couple to the system and—

"I'm there already, Burma. My essence is back in the control seat. And I can see that the Defense of Humanity urgently needs my full attention. We shall speak again soon."

Burma vanished from her thoughts. She took command again of her Coordinator's post. The mystery of the parallel times needed pressing analysis. She convened a scientific and engineering team to study the matter without delay.

— ∞ —

## CHAPTER XVI

## 4070: Red and Chantal

When Red woke he sensed time having passed, amid the horror of dreams of mutilation, but with no intervening awareness. For a few moments he simply lay still, wondering what had happened in his head. His heart should be pounding, he knew that much, but something was holding it to its regular slow beat. Drugs suffusing his blood and tissues from the machine clamped to the stump of his missing leg?

The strangest aspect, it suddenly struck him, was that after six or perhaps eight hours flat on his back he felt no urgent need to urinate. He sent his hand down. They had not intubated him, or if Teula had she'd already withdrawn the urinary catheter. For a moment he felt his ears warm in embarrassment.

"So you're conscious," said Teula's voice from behind him.

"What the hell did you do to us?" Red asked in a confrontingly rough tone, but was interrupted by a cry from Chantal.

"Red! You're talking Speech."

"What? Oh. So are you." They gazed at each other in amazement for a moment, and then he turned to Teula. "Is it hypnosis?"

"Partly."

"But—no, damn it, you can't teach a language in six hours."

"True. But Speech is developed from English according to certain very inflexible rules. Those grammatical rules have been written into the language centers of your brains so thoroughly that you automatically use Speech. It's similar to the process involved in learning to express yourself as an infant, but much more efficient. A few weeks will be needed for you to acquire a full working vocabulary, just as you needed years to learn how best to combine the symbols of speech and writing. But you can make yourselves understood anywhere from now on. Excuse me—I must notify Magwareet that you're ready to see him."

She left them alone. Turning to Chantal, Red found himself at a loss for words.

"I'm sorry," he said at length. "I was very rude to you, and inconsiderate—"

"I understand why," Chantal answered softly, and it was astonishing how much more complete and precise her meaning was in this new tongue. "How's your leg?"

"Why—why, I—I'd forgotten about it...."The black box and clear tube had been removed. As in a dream, he looked down at a pair of healthy limbs, Delighted, Red swung his *legs*—for the first time since Korea he could think that—to the floor, and walked up and down staring at a pair of living feet. After a moment, Chantal spoke again.

"Red, I was scared for a while. I was afraid of what people might be like in this age. But if they could make you *forget* something that has obsessed you and blinded you for years—just like that—" She gained assurance and spoke up boldly. "I have never dreamed that anyone could be cured so swiftly."

And I *was* ill, thought Red. I was more crippled in my mind than in my body, and I wouldn't admit it.

Now, though, he could confess it to himself without pain, and he was very glad.


"Our visitors must be famished," Artesha's disembodied voice suddenly announced. "I find there is a two hour window of opportunity, so I'm arranging dinner. Please all go, use the facilities, dress, and gather in the wardroom within twenty minutes. Chantal and Red, my staff will assist you both."

Formal dinner? In a spaceship, or whatever this was? In the middle of a war? Red shook his head and found himself grinning. That would work.

A uniformed steward took him to a small cabin, showed him the toilet and shower and how to work them—obvious, on the one hand, yet weirdly unfamiliar, on the other—and told him a machine would compile clothing for him suitable for a formal meal. "Since you are not a member of the crew, sir, you are not required to wear dress uniform." Not *permitted* to do so, Red thought with a smile, He threw his own clothes on the bed, bent automatically to remove the aluminum leg before he remembered with incredulous joy that his leg was now whole, and stepped carefully into a flow of hot water with a faint odor of…what? Eucalyptus? The liquid foamed slightly, was replaced by a sort of mist, and then drafts of warmth. A jangle of bells attended the arrival of his freshly created garments, neatly wrapped in something transparent. So this was the future, where the machines thought of everything.

He rebuked himself, pulling on underwear and slipping into a kind of relaxed midnight black dinner suit with crisp white collarless shirt. It was utterly unfair to consider Artesha a machine, he told himself. Perhaps the best way to think about her situation was that she lived *inside* a machine, a spectacular advanced device that was the two millennia descendant of Univac or one of those other gigantic computers Sperry Rand had developed in his home century. He smiled at that.

The steward was standing patiently outside his door, nodded politely, took the opportunity to straighten Red's jacket, and led him into a larger room with a table covered in crisp white linen, or something that looked like it, bowls of fragrant curries and salads, plates and utensils, goblets, and chairs sufficient for a small party. Magwareet stood in clean new dress whites, chatting with Chantal who wore a long golden skirt and jacket.

Several members of the crew, also dressed formally, looked a little nervous. Red joined them and was poured a crisp wine that cleansed his tongue and palate. He choked slightly on it a moment later, alerted by Chantal's gasp to the arrival of a marvelous sight. Burma entered the room clad in formal white, floor-length gown cinched at the waist by a red cummerbund. Perhaps Burma *was* a princess in this world, Red thought. Certainly she carried herself with as much contained force as any General he'd ever met in Korea or afterward. He noticed then, with a start, the blue-green slash of color in Burma's upbrushed hair, an exact counterpoint to Chantal's.

A burn of jealousy rushed through him, and he did what he could to dismiss it. Neither woman was interested in him in that way, nor were they likely to change for his convenience, and besides, Burma was married. To, he thought with a touch of spite, a machine.

An oboe sounded, and the men in the room straightened. A doorway appeared in the middle of a wall, and another woman stepped through, halting just beyond the threshold. She was not old, but not young either, perhaps, to look at her, ten years or so more than Burma's age. Her deep green command dress was dignified but the very opposite of frumpish. Her silver hair was worn up, and danced with specks of luminous fire.

Magwareet stepped forward and bowed. "Madam, you do us honor." She smiled at him and said nothing. In her silence was authority and power, but no lack of humor. He turned to the time travelers. "Allow me to introduce you formally to our leader, Artesha Wong."

My god, Red thought. She's a mirage, an apparition, a magnificent art work in three dimensions. My hand would pass through her, he told himself. Frozen, he watched Burma cross the room and stand beside her magical wife. When she reached out one hand to Artesha, some marvel of responsive technology matched the illusion to the living woman, and their hands seemed to close warmly upon each other.

"How do you do, Madam Wong," he said, bowing slightly.

"Madam, you look beautiful," Chantal said.

"Let us not stand on ceremony. I am still Artesha, even at table. Come, let's sit."

They took their places, guided unobtrusively by stewards. Without crossing the intervening space, Artesha was suddenly at one end of the table. "Here, sit beside me, Paulo." Magwareet drew out her chair, and the illusion of a living woman seated herself. She gestured to her right; he stood in place while Burma was seated at the other end of the table, Red to her left, Chantal to her right. Not the typical order of courtesy, Red thought, recalling tedious military dinners at which he'd served food and wine to bumptious officers, their guests and occasionally their ladies.

No, enough, he rebuked himself. That was another place and time. These are the customs of a world or worlds as distant from his as the Roman Republic had been from his own birthplace. That echoing insight in turn dazed him. He dipped into a kind of curry, fumbled his cutlery, caught himself (fool! fool! what is *wrong* with you?) and was snared by Teula's eyes. She sent back a friendly grin.

The fellow at his left was a weapons specialist from a distant star system who seemed entirely at a loss with this relic of Earth. Even his miraculous new mastery of Speech failed to provide enough information to Red, including the fine details of etiquette, to allow a fluent conversation. For a start, back in Korea a specialist in weapons would be a non-com, and hence would never have been invited to join this reception. Burma, meanwhile, at his right, was chatting in a lively way to Chantal, who gave every indication of being enchanted. Red bit his lip, and was careful to drink moderately. There had been more than one occasion in the past when this sort of situation had plunged him into a sort of loud oafishness. He shook his head slightly, and looked again at Teula, who sent him a merry wink.

At length they rose and moved into a neighboring lounge, where a kind of Asian music played: reed pipes, by the sound of it, and gongs, and drums, and sweet high-pitched voices. People bowed to one another, offered an arm, women as often as men making the first move. Red edged toward a couch. Teula intercepted him.

"Come, sir, let us try out your fine new leg."

"Sorry," he muttered. "This music is very different from the dance tunes of my time."

"You'll soon get used to it. Here, let me guide you. The steps of the dance are imbedded in your motor centers, sir, along with our language."

Agonized, he stood there as couples moved gracefully about them. He saw Artesha seated, or "seated," in a place of honor, and two women with blue streaks in their hair dancing together and laughing. Chantal had picked up the dance steps with apparent ease, and threw in some arm motions that caused the others to nod and smile as they passed. "I haven't danced in years," Red said defensively. "You...forget."

"Now you can remember again," Teula said, taking his left hand and drawing him to her. He felt a jolt of arousal. "Come now, sir, lean into me. I wish to feel proud of my medical work, and I will show you the way."

Abandoning all hope, Red stepped forward and back, his new limb slightly paralyzed. He saw himself suddenly as one of his own sculptures, metallic and angular, but containing trapped motion, a sort of locked kinesis. With an effort of will he broke the bonds, and began to move more freely, taking the steps his sculpture yearned to take. With a sudden laugh, he adopted the posture of a steel gryphon poised to leap, sejant guardant. And leaped in truth, dancing.

— ∞ —

## CHAPTER XVII

# 4070: Magwareet

Embedded in immense computational spaces, Artesha said. "They've stepped up the power of a map past the safety limit, and it seems that there's been anachronistic exchange between several of the peaks in the far past."

"Dangerous?"

"Probably. Magwareet, get up a team quickly and go look for Wymarin. Burma, take over what you think is the most promising remaining anchor team and try to duplicate Wymarin's work, in case we don't find him."

Burma said sharply, "Are you saying that to keep me out of harm?".

"I love you," Artesha said. Sincerity formed the words. "But I could not do anything I thought was not the best course for the human species."

Burma bowed her head and went out, leaving Magwareet to look thoughtful.

"How about this specimen of the Enemy?" he said. "It worries me—"

"Qepthin is coming up to see us now," Artesha reported, and almost as she spoke the little biologist entered.

"We've got our Enemy alive," he said proudly. "Its metabolism is oxygen-using, fortunately, so it didn't stifle when its spacesuit was punctured. We think we've figured out how it got into the city. Vantchuk has been over the information, and he thinks that the Enemy abandoned its scout, boarded the city through the sheath holding the foundations, and made its way up to the control center to destroy the communication equipment. Unfortunately for it, someone realized what was happening and sent the city deliberately out of control. The Enemy seems to have lost its temper at that, and killed the survivors."

"What did it hope to gain?" asked Magwareet.

"We haven't begun to communicate with it yet. Vantchuk points out, though, that it could instead have turned on the star drive and crashed billions of tons of matter either into the atmosphere of Earth or even, possibly, into the Sun. And that much relativistic mass might—possibly—have triggered a fatal solar flare."

"This presupposes that they're capable of suicide to gain an advantage," Magwareet pointed out. "Artesha, how does that tie in with our theory of their psychology?"

"Doesn't," said Artesha bluntly. "It's either all wrong, or there was another reason for the Enemy's action. As we have it figured, the Enemy is capable of extreme action only out of desperation." She sounded more cheerful.

"And that," Magwareet said, "implies that we are doing them more damage than we believed."

The relief was amazing. He set his shoulders back.

"All right, Artesha. I'll go assemble my team—I'll be taking Red and Chantal, of course—and we'll ride that same temporal surge that Burma was thrown out on. Wymarin must have surfaced at one of the secondary peaks, surely."

"If his time map isn't operating, you're going to have to find him by using only trace instability. Admittedly, it will be strong if he's been thrown more than two thousand years, but there'll be a lot of interference from your instruments, after they've done the same distance."

"If necessary, we'll land and make up fresh ones with native materials," Magwareet answered. "Keep us posted about the Enemy if you can."

"Good luck," said Artesha.


The organization of his project presented Magwareet with little difficulty—except lack of resources. Fresh possibilities came to him even as he was issuing orders.

Essentially, the plan was simple. The recent temporal surges had tended to break—like waves—into two or more branches at either end of their millennium-long sweep. Anything absorbed at either end was transposed by a mechanism no one quite understood to the opposite one. Limited time travel had been one of the first by-products of the study of the Being, but it took tremendous power. They could afford enough to return Magwareet's team to one of the peaks of the temporal surge that had tossed Burma and her team far into the past. They would break out at one of the other earlier peaks.

And it was not so difficult to pick one stranded time-traveler out of Earth's teaming hundreds or thousands of millions, because any matter displaced in time acquired a certain characteristic surplus of resonance energy that could be detected over a range of millions of kilometers. It looked on a time map like a tiny whirlpool.

Of course, the instruments with which this energy was detected would be carrying a similar charge, but it was a peculiar aspect of the temporal surges that they affected organic matter more readily than inorganic, and even human beings more readily than animals. Why was one of the million unanswered problems that had been shelved as less urgent than others.

It would take a while to make the expedition ready, and he would not have to supervise everything. In accordance with the precept that it was a Coordinator's business to know all he could, he went to see what was happening to the imprisoned Enemy.

— ∞ —

## CHAPTER XVIII

### 4070: Enemy

They had placed the alien in what researchers estimated to be ideal interrogation conditions for it, in a large open room somewhere in Center's sprawling complex. Then they had collected every available spare man or woman who might contribute to the effort, and gone ahead studying the captive.

When Magwareet entered, he was shaken to find the result so impressive. It's fantastic how much the human species has learned! he reflected. Surely we don't deserve to go under.

The Enemy was large, he already knew, but stripped of its bulky spacesuit it appeared somehow more impressive. Its five-limbed, pale golden bulk lay on a specially designed support; artificial feeding devices poured hastily synthesized nourishment into its body. People milling about were studying the wound left by the blaster shot and carefully repairing it.

But there were strong bands holding down those five thick limbs.

Magwareet mingled with the crowd and sought out Qepthin to ask about progress.

"It's unwilling to communicate, of course, but we're working on something to relax the higher nervous centers. They're trying hypnosis over there, you notice?"

"How's that possible?" said Magwareet, staring. "You don't know that much about its brain yet, do you?"

"Brain?" Qepthin chuckled. "This thing has a mixture of memory-devices that beats even Regulan life-forms."

"Precisely my point. You might as well try to hypnotize a computer."

"You could, if the computer held a human's consciousness." There was no need for Qepthin to add *Such as Artesha's.* "Hypnosis is only a way of confusing someone's interpretation of external reality. If we can find characteristic rhythms in the Enemy's metabolism, we can heterodyne them. Failing that, we'll just have to synthesize the right kind of printed neuromodulator molecules to make it obey our wishes."

Excusing himself, he hurried off, but his last remark sounded so confident and matter-of-fact that Magwareet stood gazing after him.

—— ∞ ——

## CHAPTER XIX

## 1847: TIME SURGE Kaspar Hauser

The boy was strange. When asked his name, he said something that the English maid thought was "Caspian" but seemed to the master of the house obviously "Kaspar," a good solid German name. As for his parental nomenclature, he could only say in a muffed way

"Hauser! Hauser!" which again the wayward Englisher girl insisted was his attempt to utter the English word "House," or perhaps "Horse." This latter conjecture was corroborated in some measure by the small infantile toy he clutched to his chest, a horse carved rudely from wood.

This former foundling was perhaps, in that year 1828, and in Nuremberg, some sixteen years of age, and plainly retarded. He answered intelligibly to neither German nor English, and certainly showed no familiarity with French or Italian, or such outlandish tongues as Japanese and Mandarin Chinese, when speakers of those languages were presented before him by Mayor Binder. The Mayor took a keen interest in this case, which he found inexplicable.

"See here," Binder would tell the police authorities, "he has a document alleging to represent the wishes of his father, a cavalryman of the sixth regiment in Bavaria, now passed away, and indeed the youth will chant in Old Bavarian the words 'I wish to become a cavalryman, like my father.' Plainly he has been taught this by rote. Yet he is frightened when he is shown my own steed, and hides his face in Nanny's skirts, holding out all five fingers of his left hand, spread wide. 'Horse, horse,' he whimpers, but not 'Pferd' in good German, keeping the hand far from his shielded eyes."

Hauser was confined for two months in Luginsland Tower, for his own protection, under the care of a jailer named Andreas Hitler, or perhaps Hiltel. He had suffered shock, and even malign treatment at the hands of a brutal disciplinarian, but here is the strangest aspect of this strange boy: while seeming to possess a gravely impaired intellect (he sang to himself in a language a little like Chinese, which is why those Oriental worthies were introduced to him), he began to acquire the elements of German quickly, but had nothing but absurd lies and foolishness to report.

He claimed, for example, to have been held captive from earliest childhood in a dark box or container, fed each day on rye bread and water only—a palpable untruth, since he showed no sign of malnutrition nor the other bodily disorders typical of those long incarcerated away from healthy sunlight. From time to time, he claimed, a nasty taste in the day's water was followed by unconsciousness, and he awoke next day to find his hair and nails trimmed, his body washed and his bedding replaced.

After he had been released, a philosophical school master, Herr Friedrich Daumer, took charge of his case, employing magnetic healing which somewhat distressed the lad, as if his body contained an equal and opposite magnetic force. He later fell victim to stabbings and a bullet wound, possibly self-inflicted. Certainly he was often in an agony of dispossession, even after his case and care were seconded to the Baron von Tucher, and subsequently the British Lord Stanhope. Yet his absurd tales and pretensions irked everyone. A Frau Biberback was outspoken, condemning his "horrendous mendacity," his "art of dissimulation," and in general what she asserted were his spite and vanity, as if he supposed himself the heir to some distant and far superior realm.

Throughout all of this, he retained his terror of the horses with five legs, while clutching his toy as a kind of amulet warding off that hallucinatory horror.

After the death of another patron, Anselm von Feuerbach, Hauser soon died from wounds on December 17, 1833, leaving behind a handwritten note, perhaps in code, and certainly in reverse or mirror writing, that has never been satisfactorily deciphered. Perhaps it related to the mystery of the dreadful headless horses with five great legs, as if they were not *Equus ferus caballus* (it seemed from the drawings he made obsessively) but a species of starfish. Certainly that is compatible with his absurd claim to be "from the stars" and "lost in the seas of time."

We hope to be informed of any further mysterious events and personages of this kind, although we doubt that such a disturbing wonder will occur again in our lifetime.

—— ∞ ——

## CHAPTER XX

## 1872: TIME SURGE *Mary Celeste*

*There was a ship. She was found silent and abandoned in mid-ocean—fires burning, tables laid, but crewless and adrift. Her name was the* Mary Celeste.

Heavy seas had rocked the newly refitted brigantine the day before, and winds had shaken the sails and rigging at 35 knots, but waters were calmer today. Captain Benjamin Spooner Briggs made his log entry at two bells in the pale morning light of November 25, 1872. In the recently expanded master's quarters, his wife Sarah slept beside little Sophia Matilda, less troubled now by the constant pitch and roll of the ship after two weeks voyage from New York. He was mostly satisfied, now that they were within sight of Santa Maria island in the Azores. He made a final note of the coal dust slurry, remnants of their previous cargo, that clogged one of the bilge pumps. The German boys were working even now to clean the disassembled equipment, eager to clean out sea water flung by the storm into his vessel's hold. It was unlikely to be a threatening quantity, although the heavily packed goods below—all 1709 barrels of industrial grain alcohol—made it hard to be certain how much damage had been done.

"Breakfast will be ready in thirty minutes, sir," reported Eddie Head, his steward.

"I'll rouse my good lady and the child, they did not have an easy night of it. We shall break our fast in my cabin at that time. Send Mr. Richardson to me, if you would."

His First Officer was a reliable fellow; they had sailed together before. Albert Richardson entered and reported that the wind was quickening again. "Sir, I have reason to suspect that the chronometer is slow, so it has been giving us faulty readings."

"May God help us, then," the captain said, heart sinking. If the calculations were seriously astray, they might be a hundred or more miles off course. By the steady light of the oil lamp in the binnacle he checked the reading of the compass. "Albert, if that fresh gale returns we must be ready." He raised one hand. "I fear we'll need the yawl."

Briggs was a sober man of thirty-seven years, master now of this sturdy brigantine ("Mr. Briggs of the brig, may he never be thrown in the brig," Sarah had said with a laugh). He was father to two bright children, and wished that he might have brought with them as well as his seven-year-old son Arthur, who had remained at home with his grandmother to continue his schooling. Overhead, he heard thudding as the yawl, lashed to the main hatch, was cut free with an axe.

"Daddy, Daddy," cried little Sophia, and flung herself into his arms. The sound of the yawl must have woken his family. He kissed her locks, and placed one hand reassuringly on his wife's waist.

Albert Richardson, the first mate, went down to the mess where a cheery fire had been laid in the brazier and the steward had set out bowls and spoons—but there was not yet the encouraging odor of hot food from the galley. In a gabble of friendly German, the four Frisian general seamen came into the mess, hands newly washed after their exertions with the bilge pump and the lifeboat. He nodded to them. "Volkert, Boz," the Lorensen brothers, "Arian, Gottlieb," young Martens and Goodschaard.

"Sir," said Volkert Lorensen in his accented English, "the pump should be ready for service by 1600 hours—"

And an unpleasant blurring interfered with his eyes, a rumble as of great sudden winds in his ears, and his stomach made as if to heave. Richardson lurched, grabbed with one hand at the edge of the table. He retained sufficient presence of mind to note the pale and horrified faces of the other crew members. It was a wind but, impossibly, nothing stirred. The brig seemed to pitch sharply from bow to stern and yet the sea remained calm. The very world seemed torn asunder, or rather one stable marine landscape was overlain by a monstrous upheaval of silent storming ocean. Impossible! Terrifying! Was this, then, the coming of the Last Days, prophesied in the Good Book?

"Mr. Richardson," he heard Briggs cry, "to the yawl!" Richardson tried to compose himself, ran up the steps of the companionway and saw the captain tuck Sophia firmly under one arm and hoist Mrs. Briggs unceremoniously to her feet, hauling them to the weather deck. The crewmen, one weeping in uncanny fear, winched the yawl over the starboard side to the surface of the light swell. Part of the railing had been axed away to facilitate this hasty launching. "Quick, bring supplies," Richardson called. "And weapons."

"My harmonium," cried Sarah, but of course it had to be abandoned. The men scurried away.

It felt to Briggs as if they were under attack by Lucifer and his invisible demonic angels, for there was no sign of an earthly enemy. Yet he was determined to confront whatever awaited them. Gilling and the steward returned with sacks of salt beef and hard tack. Richardson brought a gun apiece for the captain, himself and the second mate, a sword, an axe. They clambered down into the lifeboat, Briggs last of all, cluttered with the tools of his trade: chronometer, sextant, the ship's papers and compass. "Mr. First," he called, "do you have the log?" Briggs felt his heart clench, and his bowels, as another wave of double vision and impossible echoes tormented his senses and the very balance of his mind.

"I'm sorry, sir, no time. What is happening? Oh, saints preserve us, this is the devil's own weather."

The boat broke free of the brigantine tow rope.

In that instant, Briggs and his party were flung not into the brig—his wife's gentle whimsy—but into the very world's most ancient history. He cried out piously to the mercy of Christ and—

—the boat slammed down hard, with a loud splash and howls from its crew, into shallow water freckled with brown and yellow plant life. Strange birds flung themselves up from the water in a typhoon of wings, screeching.

The sea was gone.

Briggs stared about him wildly. A hundred yards distant, at the edge of the swamp, conifers towered. Between their branches hot sunlight struck. Animals of some arboreal variety barked and screamed in the conical trees and in the matted brush. It was all utterly impossible.

I have been struck on the head, Briggs told himself woozily. This is an hallucination. He had rarely taken drink, but from the ample reports of seamen he knew that this kind of demented vision came commonly at the end of a week-long bender. Yet his head did not ache. He thrust these useless lucubrations aside and turned to his family. Sarah had not fainted. She held his daughter to her sturdy breast, and looked about her with a determined mien. The men were in worse shape. One cried, "Is this *Hölle*?" Hell, the German plainly meant. Another, slightly more robust, said, "No, but not *Himmel*, neither, nor anywhere in our world."

"Sir," said Richardson, "I fear this boat is holed. That was an almighty drop into the swamp beneath us. Begging your pardon."

"Men, all out. Now!" Briggs barked. "Remain seated, Mrs. Briggs," he told his wife, "and see to little Sophia Matilda. Look to the perishables also, if you would be so kind." The yawl was a large, heavy boat, and it seemed the keel was jammed into the muck beneath the shallow water. Heedless of boots and trousers, his crew clambered into the mild water and dragged the boat toward the nearest shore.

Later, rain fell and was not very cold, but it drenched them and put out the small fire Richardson had raised with the flint providentially preserved in a deep pocket of his breeks. Discovery of the flint was met with cries of delight, followed at once by laments as each man admitted leaving his pipe and fixings beside his bed as they made their escape. If escape it was—how did the good ship fare, in their absence? That had been no ordinary storm or seaquake, they muttered among themselves as they built two hasty tents with the canvas of the yawl's main and mizzen sails. Mrs. Briggs turned away the steward to more masculine tasks such as gathering unwetted branches, and when the rain ceased she boiled up a soup in their single pot. Crew and passengers watched it anxiously as it cooled enough to take a gulp or two each from the pot, and voted hers the best soup they had ever tasted.

When night fell, and the sky cleared, their moans of terror rose into the sky where the stars were jumbled into meaningless patterns.

"God has shaken them like a million dice and flung them anew into the sky," said one of the German boys.

"Belay that blasphemy," Briggs said. But he wondered as he drew out his glass. Venus he found quickly, burning with rarest clarity in this pure air. And Jupiter, yes, near the dark horizon. All the rest of the heavens were scattered.

"Perhaps we have slept, somehow," he muttered in a speculative tone, "and awoken deep into the future. I have read that the stars wander over the eons."

"Or sir, another dreadful proposition," said Gilling, "if I may have your permission to voice it?"

"Very well, speak up, man, We seem to me to be truly lost, more than any man ever before in history."

"Earlier than history is my conjecture, sir, and ladies." He gave the child a nod, and her mother. "What if we have been purloined into the Garden of Eden before Adam and Eve? Or stranger still, after their expulsion?"

"Back to blasphemy again, then," Briggs said curtly. "We have certainly been cast ashore here for some divine purpose. I do not yet perceive what it might be, but I shall. Enough. We must now sleep as best we may, and tomorrow begin the work of finding other men, or, if they are not to be found, of gathering wild food and then building ourselves a number of sturdy huts."


Briggs nervously awaited, for the interval of several months, the arrival of natives armed with spears or worse, or perhaps plantation owners, or even rescue from the sea. But here was no sea, only swamp and strange animals.

Nobody ever came.

—— ∞ ——

## CHAPTER XXI

## 54 million BCE: *Mary Celeste*

*It is our expression that nothing can attempt to be, except by attempting to exclude something else: that that which is commonly called "being" is a state that is wrought more or less definitely proportionately to the appearance of positive difference between that which is included and that which is excluded.*

### *Charles Fort,* The Book of the Damned

The day after her thirteenth birthday (marked on the captain's meticulous calendar carved daily on the trunk of a broad tree), Sophia Matilda Briggs was attacked by one of the Germans. He stripped open her skirt of fronds, dragged down the undergarment stitched and restitched by her mother and herself from several of the men's undershirts, and attempted to mount her. Feet trapped by the threadbare cloth at her ankles, she twisted and dealt him a most satisfactory knee to the testicles, and a hard smack in the ear for good measure, pulled free, then ran quickly to the security of her parents.

Of all the company she was best-suited to this uninhabited landscape none of them understood. Smoke rose from the firepit, blown toward the swamp by a light breeze. Her father, in clothing even more tattered than hers, rose from the tangled net of vines he was trying yet again to use to trawl for uncouth but barely edible sea life. He tore off his brutally worn jacket and wrapped it around her waist, sunburned face darkened further by his rage, shouting for the other men. He bundled his daughter into the spare arm of his nursing wife, and ran with them toward the path from which she had emerged.

Within minutes, there were cries, a barrage of dull thuds, terrible screams, and then silence. After a time the men returned to the cabins, their hands covered in blood. One of the Germans was not with them. Eyes wide, Matilda shrieked, "O dear Lord, have you killed him? Have you killed him?"

Only her father could meet her eyes. He nodded.

"O father, this was wrong. I had dealt with the matter. He would not have troubled me again."

"Daughter, go to your cabin. These are lifeboat rules, and I will not have such vile affronts from any of us. There is only one penalty."

"Sir, that is not lifeboat rules." She had learned those rules from childhood, at her father's knee. "You are the captain, sir, and should have brought him back and put him on trial, and if he was found guilty you would have hanged him."

"Go to your cabin, I say. You also, men, to your quarters after you have cleaned yourselves." He stared from one of the men to the next, and with shame and guilt they nodded, and turned away.

Sophia Matilda wept, and went without another word to the wooden cabin where her father had used his axe and knife to carve above the entrance the name of their pitiful, doomed village.


A month later, Matilda pressed through the primitive Paleocene forest she did not know would be given that appellation fifty-four million years in her future. She was alone, despite her father's ruling that she must go nowhere without first gaining his permission and the protective company of second mate Gilling, a serious man of some forty years. Matilda had shaken him off her trail, and went forward now, as always, with joy in her heart at the beauty of everything she saw.

A flash of color caught her eye. At first she took it for a scarlet leaf trapped in the heavy spider's web stretched between branches. It moved, then, flapping, but there was no breeze today. Curious, delighted by the vivid wings, she approached the butterfly. Her father had told her that name, and the word *Lepidoptera*, but she had never seen nor tasted butter, unless it was when she was too young to remember it. The poor creature was restrained by sticky strands. A huge black and gold spider sat out of the sunlight, strumming a link of the web. As Sophia Matilda stood quietly, it began to move toward the lovely creature.

"Oh no you do not," muttered Matilda, and picked up a slender fallen branch. Taking care not to damage the web, she eased the trapped butterfly away from captivity, and let it settle on the back on her hand. After a moment it stirred, opened its radiant wings, and lofted into the air. And was gone.

Sophia Matilda was glad. She had no way of knowing the consequences of her act: the mutated gene nestled deep in every cell of the insect, the offspring it would produce, the slow but relentless swerve they would introduce into their species. The amplified consequences, flowing outward into eternity, of this one simple act of kindness.

Her baby brother was the last of them. All the crew grew old, finally, or injured themselves fatally, and were buried one by one in the plot of land which held first the would-be rapist and then all the others. Within forty years Sophia Matilda followed her parents and the male crew into the ground, into a shallow grave she had dug for herself. Sarah's only other surviving baby, little Rollie, had grown to sturdy manhood as Roland. He knew even less of the past and future than his sister, and in his turn lay down in a bed of leaves to die. What purpose a grave, he thought dismissively. There will be no others in this world to mourn my passing. He heard a distant sound of thunder, and light cool rain began to fall on his bearded face as he watched the scarlet creatures flocking in the air, and turned his gaze for one final glimpse of the sign he could not read, yet knew by heart, carved by his stern, beloved father before Roland was born: the name of their lost ship and heroic settlement:

MARY CELESTE

—— ∞ ——

## CHAPTER XXII

### 4070: Magwareet

Ezekiel, prophet of the Most High among the people of Israel: *Under the firmament were their wings straight…every one had two, which covered on this side, and every one had two, which covered on that side, their bodies. And when they went, I heard the noise, of their wings, like the noise of great waters.*

Commander of an Italian air force squadron, North Africa, 1941: *Four Savoia-Marchetti biplanes failed to return from reconnaissance flight....*

A panel slid back, and Magwareet appeared in the gap. He looked tired, but there was confidence in his bearing.

"I saw that your new leg was doing sterling service at the after-dinner dancing, Red," he said. "Congratulations! You, too, Chantal. You're both fitting in here quite nicely."

"Thank you. Are you taking us somewhere now?"

"To the observation room. I don't know if you've been told, but you're already aboard the ship that is taking us back to your time." Chantal blinked, and he chuckled. "No, we are not going to return you summarily! You are going to be useful, both of you." He beckoned, and they followed him from the room.

"We're headed for the nearest peak of the same temporal surge that threw Burma into your time," Magwareet explained as they went along. "There was a man working with the same team—called Wymarin—who had achieved the best results so far on understanding the nature of the Being. We've got to look for him. It may be futile, but it's a chance, at least."

They came into the observation room. It was small, but it had a view onto infinity.

This time, they could enjoy looking at the stars.

There was only one other person in the room—a youthful man before a group of lighted control panels. Magwareet presented him as Arafan, their pilot.

And at the same instant an amplified sound source came to frantic life.

"Magwareet! Magwareet! Artesha here! There's an Enemy raider—a big one—heading for you at top speed."

Magwareet hardly changed externally, but his relaxed attitude tensed indefinably. There was a short pause.

"I see him now," he answered. There was nothing but a smear of red on the illuminated plate he was staring at. "Arafan, what's his course like?"

"If he carries on as he is," the pilot reported unemotionally, "he'll sink right into this end of the temporal surge."

"Artesha, we'll have to get something after him—catch him! We don't dare have an Enemy raider loose in an earlier millennium."

"Agreed." Artesha's voice was inhumanly level. "Magwareet, step up your generators to maximum. I want as much trace instability as possible on the maps. I'll have a squadron of ships after you as fast as possible."

"Right." Magwareet moved across the room in one easy bound, and his hands began to move like water rippling on a bank of controls. Arafan tensed, watching the monitor.

"There he goes," he said, and touched a control icon.

"Is this the first time anything like this has happened?" Chantal asked, and Magwareet replied without turning.

"Yes. As far as I know, the Enemy has never before struck the end of a temporal surge."

He glanced at Arafan's screen. "Anything following us?"

"Can't tell! We're co-existing with the anchor team Burma was with, now. It'll be impossible to sort out anything else till either we or they drop into normal space again."

"Then there's nothing else we can do," Magwareet said. He turned on his heel and stared at Red and Chantal. "I suppose you want to be told what's happening. Well, somewhere 'behind' us there ought to be enough ships to take that Enemy raider apart. But—it's difficult to make it clear—roughly, things go through a temporal surge in the order they enter it in real time, and original relationships are preserved. I think by your time it had been discovered that there are things called operators—actions that have equal reality with the things they affect. Our relationship with the Enemy is unchanged because the operator that has been applied to us—the temporal surge—acts only *along* the world-line, and not across it."

He shrugged. "So until we return to normal space, we don't know what's happening to us, or the Enemy, or the ships following us. What's worse, there has never been a chase like this before."

"Why can't the ships following do what we did—enter the surge at the same moment as us? You can jump in time—"

"That jump gives a surplus of temporal energy, which is what we use to detect something out of its original time. The more you have, the slower you pass through the surge. The Enemy has none except what it's getting now; we have twenty hours' worth, and we can't tell how much the ships behind us have because we don't know how far they had to jump in time to enter the surge."

"Anchor team's splitting," reported Arafan.

"What?"

"They've hit a sort of eddy! It's tossed some of them back into normal space."

"When the fleet gets here, we'll have to pick up anyone we can." Magwareet looked sour, then brightened. "Maybe Wymarin or one of his staff will be among them."

"We're going to emerge," warned Arafan. "*And there's the Enemy.*"

It was vast beyond imagination. It lay across the Milky Way like a black rod, and it was like no ship Red and Chantal had ever imagined. It was pentagonal in section, and the ends of its long shaft were multifaceted lenses gleaming with cold fire.

"Do you imagine they know where—*when* they are?" Chantal murmured.

Magwareet shot her a glance and spoke dryly. "It took us years to figure out about the Being. If they've solved the problem this soon, they're cleverer than we are."

The Enemy raider rolled, slowly, it seemed. As it turned, something that glinted rushed across the sky—out of control.

"That must be one of the anchor team's ships," said Magwareet.

There was no sign from the Enemy, except that one facet of one jeweled end blazed like a sun, but the racing ship became a Catherine wheel of incandescence and bloomed into a flower of yellow fire.

"If Wymarin was aboard—" said Magwareet, biting his lip. Arafan leaned forward, turning to the viewport as if to confirm what his instruments reported.

"They know *where* they are, at any rate," he said. "Look."

Again the huge ship was turning, this time so that its axis lay along a line that intersected a tiny blue-green disc in the sky. Red realized in sick horror what it must be, even as Chantal uttered the words.

"Red, surely—that's Earth."

A thousand fantasies filled their minds. Were they back in their own time? If so, then they themselves, before they met each other, were walking about on that tiny planet. If the Enemy struck—if it did damage—what would result? Paradox!

Incoherently Red asked the question. Magwareet snapped at Arafan, "Go after them," and wiped his forehead on the back of his hand. "I don't know," he confessed to Red. "We think that our interference with the past is already accounted for, but we have never had outside intrusion before. And there's the fact that we can't detect what happens in the past as the result of a temporal surge until it's peaked in real time."

The minute disc that was Earth grew larger. Magwareet came to a decision. "Arafan, we'll have to decoy them. Why didn't I have this ship armed? Oh, what a mess!"

Red had been wondering why they themselves had not shared the fate of the anchor team's ship. He had his answer in Magwareet's next utterance.

"Are you screening out everything, Arafan?"

The pilot nodded.

"Can you drop the screens so that they catch sight of us and get them back up before they can fire on us?"

"No," said Arafan.

"I suppose not...." Magwareet went to the viewport and leaned against it on his outstretched arms, palms flat. He stared at the Enemy, as if working a complex calculation.

"Arafan, that ship has a blind spot. It's a belt round the middle of the shaft. The facets only radiate normal to their plane surface, don't they? They can't fire on anything subtending an angle smaller than—oh, about nine and a quarter degrees is my guess—to the two ends. Could you get that close?"

"We'd have to creep up," the pilot answered. "I'm not sure our screens would mask the drive energy at short range. Want me to try?"

"We've *got* to try," said Magwareet. "Where are those *ships*?"

Arafan's face was quite composed as he turned the ship. The Enemy grew abruptly larger, until it almost filled the viewport, its faceted ends just touching the edges of the holographic screen. Then he shut off the power, and they began to drift towards the mid-point of the vast pentagonal shaft.

The tension climbed steadily towards the intolerable. Red felt he must scream in another second, or hide his eyes, or—best of all—run. Somewhere. Anywhere.

Chantal, when he stole a look at her, was gazing through the port with fascination, as if hypnotized. Arafan had somehow managed to lose himself in the symbols on his instruments and forget reality, but Magwareet knew he was risking their lives on guesswork, and even though he had been trained for years to guess, and guess right, he still suffered that terrifying fear of being mistaken.

"Arafan," he said softly. The pilot inclined his head. "When I say *now*, drop the screens. Wait a moment. Let them get a good sight of us. Then raise the screens again and head directly outwards."

Arafan's head swung round as if jerked by a rope. "Are you crazy, Magwareet? Straight into the full blast of their armament?"

"Do as I say! All right—now."

And an indefinable mist cleared from the viewport, so that they saw the Enemy apparently close enough to touch.

"They're nearly within range of Earth," Red heard Arafan say in that long moment when they lay naked and defenseless. Magwareet gazed at the broad expanse of metal, thinking of the big, five-limbed creatures inhabiting it.

He grew aware that they had been dangerously long here. "Arafan," he rapped. "Screens up! Head outbound."

The pilot's face had gone completely white. His hand reached out towards a control icon, and remained, shaking like a leaf, inches from it.

"I—I can't do it," he said, with a moan.

Red glanced at the side of the Enemy ship, and saw with blank despair that it had already begun to change position and bring them within the field of fire of its weapons. If that sunlike power struck them when the screens were down—

Magwareet waited the instant necessary to think out and coordinate all his movements. Then he leapt across the room and slammed into the control board, falling on to it as on to a floor, face down. His head struck the screen control, one hand found the power and the other the course director. He was barely in time.

The viewport was suddenly blinding with red light, and a shrill alarm rattled at the edge of hearing. Fatalistically, they waited for disaster. All except Magwareet, who had slumped to the floor with blood crawling down his face.

Arafan recovered slowly and rose to his feet, looking at the injured Magwareet with awe. "I should have known better than to distrust a Coordinator," he said.

Red and Chantal spoke together:

"Why?"

"What's happening?".

"The radiation pressure is pushing us back! There's power equivalent to a small star driving against us. In a moment, we'll be able to start our own engines and get out of harm's way." He dropped back into the pilot's seat.

Sure enough, after another few seconds the red against the port faded and vanished, and the Enemy was no more than a stroke against the stars.

Magwareet stirred and picked himself up. Chantal ran to help him, but he shook his head when she asked if he was badly hurt. He looked meaningfully at Arafan, who bent his head in acknowledgment, and then, wiping blood from the cut on his head, turned to the port.

"Here they come," he said with infinite relief.

Like a checkerboard of multiple suns the ships of Earth sprang into being.

They caught their breath at the sight. There were hundreds of ships, bringing an overwhelming impression of power. It was very comforting. But it seemed the ships had no more than appeared when they returned into nothing.

"What—" began Red.

Again the Enemy had turned, and now it was clear that the blue-green disc aligned with it was really a round planet rolling about the sun. The polyfaceted end of the Enemy craft looked like the eye of an evil insect focused on its prey.

A transient flicker illumined the interior of the eye.

And the defending ships were back. But this time they were like novae erupting, and the Enemy glowed.

It shone like a red-hot wire, except for its ends, which almost instantly began to swing again, but more swiftly, while each of their facets became a piece of a star. One of the novae flared up and winked out.

But the glow whitened.

The lensed ends became uniform masses of intolerable light, and Red noticed with a start that the viewport had darkened until the stars were no longer visible—only the greater-than-sunpower of the fighting ships.

A dozen of the circling attackers passed into nothing, and there was a shift that altered their arrangement. But they had also closed in.

"How come they are destroyed so far away when we took all they could give at close range?" Red wanted to know.

Magwareet answered absently, "We have a lot of delicate equipment on board. The energies in a temporal surge wipe clean the electronic patterns in computer memories unless the insulation is very good indeed. So we're carrying at least ten times as much screening as any of those ships out there."

The circling novae were definitely fewer now. Some twenty or thirty of them must have been seared into nothing by the mighty alien. Their pattern changed again. Red felt Chantal shiver as she stood close to him.

Unexpectedly Magwareet uttered a jubilant cry. "We've got them."

Almost imperceptibly the balance had shifted, and the central shaft of the Enemy ship was now noticeably brighter than its ends. At the same time a bluish tinge crept into the luminescence.

"What do you mean?"

"They're having to switch their available power from attack to defense. Once they do that, it's only a matter of time."

The blue glow spread steadily until it covered even the ends of the Enemy. Blazing, the attackers moved in for the kill.

Finally, the blue light began to shift back down the spectrum, becoming yellower, and at last taking on a hint of red. Finally, it sank beyond the visible, and the remnants of the mighty ship turned into a cloud of dust.

There was complete silence in the room.

"Won't they have seen that back on Earth?" Chantal said eventually, and Magwareet shook his head.

"There was a ship standing by between us and Earth doing nothing but shift radiant energy up the scale and convert it into high energy particles. All Earth will have detected is a slight increase in cosmic rays." He went across the cabin, muttering, "Excuse me."

There was a blank screen set in the wall, with press icons under it. He touched one of them and said, "Commanding officer, please."

The screen lit to show a fat woman in a coverall soaked with sweat until it clung to her like a second skin. She gave Magwareet a wry smile.

"Think I'm the senior surviving officer. That was a hell of a ship, Coordinator. Must be their biggest and latest design."

"It could be. I want you to give a detailed report to Artesha on your return. I also want your ships—when they re-enter the temporal surge—to look out for the other peak we passed shortly before emerging. There's an eddy close to it, and some of the anchor team Burma got lost with have been thrown out into normal space nearby. Check on them and if Wymarin or one of his assistants is among them, let me know. Okay?"

"Agreed," said the fat woman. She gave another wan smile, said, "A hell of a fight!" and disappeared.

"It was indeed," said Magwareet to the air. "I hope I never have a closer call. Well, I wonder what the detector teams have come up with. You might as well come down with me, Red and Chantal."

"There *are* other people on board?" Red said haltingly.

"Eight of them."

"Did they know what was going on?"

"No…. They were studying temporal maps, so they'll have registered the appearance of the Enemy raider and of the fleet, but they don't have details. This way."

The room was directly beneath the pilot's station; its walls were lined with green-glowing time maps. Five women and three men listened quietly as Magwareet recounted the history of the past few minutes, but made no comment. Red remembered that these were people fighting for existence, who had been schooled out of wasting their time.

"Found anything?" Magwareet asked when he had finished.

"Here," said a woman with dark hair, and pointed. "This is anachronistic, but it's an exchange with the close peak where the anchor team was broken up. See?"

"Oho no," said Magwareet slowly, studying the green pattern. "Yes, it's right in this moment, isn't it?"

"Is it bad?" Red said tentatively.

"It may be. It may be very bad. For some reason we can't fathom, anything picked up in a temporal surge is more likely to be organic than inorganic, and most likely to be human. The mass of this one is comparatively small, but diffuse—which means perhaps hundreds of people or animals. And there is a strong indication that one of them is a magician—"

"A *what?*"

"The 21$^{st}$ century has been invaded by a bunch of the most bloodthirsty savages in history—a war party from the 26$^{th}$ century Croceraunian Empire."

— ∞ —

## CHAPTER XXIII

## 26$^{th}$ Century: TIME SURGE Raiders of the Croceraunian Empire

Andrevas, High Priest of the most exoteric circle of magicians around the Imperial Presence in the Croceraunian Empire: *It is not seemly for any magician to appear awed by a perfectly normal miracle.*

Conyul, Astrologer Imperial to the Court of the Croceraunian Empire: (*Incomprehensible*).

Khasnik, commander of the war party, would have been perfectly invisible to anyone in the Dead Place at the foot of the hill. But it was said that there were still people in some of the ruined cities who knew the sorcery of the Old Days, and Khasnik had a powerful re-

107

spect for magic of the kind that had produced the prismatic binocular periscope through which he was surveying the scene. Therefore he kept as much of the rock between him and the Dead Place as possible.

The Fist of Heaven had been merciful here; it had struck not the city itself but the low ground on the other side of the river. Probably the rush of air and the wild-fire had done more damage than the actual blow. Some twenty or twenty-five of the towers were still standing.

A hint of movement at his side disturbed him, and he scowled down at the smooth-faced boy of nineteen who crouched there. Khasnik had not yet figured out exactly what he was going to do to the official who had ensured that he—he, Khasnik, fourteenth in the roster of raider captains of the Croceraunian Empire!—was sent out this time with a freshly graduated magician.

Still, he wore the symbols: there was power in the blue tattoos across his body and arms, and obviously someone thought highly of his ability.

Grudgingly, Khasnik stepped aside and let Vyko get at the eyepiece of the periscope. After a quick look, the boy nodded. "Quiet enough," he said. "My bones don't show any risk in the near future, but—"

"But what?" Khasnik demanded harshly. "There have been too many reports of miracles lately, Vyko! I'm not going into any Dead Places, no matter how nearly intact they may seem, until I'm trebly sure of what I'm doing."

Vyko colored slightly, but he answered boldly enough. "Do you not see this?" he demanded, bunching his right fist and raising it towards Khasnik's face. "Do you not know the mark of the Eyes that See? I tell you, Khasnik, that there is no danger in the immediate future for me or anyone who is with me."

Khasnik grumbled; he had never really liked the fact that it was not the commander of the party but the magician-who-could-see-ahead who made the plans.

"In fact," Vyko said, almost to himself, "*I* have never known the future seem so uneventful."

"Nevertheless, I wish to try it for myself," said Khasnik. "Crellan!"

"Captain?" A man slid down the side of the hill like a ghost.

"Cross the valley and breathe on the Dead Place with the Breath of Terror. That way we shall know if there is anyone with power there."

"Aye, Captain," said Crellan. He didn't look pleased, and Khasnik eyed him sharply.

"Well, what is it?'

"This Dead Place is largely undamaged," said Crellan haltingly. "I have heard that—suppose there are—suppose they strike me with the Fist of Heaven."

"Blasphemy," said Vyko quietly, before Khasnik could reply. "The Fist of Heaven is not at the call of men. I shall require an hour of penance from you at camp-time tonight." Crellan scowled and withdrew. In a few minutes they saw his horse, laden with the generator of the Breath of Terror, slip away into the hills.

There was nothing to do now for a while but wait. Khasnik whispered orders up the hillside, and the party of men relaxed into comfortable positions. Then he found himself a spot and was annoyed when Vyko dropped beside him,

"Sorry about that, Khasnik," said the magician informally. "This stuff is all very well for the men—I had to drive the point home—but it's a nuisance."

Khasnik could never get to enjoy the casual way in which Vyko, a beardless boy, assumed equality with him. He only grunted in reply.


Seeing that the captain was not in a talkative mood, Vyko bent to the periscope and studied the Dead Place.

His heart pounded. This was the first time he had come out as staff magician for a war party, though of course he had made a few trips as a novice. Furthermore, this was the first nearly intact Dead Place he had approached, and he longed to find out what those enigmatic ruins concealed.

Oh, there would be the obvious things, naturally—it was the war party's main purpose to discover and scout the sources of metal, plastic and other materials in such ruins. But Vyko, despite his education, despite his carefully nurtured ability to see the future, still wondered how right the stories were....

These people—of the Dead Places—had angered Heaven, so it was said, and been struck down for their arrogance. Their seed—himself and Crellan and Khasnik and the rest—had been scattered abroad.

But there were books, a few carefully preserved volumes, which hinted at something else. Vyko wanted to find more of those books.

And of course there were the flying things. Vyko had been present at the burning of one of them. It had been huge and silvery, and made a great noise as it came to Earth, but before any sign had come from it, the senior officer present had given a slight nod, and the Breath of Terror had eaten it up. Occasionally, they were still seen, but they no longer landed if they could help it.

An hour passed. At last, from the other side of the Dead Place, the Breath of Terror wafted gently across an acre of shattered brickwork and concrete. Vyko found himself hoping that there had been no valuable books in that part of the Dead Place.

"Now," said Khasnik eagerly. "Now we shall see."

They waited for a tense minute to see an answering weapon strike from one of the broken towers. Nothing happened. Nothing—

Except a sudden intolerable pressure, a wind that seemed to toss them about like chips of wind and yet left them unmoved. And when it passed, and Khasnik's best warriors had wailed aloud in terror, there was no Dead Place before them.

There was, instead, a broad tract of cultivated land, a grove of nearby trees, long straggly grasses. In their lungs, the air was cold and dry.

The broken towers were gone, had never been.

The troop were no longer sheltered by smashed rock. They lay scattered about, some beneath foliage, some exposed on a grassy hillside.


In the valley beyond the trees, a machine was at work—if it was work, for it seemed to consist entirely of traveling back and forth, leaving the turned brown soil a dusty gray when it had passed. Even as they watched, a big black carriage that traveled at enormous speed, pulled by no draft animals, tore by on a brown track between the fields.

Khasnik's military training asserted itself; a few quick orders before anyone had time to think, and they were safe behind or under cover. Then he looked around, seeing Vyko nearby.

"What can have happened?" Vyko said in wonder.

"That's a fine question for you to ask," Khasnik said with a snarl. "You're supposed to *know* all that."

From up the hill came a keening, as several men took in what had happened. Someone cried, "A miracle!" and Khasnik yelled at him to shut his mouth.

"Well?" he asked Vyko. "You said the future was uneventful. Now a sorcerer in that Dead Place has picked us up by magic and flung us down somewhere else. I call *that* an event." His tone was heavily ironic, helping to contain the nervousness that shook him.

Vyko indicated negation with a motion of his tattooed hand. "I don't think so," he said. "Khasnik, I believe a great boon has been granted to us." His eyes shone. "I haven't yet got the feel of what is to come, except that it is great and terrible. But look yonder—did you ever see such a machine? There are men with it, too! And the black carriage that passed so swiftly—there's only one answer."

"That being?"

"We are being granted a sight of the Old Days! We have been translated in time."

Fear showed in Khasnik's black eyes for a moment, but he answered harshly. "Magicians' jargon! Nonsense! I'll accept that a sorcerer can move men in space—I've heard of such things often enough—but in time? No, we must have been sent to one of those places beyond the east of the Empire where these men with strange powers live. And therefore we have a fine chance to add territory to the Empire."

That'll teach them to send me out with a freshly qualified Staff magician, he added to himself, and went on to picture the advance in status a whole new province of the Empire would get him—especially one with so many secrets.

"It's something I've always dreamed of," Vyko went on, but Khasnik flung up a hand and almost started out from cover at what he saw.

Panicked—presumably—Crellan had again loosed the Breath of Terror, and the strange machine and its attendants had flared to nothing. The ground about it was charred.

"Idiot," said Vyko softly. Crellan's racing horse now came into sight, being ridden as if he were fleeing a thousand devils. "Oh, the idiot! Khasnik, he will give away our position if he comes charging up that way."

Khasnik nodded. He glanced up automatically to note the position of the Sun—which was bright in a cold clear sky—set the range of his gun to maximum, and aligned it on Crellan's body.

They were beautiful weapons, these, Khasnik thought, as the man and horse tumbled together in death. He did not understand quite how they operated—something about total conversion of incident illumination into beamed sonic frequencies capable of disrupting protein molecules was how the magicians referred to it. They were little use at night or on a cloudy day, of course, but for ordinary occasions, sighting one of them on a man's neck or skull was enough to dispose of him in a second.

Maybe—one day—they'd discover how to make them again.

"Conference," said Khasnik shortly, and the section leaders slid down the hill towards him.

"Sorcerers must have lived in that Dead Place," he began, glancing at Vyko as if challenging him to contradict. "We seem to have been carried somewhere else by magic."

The NCOs stiffened and made as if to move closer together.

"However!" said Khasnik. "This has great possibilities."

He went on to paint the rosy future awaiting men who added new ground to the Empire—skillfully, Vyko had to admit so that soon enough this apparent disaster had become an apparent blessing.

Not entirely, though; a few of the older NCOs looked keenly at their young staff magician while Khasnik was speaking—wondering, perhaps, whether he was competent to protect them after they had been abducted by this kind of magic.

"We will range out until we discover a center of population," Khasnik finished, "and base our further moves on what we discover there."

It took them only minutes to assemble and move off. Vyko cantered thoughtfully at Khasnik's side as they made for the track leading through the fields.

For fifteen minutes or so they progressed warily, sometimes at a half-gallop, seeing little sign of life.

Then a strange noise on the track ahead warned them of the approach of another of the carriages without draft animals. This one was going too fast for them to hide; a hundred-man war party on horseback could not melt instantly into the landscape.

The car halted with a screech of brakes, and a scowling man looked from one of the rear windows, his mouth opening in astonishment at the sight of Khasnik's men. He called out.

"Why—he speaks almost our language," remarked Vyko.

"Is that so peculiar?" said Khasnik. Tension showed in his voice, and several of the men seemed to be drawing back from the apparent power the car represented. Assuming a bold front, he rode forward to the car.

"Who the hell are you?" the scowling man demanded in an abominable accent.

"Khasnik, fourteenth captain of the Croceraunian Empire," said Khasnik shortly.

The man blinked. "The what? Show me your identification papers!"

"Men do not address an Imperial officer that way."

"Why, you impertinent—" The man started to get out. Khasnik motioned, and at once a dozen men raised weapons aimed towards the car.

"That's right," said Khasnik silkily. "You are plainly a man of some authority. You will get out and come with us."

Two raiders advanced and took the scowling man roughly by the arms; another pulled out the man from the front compartment. It was standard policy to obtain hostages as early as might be. They made a useful bargaining point. The man stared wildly.

"Saint Kiril, who are you people? What have you done to your teeth?"

Khasnik smiled savagely, and bared his filed teeth.

"And the carriage?" said Vyko wistfully.

"Destroy it." Khasnik signaled the man holding the Breath of Terror, and the carriage flared up.

"My god, how did you do that?" the scowling man said, panting, sweat on his face. After a shuddering moment, he rallied. "You won't get away with this. If I do not return on schedule, I will be missed. There will be search parties, and when you're caught—"

"Just as I want it," Khasnik replied. "Back to the trees, men, and camp down. Full defensive circle. It's easier for them to come to us than for us to go to them."

With quiet efficiency the circle was made. In twenty minutes the war party commanded a significant area. Securely bound, the strangers were thrown to the ground in the middle of the ring.

But before the warriors could vanish behind their improvised screens of tree and rock, there was a howling overhead and one of the flying things circled them three times. On the third pass Khasnik lost patience and ordered it fired on. It immediately flew off.

"That will bring them," said the bumptious captive, again in command of himself. The sweat had dried on his forehead. Vyko turned to him.

"You mean there are *men* in those things?"

The captive stared, and then laughed. Vyko tried to press him, but the fellow was not willing to answer, and when Khasnik saw what was happening, he silenced his magician.

The captive, though, was right. Barely half an hour had passed when there were rumblings from up the valley, and a scout came in to report that wagons bearing troops were on the way along the road. Khasnik nodded, and ordered fire to be held for the time being.

"Oh, but this can only be the Old Days," said Vyko as he studied the transport arriving, the strangely armed men deploying into the landscape. Another aircraft swooped overhead; Khasnik had not been counting on the need to be masked from the air as well as the ground, but he had done his best to rectify his earlier mistake, his men drawing together under tree cover.

"You're the expert on them," said Khasnik bitingly. "Look yonder! Does that not seem like an officer?"

Vyko studied a trio of men who had emerged into plain sight and were walking in irregular echelon in their direction, weapons in hand. "It does," he agreed, meaning the leader.

"Go and see what they want, then," said Khasnik.

For a horrible moment Vyko felt himself on the brink of a precipice. He recalled what was most likely to happen to anyone attempting a parley with Croceraunians. But then his strong urge to find out more of this wonderful age triumphed. If he only got a chance to ask some questions!

With an almost happy smile at Khasnik, he rose out of the long shaggy grass into sight.

The trio ahead stiffened and halted. The officer was the first to regain himself after seeing Vyko's odd clothing, and the outlandish tattooing on his body. "Come forward without hurrying," he directed.

Vyko did so, heart hammering. The others made no move until he was thirty feet from them, when the officer gestured. "All right, stop there. Who are you and where do you come from?"

Vyko debated his answer for an instant. There was one possibility, of course; this man might understand some of the esoteric signs used by magicians, and see the necessity for talking privately, away from Khasnik's suspicious eyes.

He started to make the sign demanding secret conference, but the soldier on the officer's right drew out a weapon and fired it. An enormous fist seemed to slam Vyko in the stomach, and he dropped to the earth in a black haze.

Khasnik, watching, rapped the order to strike, and in a few moments the war party had all but wiped out their opponents.

Before the Sun set, they were masters of the countryside as far as they could see, including two unsuspecting villages and several miles of metaled road.

—— ∞ ——

## CHAPTER XXIV

## 4070: Enemy

Master Cleaner Yeptverki hunched up, against its restraints, on all five painfully dry limbs. Its mood swung between rage and dismay. To be isolated from its quinque was physically painful, and spiritually draining. Sometimes it seemed that the True God had abandoned it, in this vile cell, and that the True Way had failed. No! That was heresy of the bleakest kind, precisely the sort of spiritual enfeebling the vermin hoped to impose. The stench of the Beast was everywhere, oppressive, loathsome.

Without its suit, the Master Cleaner was seriously compromised. The vermin provided disgusting food and drink, enough to sustain life, but neglected the emollients required to moisten and revive the outer integument. Of course this might not be simple stupidity or cruelty. They might guess that returning the suit, damaged as it was by the beam that slashed the tough skin, would also make its weapons and communicator available to it.

The visible lights went out, and the noise of the vermin's' high-pitched squealing subsided. But heat radiation crisscrossed the transparent cage, plainly a system of sensors. In the near darkness, Yeptverki settled in discomfort and tried to find a way to free itself and wreak its vengeance.

Light again, then, and thin flexible tubes entered the cage from above and inserted themselves into its arboreal surface, twisting and turning along the pyloric caeca of its symmetrical rays, probing the delicate network of its macromolecules. It felt the bulb in each tube foot invaded, ampulla at the top, suckers at the base. Chemicals infused the lateral canals in its jerking rays, flushing inward to infiltrate the ring canal and at last the madreporite where water usually entered its central core. The invasion was not painful, exactly, the investigative tubes were thin and avoided the nerves in the rays.

At first.

Then the itching began, the convulsive twitching at the end of each foot, the gastric heaving, the spontaneous evulsion from the anus, the pains, the pain. In the final indignity, gonads in each arm were provoked, spilling spawn gametes into the absent water, to perish, lost forever from their future each in a quinque of its own. The horror and shame at this horrible and shameless rape filled Yeptverki with incensed fury, and it heaved itself against its own massive weight to batter uselessly against the walls of the cage.

That repulsive squeaking, it had decided light-and-dark days ago, was surely their sonic means of expression and communication. It watched obsessively from five points of witness, each eyespot adding its perspective to a rounded portrait of its cage and the vermin beyond the circular wall. How had they got it in here? No opening other than tiny apertures above and below for the provision of rank food and water. Lowered in? Antigrav dependencies? Or had they dragged it in by brute force, drugged and ill, and built or grown the prison? That last seemed most plausible.

How, then, to remove it, gain access to the small dreadful vermin? Physical blows had no success at all, merely bruising to its heavy unprotected rays. Chemical attack? It had only its own excrement slime, and that, it now knew, was worthless for the task. In an extremity it might bite through a limb and spray out transparent circulatory fluid from its hemal system. But what good might come of that, other than to weaken it still further.

Despair again. It flattened itself on the floor of the cage, pressed its central core to the insipid water outlet, sucked in a dribble of moisture. In torpor, it watched one of the vermin, apparently a creature in command of the others. The mouth moved, sounds came from it that passed the walls of the cage as easily as light did. Yeptverki resigned itself to the futility of learning the things' language, the encoded messages of those tweets and clicks. There seemed no way it might emulate those noises, but even if it learned some way to generate the form of messages it would yet have to assimilate the semiotics, the meaningful signification, of these small brutish things. Perhaps it could do that in a century. Perhaps in a century the war against the Beast and its acolytes would be won. Perhaps it would die voiceless and alone, its quinque reduced to a sorrowing quattuor, but at last regrown with a fifth invited to their company.

The Master Cleaner roared at that melancholy, intolerable thought, hoisted itself high on its rays. Beyond the glass the vermin stopped and stared, or dashed together in fright. So it would be on a day of reckoning! Under the protection and guidance of the True God, it would tear them asunder and—

The tubes thrust into the spiky plates of its dorsal surface washed it with synthetic proteins. It collapsed to the floor, numbed and blurred, and was almost instantly unconscious.

—— ∞ ——

## CHAPTER XXV

## 4070: Burma

Extract from a 300th anniversary paper read to the British Science Society, Physical Division, September 27, 2031: *"It is proposed to substitute an equation defining the conditions proper to the displacement of energy from To or 'now'.... This suggests that what to us in 4-space phenomenal reality appears as the destruction or creation of matter and energy is due simply to a sudden reversal of the entropy of wavicles over a sharply delineated area of the continuum.... The advanced or 'backwards' path through time as an anti-particle, despite Feynman's and Cramer's traditional analyses, need not coincide with the visible retarded or 'forward' trajectory, which explains why they are not self-interacting...."*

The arrangement of the half-dozen small ships aboard which an anchor team carried out its work was always haphazard, depending on the whim and conveniences of the team's director. It did not much matter, since the Being's "substance" was reasonably homogeneous over any given volume. Its presence could only be detected by the most sensitive instruments, though; it registered on them more as a tendency to displacement in time than as anything more tangible.

Still, as Burma pushed her way through the airlock of the nearest ship belonging to the team she had selected, she could not help wondering what kind of configuration the local director had adopted this time. It was a fine team—that was why she had picked it—but from the arrangement of the ships it looked as if they had simply been allowed to drift in a circular orbit until they were haphazardly placed.

It was good to have the familiar tools of her trade about her again, after that nightmare plunge into what she could not help regarding, despite her growing friendship with Chantal, as a barbarian era. It almost, but not quite, stopped her wishing that it had not been necessary to do away with sleep. The combination of hypnotic relaxation and selective removal of fatigue poisons that the species had been forced to develop doubled an individual's thinking time, was completely harmless and even aided longevity. But she missed—how she missed!—the ability simply to turn herself off for a while.

We never knew, her mind ran on idly. We never knew just what a human being could be made to do until we *had* to find out. Yet and still we're being *made to do it. How long can we stand the strain?*

She came into what should have been the busiest part of the ship, and stopped dead in her tracks.

Among the elaborate and immensely valuable array of equipment, there was one weary-looking woman monitoring a single input trace on the temporal band.

Burma spoke with a kind of controlled fury. "What is going on here?"

The woman looked up, clearly distraught. "So they finally remembered us!"

Burma said, "This is supposed to be a fully operating anchor team. Where is everyone? How can you possibly be expected to monitor all these display stations by yourself?"

Stung, the woman retorted, "Ask Artesha! They put out a call yesterday for the top crew in alien psychology to investigate this Enemy they'd captured, and every Being-blasted member of this team was sent for, except me."

Burma forced herself to calm down, but she was still fumbling. Mistakes like this were inevitable when you were trying to administer the fighting efforts of a race of some quintillion-odd individuals through a central agency. "All right," she said, and gave her name and station. "I'll have this settled in quick time. Artesha!" she added, opening the communicator on the wall.

"I'm sorry," said Artesha when she had explained the situation. "I was getting around to that—I wanted to break up the team and disperse it because the odds are slightly in favor of our getting results with the Enemy before we get them with the Being. After all, we have more knowledge of their psychology—"

"We did have," said Burma. "Artesha, you aren't computing with the fact that Wymarin stimulated the Being, are you? I have only the faintest idea how he managed it, but I know he was pursuing a brand new line. Listen! We've found only one way of directly affecting the Being—that's by a nuclear explosion. It doesn't like high energy levels. Maybe they affect it as a hot fire does us. Anyway, we can't find traces of its presence much closer than Mercury to the Sun, and every time there's a really big explosion it…*writhes*.

"But Wymarin had an idea. He's been probing the possibility that the thing is intelligent in a way comprehensible to us. Mostly, we've been assuming it's the four-dimensional equivalent of an amoeba, because it exhibits the same kind of actions so far as we can determine and is equally shapeless.

"He tried to *communicate* with it. He wanted to see if we could explain to it what it was doing to us, so that it would help us to move it out of this area of space. And if it was the result of his communicating with it that caused that last outsize temporal surge—the one that caught me—"

"I see," said Artesha. She sounded as nearly excited as she could get. "I can't return all your experts, but there must be some who've completed their contribution to the study of the Enemy. Why did you pick that team, anyway?"

"Because there were experts in psychology here as well as in continuum mathematics," Burma answered. "The same reason you took them for the study of the Enemy."

"I'll have your people with you in quick time," Artesha said, and signed off.

Burma turned from the communicator to find the older woman eying her.

"I'm sorry, ma'am," she said. "I didn't realize who you were. I'm Lalitha Benoni."

Burma acknowledged the introduction. "Had your team been attempting anything on the lines Wymarin tried?" she demanded.

"No. We were thinking in terms of the Being reacting to stimuli. Mainly, we were trying to set up a pattern that fitted the way it pulls away fast from atomic explosions and suchlike. We hoped to find a stimulus that would drive it away for good. Owing to the Being's four-dimensional nature, we assumed the stimulus would have to be powerful and complex."

"I wish coordination wasn't so difficult," said Burma feelingly. "We've got nine thousand-odd anchor teams all over the Solar System, and we haven't yet solved the problem of aggregating the deep information obtained by one immediately available to all without running into informational overload. When did you last check your digest?"

"Yesterday. I haven't had a red-tabbed signal in since, though." Lalitha spoke defensively.

"One of the mathematicians on another team worked out the end results of driving the Being away." Burma was surveying the equipment as she spoke; it seemed in good order. "It might literally wreck the Solar System. At worst, the Sun would flare and deform; the planets would leave their orbits. But of course it wouldn't be red-tabbed, since this was probably the only team that really needed the information. No, it's as well the pattern has been broken. We'll be able to get down to our own problem with fresh minds."

It was a damnable conundrum. Whenever one of the anchor teams—or indeed any of the groups of super-specialists who were the brain of the species working as a whole—had functioned smoothly together for some time, there grew up among them a mutual understanding that approached telepathy. That was wonderful so long as they remained on the same task, but made it appallingly difficult to change their line of research.

"Have the information system sift the data of the last year for items regarding communication with the Being," Burma said. Nodding, Lalitha did so. Burma began to hum to herself as she continued studying the machinery. It was good; the former director of this team had been an imaginative man.

"What a hell of a waste," she burst out suddenly. Lalitha made an inquiring noise, and she went on, "Sorry. Your team has done some fine work. I was just thinking it was a shame that driving the Being away should turn out to be too big a risk after all."

Lalitha nodded, and the digest computer sang its little ready signal. "Already?" said Burma, alarmed. "I expected there wouldn't be much on the subject, but if the computer got through a year's aggregated data so fast there can be hardly anything salient."

There was indeed hardly anything—four completed preliminary studies, two of which she had helped Wymarin to program for their own team's computers, and an unfinished simultaneous broadcast that had been recorded while Wymarin was actually carrying out his experiment.

"Oh, good man, Wy," said Burma, clicking on it. "This is like finding treasure."

The data stream was notated in the arcane markings of instrument readings, but she could follow it without trouble. At the end, she frowned. "Tantalizing," she exclaimed. "Just when it started to show a response, the temporal surge built up and its energies jammed the broadcast! Lalitha, put a chaos package onto analyzing the trend of these recordings, will you? I can't see a predictable pattern, but it's worth trying, I suppose. Wymarin's such a brilliant intuitive reasoner, though, I suspect he would just have been relying on his unconscious to lead him on until he found something that worked."

There was a cough at the door and a man entered. He looked around before coming over. "Gevolan," he introduced himself. "Artesha told me you were starting something big here?" The sentence ended in the faintest of inquiries.

"As soon as possible. How's the study of the Enemy coming along?"

Gevolan shrugged. "We can't hypnotize it, so now it's up to the neurochemists to synthesize something we can use to inject our commands into it." He wiped his face. "It's made me wonder what would happen to any poor human being who fell into Enemy clutches—"

"None have, to our knowledge, with the possible exception of one small child," said Burma. "All right, Gevolan. I'll give you the set-up. After that, it's over to you. I hope that search party of Magwareet's does find Wymarin—otherwise we'll have as much chance as a bunch of blind men trying to find a black hole in the Coal Sack."

Gevolan stared, and then laughed. "I come from around there," he said. "I was evacuated from Arauk. We never used that simile, because it's a matter of record that a blind man *did* once find a black hole in the Coal Sack."

"I hope we have that kind of luck," said Burma flatly.

—— ∞ ——

# CHAPTER XXVI

## 2144: TIME SURGE *Betelgeuse*

*The first sailors ever to see a sea-serpent and bring in proof* (reported Reuters) *were the crew of the Panamanian trader* Hargreaves Halliday *who docked at Capetown today with a strange animal found floating in the Indian Ocean. Scientists say it resembles a prehistoric dinosaur, but are at a loss to understand how an air-breathing creature in freshly killed condition....*

The first commercial flight on April 22, 2144 of Virgin Starflight's spacetwister *Betelgeuse* launched perfectly from atop the Storrs Hall platform perched 100 kilometers above Mauna Kea. She was sent on her way with the blessings of the spirits of the mountain, and ample media coverage on what was to be a relatively short maiden voyage into the outer Solar System and back.

Docking at the selenocentric orbital station, the crew of fifteen checked their programmed route through higher space a final time, smiled at the rollicking applause of their three hundred intensely wealthy passengers, and hit the gas at exactly 8:05 p.m. Eastern Standard Time in the Rim States of America. Designed as much to capture the imagination of its clientele as for function, the Captain's command and control center extended well forward of the main fuselage on a slender ellipsoidal extension, which, merged and blended with the craft's deeply swept wings, presented a planform glorious in the retina feeds of that nation and the world.

*Betelgeuse* went critical seven minutes and thirty-six seconds later, as programmed, and was never seen again, not at all as programmed.

The craft's goal was not, of course, the red supergiant star, Alpha Orionis, of its name. While that destination was perfectly feasible with such devices, according to the engineers, going 642 light years and back for a public relations jaunt was deemed reckless. Instead, the craft flew at superluminal pseudo-velocity to the Oort Cloud's largest planet, the subJovian Supay. That frigid world was named for the Incan god of death and the underworld, which would prove eerily apt.

*Betelgeuse* passed across the orbit of Supay, taking a gravity assist to return them to Earth. As the craft went back into superlight space, without warning the vessel abruptly began radical and un-commanded pitching and rolling motions, setting off alarms as she moved outside never-to-exceed parameters. Neither captain nor flight crew recognized the cause as they battled to remain sane and in command of the vessel. Time seemed to blur and shatter, twist even more recklessly than the spacetwist they anticipated. What they had flown into was a temporal surge of colossal force, and nobody aboard the *Betelgeuse* or on all of Earth knew anything, yet, about time surges.

Struggling to maintain an appearance of composure while fighting off their own panic, the lissome male and female stewards went through the prepared patter, and automated cameras captured every heartwarming moment for the media outlets at home. Sixteen billion new dollars were wrapped up in this extravaganza. It would never be realized, which was fair because the recordings would never be seen.


Minor mission anomalies had been anticipated with the new design, as always, but encounters with the unknown could not possibly be planned for. Decades of incident reconstruction efforts were conducted, but ultimately engineers and astrophysicists were unable to establish a plausible, let alone probable, cause for the disappearance of the ship, all its passengers, and crew. In the spring of 2145, the Rim States CEO declared *Betelgeuse* lost, and all aboard declared dead. During the same speech he also announced cancelation of Virgin Starflight's licenses to experiment at speeds even approaching the transluminal range.


Captain Drishti Lavanya, an intersex sensation, PhD engineer and former starship test pilot, retarded thrust and took *Betelgeuse* out of superspace and into Hell.

Suddenly and impossibly, the starship was deep in atmosphere, buffeted by a dreadful storm. It should not have been in atmosphere at such speed. To maximize drag and slow their headlong plunge, Capt. Drishti immediately commanded extension of every surface that would tolerate the current airspeed. They cut off the ion drives and engaged the air-breathing turbine engines. They found all other controls either inoperative, or stiff and only marginally effective.

The elite passengers laughed and clapped for a few moments, thinking this a superlative special effect. Then the screams and wailing and weeping started, as it dawned on many that what they were seeing was real, however impossible.

Grim-face men unbuckled with difficulty and ran back and forth in the aisle. The Captain spoke soothingly, to little avail. The crew shut off the direct feed from the cameras and combated the shrieking acoustics with soothing classical spaceflight music by the old composer Richard Strauss. The air outside the shell was blazingly hot. Clouds boiled in the heavens. Was this Earth or Venus? Temperature on the outer skin was some 340 degrees Celsius. In the command and control center, radio scans discovered no signals on any band, just crackling noise. *Betelgeuse* dropped below cloud cover on its own, and sea stretched beneath them, curdled and frothing. To port, a cone of fire rose above the silent seascape, sulfurously red and yellow with erupting lava.

The craft was out of all human control now, stable only because of the adaptive programming in its autopilot and guidance system software. The needle prow dipped inexorably toward the water, decreasing altitude but increasing speed. To retard the airspeed, the Captain extended the landing skids to add extra drag.

A second fearful shudder of time storm filled every eye with three or four blurred images of their surroundings. Men clutched at women and men. Women hung weeping together, or pressed against men. Hell was gone, and blue water rushed by at what seemed to be just meters below. The hull cooled swiftly, thanks to a paradoxical reduction in outside air temperature that had occurred with their descent, shedding its atrocious heat.

Something large and animate and terrifying leaped from the water directly into their path. A solid impact sent a shudder through *Betelgeuse*, coupled with a terrifying yaw that the autopilot struggled to stabilize.

"Check all cameras, report external damage," commanded the pilot.

"Good god, Captain, there's a *dinosaur* hung up in the starboard skid! It's a giant goddamned reptile! It must be seven meters long."

"Easy, Number 2. Export the camera image to my side." In disbelief, they stared at the image on their control panel. The creature was still alive, snapping its terrible jaws.

"Shiva, look at the thing. Those jaws have to be a meter long. And the teeth—"

An automatic Google program was scanning everything beyond the hull, including accidental dinosaurs. It announced in a pleasant female voice that they had captured a Liopleurodon. There was the faintest pause as its minimal AI checked its response. "I report without prejudice that the Liopleurodon clade flourished on Earth as an apex predator during the Jurassic, approximately 145 to 200 million years ago—"

Drishti Lavanya silenced the report, struggling to lift the starcraft's nose. The ship was not well suited to this kind of flight or external burden.

A fresh surge of discomfort, dizziness, disbelief.

They still flew over water, but the light had changed again, clear noonday sky above, whitecaps below.

"Captain, it's destabilizing us. And look at those jaws! It could bite a chunk right out of our hull."

"Retract the skids," the captain ordered, and as they retracted aft the monstrous creature slipped off, tumbled away aft. The visual scanner picked up its splash.

"Good riddance, gods damn it," said the co-pilot, voice thick with the terror of aftershock. "Shiva take it!"

An equally traumatized voice came through headsets from one of the stewards, Trevor Gillespie. "Sir or madam, if you look to starboard I believe you will notice a small boat under steam heading our way."

It was so. And in the far distance, the faint green line of a coast. The southern shores of Africa, really? So the mapping system had determined from compass and other parameters. Were they home?

Time currents caught them again and flung them away.

This Sun was immense, mottled with black spots, seething with out-flung bands or curtains of dull flares, and hung high above them. Sensors showed ambient temperatures even higher than the Hell world's.

"Lord of darkness!" the Captain said, appalled. "We seem to have ended up beneath Betelgeuse after all."

"No," the navigator said, voice shaking. "I think it is our own Sun, near the end of its life. Google is suggesting some two billion years after our time."

"I thought the world and the Sun were meant to be cold and dead. Isn't that what they said in that old media? *The Time Machine*, wasn't it called?"

"Don't ask me, Captain, I just work here tending the machines. We shall have to key in a correction to Googleplex City after we deplane."

Dimly, through the heavy double wall and electronically guarded doors from the cockpit, they heard terminal cries of despair. Drishti Lavanya touched the announcement icon. "Ladies and gentlemen and others, as you will have noticed we have been experiencing some minor difficulties." The co-pilot choked, covered his mouth. Was he laughing or crying? The Captain said, "We have drifted away from our flight plan due to undisclosed difficulties, but we shall make our best efforts to have you on the ground momentarily. In the meantime, I urge you to remain seated and belted, and our hospitality staff will begin serving, um, supper immediately." They toggled a soothing melody, and turned attention to the radio search. Nothing. Always nothing but hiss and static.

There's nobody left at home, they thought with a sob. There's no way of telling where we are, or even *when* we are. They sought command of themself. I'll find a place to land, they vowed. Somebody from Virgin Starflight will come and get us. Or that strange, that horrifying flux that passed through my body on each occasion. That will return. That will take us back home.

It never did.

— ∞ —

## CHAPTER XXVII

## 2268: Red and Chantal

Mogak, Lord of the Plains, Son of the Running Horse, Paramount Chief under the Supreme Ruler of the Mertchakulun Bands, to His Most Sublime Omnipotence the Emperor of the Croceraunian Empire that stretches from dawn even unto nightfall (by courier): *Miracles are abroad in the land!*

Magwareet wished achingly for a second that he had all Artesha's resources at his command. This was too big a problem for any one man....

But he was responsible. He studied the time map for a long time before coming to his decision.

"Arafan!" he shouted, and the pilot's voice came back through the communicator. "Get us to Earth as quickly as possible."

"At once," said Arafan. Magwareet turned to look at a map of the land masses of Earth stuck on one wall, lettered in drastically abbreviated symbols. With one backward glance to make certain of the spot, he stabbed at it with his right forefinger. "Red! Whereabouts is that in your time?"

Red swallowed; the tension of their venture close to the Enemy raider was still tight in his stomach. "It looks—" he began, and had to start again. "It looks like the middle of the Soviet Union."

Magwareet nodded. "The Croceraunian Empire grew up from the wreckage of what you knew as China and Mongolia. We know more about them than we do about their predecessors, but there has always been something puzzling about their fantastically rapid expansion." He frowned. "They had a sort of bastard science that they treated as magic, but it gave them results.... I've read their scriptures—they speak of miracles and being able to see into the future."

Arafan's voice broke in on them. "We're at the edge of the atmosphere," reported the pilot.

"Trace still there?" Magwareet said, and the technician beside the time map confirmed it. "Coming up," he shouted, and made for the control cabin.

The sight from the viewport was awe-inspiring. They could see the vast spread of the Eurasian land-mass dotted with clouds like smears of dirty white paint. The terminator between night and day was creeping towards the area for which they were making.

"Are we screened?" Magwareet said absently, and Arafan nodded. "Okay, take her down. It shouldn't be hard to spot what we're looking for—if I know anything about those Croceraunians, they couldn't be in one place for ten minutes without starting a fight."

It was eerie to swoop on silent antigravs across the country whose reputation for secrecy and unapproachability had supplanted that of Tibet, looking at what might be the greatest secrets of all, unnoticed and uninterrupted.

"There," said Magwareet at last, many minutes later, and pointed. A column of trucks loaded with armed men was tearing along a poor road at the limit of safety. "Another few kilometers and—yes, that's it."

Circling under Arafan's touch, the ship surveyed the whole scene of battle. It was clear even to Red and Chantal, who knew nothing of military strategy: the ring of oddly-clad invaders, many of them sheltering behind dead horses like Indians in a Western film, was standing off an army. Every now and again there was a puff of fire that did something indistinguishable but fatal to the defending infantry.

"But there are so few of them," said Chantal. "Can they really do much damage?"

Magwareet answered wryly, "The Croceraunians are carrying probably the finest portable weapons ever developed—sonic guns, atomic grenades, and what they call the Breath of Terror—a sort of universal catalyst that accelerates natural oxidation. Look, there goes one of the tanks."

There was only a drift of mist, but the wind brought it up to the side of the tank, and in a moment it had flared brilliantly into dust. A man carrying a clumsy pack got up and ran twenty yards before dropping behind a rise and repeating the process on another tank.

Arafan swore; they had noticed nothing, but he explained, "Being screened has its disadvantages! An aircraft nearly collided with us, going like lightning."

"What are you going to do about this?" Chantal demanded in a practical tone, and Magwareet gave her a slight sad smile.

"I have a job for you and Red. I'm sorry to say it, but you're—comparatively—expendable. We carry no weapons, and it would be useless to signal one of the ships that came after us to destroy the Enemy raider—their armament is just too powerful. It would take half the countryside with it.

"I'm going to ask you to go out there—screened, so that you're invisible—pick out the Croceraunians, and render them unconscious, one by one."

"*Oui*," Chantal said, breaking the heavy seriousness of the moment with a tinkling laugh. "Yes, we shall tip-toe up to these ferocious *flics* and bash them with a hammer! You do have a spare hammer, I suppose?"

"I meant exactly what I said. Fortunately, you will be invisible."

Her face fell, and her mouth twisted in confusion. "*Merde*! But—But—if we are to attack these savages—"

"You will use medical neuromodulator injectors. The sedative works almost instantly, but we have limited supplies. This is not a warship."

"Well," Chantal said, "they worked fine on Red and me. But these men are trained warriors." She flushed. "Sorry, Red, I know that you were—"

Magwareet made an impatient sound. "We make do with what we have. That is the lesson of war."

Red was shaking his head, bemused. "All right, if that's what it takes."

"It will be dangerous, because I don't think the screens will protect you against either the Breath of Terror or a high-velocity bullet. I must be candid—it's either you doing this job, or an indispensable technician."

Red looked at Chantal. "Me, I'll go willingly," he said. With the new-found clarity in his mind, he could tell that his urge sprang from the fact that now he was a whole man he wanted to match himself against other men—violently if need be.

One of the crew came in with a pair of improvised packs, each containing dispensers.

Chantal picked one up, examined it, nodded. "Needle-free, air-punched straight through the skin. These will do, if they really work as fast as advertised," she said, and winked. "Trust me, I'm a doctor."

Magwareet laughed.

"And take these too." He held out pairs of headset goggles made of smoky gray plastic. "With these you'll be able to see each other and the ship. And hear us. *No one else can*. But they will hear you if you talk, and they'll notice any footprints you leave in soft ground.

"We'll bring the ship down to about seven feet and stay hovering in your vicinity. Knock out your men and leave them—we'll pick them up one by one with the cargo loading arms, put them in storage and figure out what to do with them later."

"And their horses?" the technician asked.

"Their what?"

"These raiders are mounted troops. They seem to have sequestered most of their animals under cover of the trees."

"And?"

"We can't just leave the poor creatures hobbled to die of thirst," Chantal said. The technician nodded. "And I'm certainly not going to help you kill them."

Magwareet looked pained. "The thought never crossed my mind. But you're right, they'll require some disposition. Obviously we can't take them with us."

"The local landowners will round them up eventually," Red said.

"And turn them into dog food," Chantal said, screwing up her face.

Now Magwareet looked physically ill. He tightened his lips. "I hope not, but really it's not our problem. Come on, time to move."

Red stepped carefully off the lowered and invisible freight access ramp, rejoicing in the equal strength of his two legs. He turned and found himself suddenly staring at Chantal with open eyes for the first time.

Like himself, she was now wearing the ubiquitous coverall that now seemed to be the human species' standard costume. But her face was flushed with excitement and nervousness, and her brown and blue-green hair was ruffled. Her right hand held an injector ampoule, and her entire appearance was purposeful.

He realized that, without noticing, he had been sensing the same air in the women he had met since his fantastic adventure hauled him across two thousand years—something quite different from most of the women he had known in his own day, aside from Joanna. This was a woman who was a partner, an equal, knowing her own capabilities and willing to make the most of them.

He barely had time to absorb the knowledge when the sharp snap of a rifle reminded him that they were in the middle of a battle.

"Down," Chantal said under her breath, and they dropped side by side into the slight dip that was the reason for their being put down here. He looked up through his goggles, seeing their ship loom over them, and then searched the area for a sign of the Croceraunians.

They did not have to look far. Moving with the skill of a practiced warrior, one of the barbarians dodged from a piece of cover that Red thought could not have concealed a mouse, and fell over them in an attempt to gain fresh protection.

The man's mouth was already opening in a scream of fear at finding invisible demons on the ground when Red jabbed him in the midriff and took the breath out of him before blasting the drug into his neck under his jaw.

"One," he said with deep satisfaction, and they moved out across the ground. "Chantal, this is incredible. That fellow had *filed teeth*."

"Hush."

Red and green arrow icons flickered inside the field of view provided by the goggles, directions from the ship that proved essential to their success. They moved cautiously around the perimeter of the defenses, where Croceraunians had taken cover from aerial observation as well as surface spotters, sedating the barbarians one by one. Behind them, loading arms noiselessly raised the unconscious warriors into the bowels of the ship.

Fortunately, the Russian attackers did not close in at once, slow to realize that barbarians were vanishing rather than lying quiet in ambush. Enjoying the effort of pitting themselves against the Croceraunians whose military expertness would have more than matched the advantage conferred by invisibility if they had understood what was happening, Red and Chantal continued their mission.

Dusk was setting in when there was nobody left except a group of three invaders at the very center of the ring, presumably the captain of the war party and his second and third in command. Two neatly barbered bodies in conventional clothing lay dead, tied together with rope.

"Chantal, Red," Magwareet whispered urgently in his ear. "We've spotted big aircraft heading this way! You'll have to clean up the rest quickly—I suspect the Russians are going to bomb the area."

Chantal drew in a quick breath.

"Okay," nodded Red. He felt very tired, but oddly exhilarated. "We can run most of the way. Look, Chantal—see that knob of ground? We'll head up that way and drop behind it."

On the last word he started forward, keeping low. The ship sidled after them.

Despite the swift, chilling fall of twilight, the three remaining Croceraunians were keeping a stern lookout. The noise of Red's awkward arrival brought one of them sharply to his feet. After he had looked around and seen nothing, he ordered one of his companions to scout the sound.

Nothing could have been more convenient. Rod's jet injector fired into the man's neck the moment he was hidden from the others by the rock.

And a howl filled the air—an aircraft, diving.

There was the buffeting crack of rapid explosions, and the ship over them staggered, exactly like a man who has taken a blow. Red's goggles slipped a little, and he was amazed to look up and find that without them he could see the retreating plane quite clearly *through* the spacecraft. The magnitude of that technical achievement shook him.

Another plane dived, and another, and the two remaining Croceraunians raised small weapons and fired on it—with no effect, of course, for they were hitting the screens of the hovering ship. Red found a stone and threw it to one side, distracting their attention. With a gesture to Chantal, he rose and ran down the slope.

But exhaustion slowed them both, and at the sound of their feet the barbarians swung around. It was very nearly dark now, and they obviously felt prepared to take on opponents they couldn't see. He thought for a horrible instant that Chantal had been hit, but she had only stumbled, and then he was on his own man in a tangle of arms and legs.

The fellow was strong, and an able fighter, but the moment he realized he could not see his antagonist he faltered long enough to allow Red to sedate him.

Rising, Red looked around for Chantal. She had been less lucky; her man, who had an air of authority, had set his jaw grimly and was throwing punches by guesswork. A blow connected just as a further blast of cannon shells hammered on the ship above, and Chantal staggered back. At the same moment a Russian sniper found the Croceraunian, but the bullet missed its target, whining off a rock into the air.

Still backing, Chantal's foot found the outstretched legs of the man lying on the ground. She fell to the earth.

The last Croceraunian's attempted blow found only air. Off balance, he too lost his footing, and Red was on top of him, injector poised. In a moment, the barbarian was hauled aboard the ship to join the rest of his war party, leaving behind only corpses marked with Russian bullets. No doubt an explanation would be found for them—somehow.

Red picked up one of the clumsy packs holding the Breath of Terror—it would not do to let *that* fall into twenty-first century hands!—and prepared to enter the ship. He looked around for Chantal, and saw her kneeling by the body she had fallen over.

"Are you all right?" he demanded anxiously, and she nodded.

"Red, I thought this man was dead. He's breathing! And look—he's no more than a boy. He's pretty badly hurt, but I think we can fix him up. Help me get him aboard."

As they had once moved Burma, they lifted him together. The memory of that first meeting made him wonder if it could really have been so recently, as he counted time. He had been a different person then, ages ago.

"Now we must deal with the horses," Chantal said. She looked as exhausted as Red felt, but determined.

"Okay, sure."

They moved through the corpses, forty, fifty, maybe more of the raiders, slain by weapons lost to their own strange future history.

The animals stirred at the synthetic odors of the protective suits and the sound of their footfalls as Red and Chantal approached them. One by one the horses were released, skittish and disturbed by the invisible humans, and ran away into the grasses, vanishing under cover of the trees.

In the ship's airlock, Magwareet was smiling. "That was great work, and quicker than I expected," he said warmly. "Do you know it's only been two and a half hours?"

"I feel tired enough to have been working for a week," said Red, wiping his forehead.

"I'll have that put right," said Magwareet. "We're already moving away from that place, you know," he added as an afterthought. "Now we've straightened out that mess, we can get on with our real job. Through there you'll find a wash-place. Clean up, and when you're done come to the control cabin—I'll fix your fatigue."

He went out, and Red and Chantal followed his directions into the washroom. It was small, but there were two basins and two of the quick, efficient hot-air dryers that had supplanted towels—there was always air available, but cloth was precious.

The water—re-cycled, absolutely pure, and just the right temperature—soaked the weariness out of their pores. Turning away after drying his face and hands, Red found himself looking straight at Chantal.

"You're—you're quite a person, aren't you?" he said awkwardly.

"I suppose my job prepares me for anything," she answered with a faint smile. "And I had done almost the same sort of thing before—I was in the Islamist riots when I was still an intern. But you did better than I did, really."

There was a pause. Red went on, "I'm surprised I can accept the reality of what's happening, you know. Thrown into a completely strange world—"

The words seemed to touch something deep in Chantal's mind. Her mouth contorted. "It's terrifying," she said. "Red, I'm so glad you're here too—someone from my own world." Her lips quirked. "Almost, anyway."

"I know what you mean," he said with deep sincerity. "And I'm glad not only because I've got someone else from my own world for company—but because the someone is someone like you."

She took a step away and looked at him.

He caught himself. "Chantal, I'm sorry—" He broke off, biting his lip.

"They've given you a lot, haven't they? Magwareet and Burma and their people?" She looked at him steadily. As a friend might. A friend who was a woman. Oh, damnation, but all right.

"So much," said Red steadily, "that I'll do anything and everything I can to recompense them."

— ∞ —

## CHAPTER XXVIII

### En route, 17<sup>th</sup> century: Red and Chantal

Anchor Command, Burma speaking, emergency: *Any team engaged in investigation of possible communication with the Being, any team having data on patterns of responses of the Being, any team having any relevant information: Notify at once!*

Defense fleet (coordinates 902634111) speaking: *Suggest investigation of possibility that Enemy found in city from 129 Lyrae, and captured, entered Solar System owing to writhing of Being. Artesha's opinion, please.*

Center, Artesha speaking: *We cannot rule out the possibility that the Being itself is being used as a weapon by the Enemy—nor, in fact, that it is an artificially created weapon. Probability low, but not negligible.*

**"S**o that definitely removes all signs of temporal displacement from this period? No indication of Wymarin?" Magwareet said, disappointment clear in his tone. The technicians nodded. "All right, where are the secondary peaks of this surge?"

"We've come so far in time that our instruments are saturated with surplus energy," said the dark haired woman standing by the time map. "There's a chance we could pick up a single individual if we matched times with the secondary peak that came up about three hundred years ago. We can't do it directly from here. The only other important peak of this surge is the one that broke up the anchor team we were chasing. I don't think Wymarin would have stood a chance if he'd been caught in that."

"All right," said Magwareet firmly. "Let's go see. And if we can't pick him out, then we'll just have to land and build ourselves new equipment out of matter that isn't overloaded with temporal interference."

"Meantime," said the woman calmly, "how about this cargo of barbarians we've just acquired?"

"Could I do anything about them?" asked Chantal, entering with Red just in time to catch the remark. "You know I was a physician back where—back when I came from."

"Fine," said Magwareet, after a slight hesitation. "Tesper! Give Chantal a brief run-down on the medical equipment aboard."

"Surely." A small man nodded, making scribbled notes on an electronic pad. "In just a moment."

"Tesper's a historian," Magwareet added, "with some knowledge of their archaic language."

Chantal accompanied Tesper through the ship to the place where forty Croceraunian barbarians lay almost literally heaped up, still torpid from the sedative. The ship was large, but the crew's quarters were cramped, and Tesper insisted that the medical equipment was hopelessly inadequate. To Chantal, it was a dream.

It took her barely ten minutes to learn the use of the regenerant and healing devices, how to administer the universal antibiotics they had met before, and how to dress bullet and shrapnel wounds with the soothing stemskin that did the job of a bandage and a graft in one. She dearly would have liked to learn *how* the devices worked, but that was for later.

Oddly, her "barbarian" methods—though they startled Tesper—came in extremely useful. The equipment was not in fact up to dealing with forty injured men, some badly hurt with wounds from their Russian assailants, but there was plenty of clean water—limited only by the speed with which it could be re-cycled and purified—and she went steadily ahead.

The Croceraunians were all finely muscled young men in their thirties, she guessed, except the captain, who was older, and the young man whose legs she had fallen over at the very end of their cleaning-up operation. He was no more than a boy—perhaps eighteen.

She lingered over him, wondering what his role was. His hands and arms were heavily tattooed with complex designs, and she puzzled over their possible meaning. Like the other warriors, he wore his long black hair in complex braids. The shape of his closed eyes, like theirs, was Asiatic—epicanthic folds smoothly covering the medial canthus of the upper eye. At length, however, giving a final glance around to see all her charges were as comfortable as possible, she returned to the main technical room.

Arafan's voice came down to them from the communicator. "We're just going into the surge again, trying for the secondary peak. I'll call you as soon as we emerge."

"Thank you," acknowledged Magwareet. "Now we can see to you, Red and Chantal, and some of the rest of us as well. I'm hungry—are you?"

"You're always hungry," Chantal said, and laughed. "I'm famished."

"I work hard. Very well, good, we might as well grab the chance of a quick meal while we're going through the surge, at that. Go and freshen up, people. You'll find suitable garments in your rooms."

Fed on strange but delicious salads, Chantal felt remarkably refreshed after a quick course of the hypnotic and anti-fatigant treatment. It was an astonishing thought that these biological developments had converted sleeping time to the thinking and working capacity of the human species,

They had emerged from the temporal surge while she was below, and she discovered Magwareet consulting worriedly with his assistants.

"What is it?" she asked, and Red, who was standing beside Magwareet, broke away and came over to her.

"We've reached the limit our equipment can compensate for," he said. "Even if Wymarin is down there, we can't detect him because the screens are saturated. There's only one thing for it—we've got to figure out a way of building new machinery. How?" he added, turning to Magwareet.

The Coordinator frowned. "You say you're no expert in history. The fact remains, you certainly know more about *this* period than I do, and probably even Tesper, and I can't compute with data I don't possess. What's our best chance of making use of whatever scientific knowledge is available?"

Red whistled. "Chemistry was the only science that had begun about this time. This is the mid-seventeenth century, isn't it?" The idea brought a chill of awe. "Even that was strictly trial-and-error. They're refining metals—some metals—down there. Is that any help?"

"A little. I had the computers run off the specifications for a thoroughly jury-rigged detector that will serve our purpose. All right, we'll have to try it. Where do you suggest? England was fairly advanced, I believe. Is—"

"England's out. I speak twentieth-century American, and they'd suspect something funny. No, it'd better be a place where I can pass as a foreigner and still get away with speaking only English. And we'll have to go very carefully—I don't know to what extent a chemist or alchemist is regarded as a witch in these days." He felt a curious stirring in the back of his mind, as if someone spoke to him at the very edge of audibility, guiding his imagination. "On the whole, I'd make a guess and say that a fair-sized town in Holland would be a reasonable bet. I'd also guess Wymarin would make the same choice for the same reasons, assuming he arrived somewhere in Europe. If so, we might be able to track him down. If he's in Japan or South America or even Africa, it will be a lot harder, I assume."

"Settled," said Magwareet. "Arafan!" He gave directions to the pilot.

"Clothing—money—an interpreter—ouf, this will be a long job." Red said ruefully. "Still, I suppose it's quicker than starting from scratch."

Chantal came up to him as he watched the European coast swell in the viewports. "Red—you'll be careful, won't you?"

"Of course," he said sincerely, and clasped her hand companionably.

But it was with trepidation that she watched him and Magwareet, carefully screened, lowered from the invisible ship. Red offered an ironic bow before they set out along a poor-surfaced road towards the flourishing township of The Hague.

"Now we have nothing to do but wait," said Tesper. "I have the oddest feeling, you know, just like Red, that if only our screens were clear we'd have no trouble. I'm certain Wymarin is actually here. I can't see there's anywhere else for him to be."

"Except several trillion cubic kilometers of empty space," put in the dark-haired woman by the time map, and Tesper was forced to nod agreement. But he grimaced as he did so.

"How are the barbarians?" he asked Chantal.

"As well as can be expected." She pushed out the cliché with no apologies. "One of them in particular interests me."

"They're all interesting," Tesper answered dryly. "The Crocerau-nian Empire is one of the most enigmatic phenomena of history. But which, in particular?"

"The very young one. He has tattoo marks all over—"

Tesper looked startled. "Can you describe them?" he said urgently, and Chantal blinked.

"Well, it'd be easier if you came down and looked," she began, but Tesper was already on his way.

She caught up with him as he was looking around and attempting to spot the tattooed boy. "Over there," she indicated, and Tesper hurried across the room. After a quick survey, he breathed a delighted sigh.

"What fantastic luck! Chantal, there's always been one outstanding puzzle about the Croceraunians—what their 'magic' was, besides bastard atomic science. Right here we have a chance to find out. This boy was the war party's magician."

Chantal digested that in silence for a moment. Tesper went on enthusiastically, "Back before the war I'd have given my arm for a chance like this. Now I can only make the most of it. I was a social historian, you see, before I was put on to the temporal survey side. Can you wake the boy up?"

She nodded, and reached for a jet injector charged with a stimulant. Meantime, Tesper fetched a chair and sat down comfortably alongside the boy's bunk.

After a pause the eyelids fluttered, and then the youth looked straight into Tesper's face. There was no sign of fear or astonishment in his reaction, and he asked a question.

There was something very attractive about his complete self-possession, and Chantal, though she could not understand what he said, felt herself warm to him at once. Tesper glanced up.

"This is remarkable. He wants to know if he's in a metal bird—he must mean an aircraft. How could he tell?" Stumblingly, he phrased a sentence in the strange tongue, and the boy answered.

"His name's Vyko, and he's the magician of the war party, as I guessed. It's his first time out. He says he told the captain that a powerful magic had sent them elsewhere in time—to the Old Days. *But how can he tell?*"

Fascinated, Chantal watched silently, occasionally venturing to interrupt and ask what was being said. She could gather only that Vyko remembered being shot, and accepted their healing him as a matter of course. But he had assumed they were powerful magicians themselves, and his terms for understanding the universe were so alien that even Tesper, who had studied the history of his time, had trouble with them.

And then he said something that made Tesper sit up and exclaim.

"What is it?" demanded Chantal.

"He's talking about looking into time. He claims he can see the future. This is wonderful…. Chantal, humans in this era experience time in a slightly extended way."

"Yes, Burma told us when we first met her. I thought she was delusional."

"She spoke the bald truth. The present moment is not a sequence of simple moving points separating past and future, as your physicists taught, but a series of overlapping possibilities from which we choose. Unconsciously, of course—usually this all happens too fast for us to control it."

"Remind me not to play poker with you for serious money."

Tesper grinned. "No, we can win and lose at games of chance. But we'd probably beat you and Red."

"I always feel slow and sluggish next to you."

"We have often tried to find where that skill arose. Some propose it was a mutation from the early nuclear era, others that it arose from genomic meddling or even directed neuronomics. Either could account for the fantastic rise of the Croceraunian Empire. With extra-temporal perceptors, perhaps specially bred, they could overcome any opposition."

Chantal frowned. She seized on the one important fact, surprised to find herself so vehement about it. "Ask him if Red and Magwareet will get back safely."

A brief exchange; then, "He can't tell. He doesn't know who they are, or anything about this time he's in. But he can tell that nothing is going to happen to harm him in the near future—that's why he's so calm and sure of himself.

"Chantal, this means that the human species can have four-dimensional awareness, and if it wasn't for the risk of monkeying with history and changing it, we'd have the perfect key to communication with the Being—right in the palms of our hands."

—— ∞ ——

## CHAPTER XXIX

## 1472 +/- 3: TIME SURGE Michoo

*This year* (according to the "Turkish Spy," Giovanni Paolo Marana, 1642–1693) *there came to Paris a man by the name of Michoo Ader, claiming to be the Wandering Jew—condemned to*

142

*walk the earth until the Second Coming because he would not let Jesus rest on his doorstep.*

Anchor team leader Ader monitored the time flux, waiting in the predicted vacuole locus for the next surge. Drawing on the information compiled by Magwareet, he felt certain that he and his crew would at the very least nudge the Being into showing itself.

"Michoo," his tectonics specialist said in a tight voice, "the disruption is only 30 seconds away now."

"I see the index rising. Very well, people, let's ride the wave."

When it came, it felt like…passing into a mirror, and out the other side. It felt like a shock of cold water that opened his eyes and blurred the world into confusion. It felt like waking from a nightmare, or into one.

He tumbled down stone steps, arms flailing, grabbing at an instrument panel that was no longer there. Head ringing, Michoo Ader fetched up sprawled full length on grimy cobblestones under a leaden sky. A child was yelling excitedly, and a woman shrieked imprecations in a language he did not know. The air smelled of rotting vegetation, burning, with a fecal overtone that brought him close to retching.

Ader clutched at his chest. The time map was there, its short smooth pipe basketed safely in its sling. Too soon to consult its data. Stand up, check for bleeding. Swaying, but hands to scalp and bruised elbows revealed no blood. Left ankle wrenched in the tumble. Limping, he tried to get his bearings.

From the gray stone house whose steps had caused his fall, at the intersection of two streets, a pair of sturdy middle-aged women with caps holding down dirty hair bustled to his rescue. Their voices were rough but curiously musical, although they lacked the tonal variety of pitch that distinguished Speech from its antecedent English. He was grateful that Burma's near-catastrophic and unprepared plunge into the epoch of Red and Chantal had led immediately to additional routine augments in anchor crews. He had an abstract of as much history as had survived the nuclear exchanges, the aborted nano-singularity, and other calamities.

As the women babbled at him, brushing away dust from his tunic and rather annoyingly propping him up, the device was sorting swiftly through its linguistics, seeking a match to their syntax, grammar, vocabulary. He thanked them in his own tongue, and they burst out laughing. Two half-naked children rushed about this novelty, offering mockery and derisive expressions with fingers, fists and tongues. The younger made noises like a chicken, and flapped her elbows. Ader sighed and waited for the machine to start translating at least the elements of the chatter.

A resonant whisper inside his head told him, "This is definitely Earth. The locale appears to be the early Renaissance city of Florence, and the year approximately 1472, plus or minus three years. The system will attempt autonomic translation between Speech and the local patois, and vice versa. Beware danger."

Ader bowed his thanks to the women, ignored the urchins, and stepped into the street. Almost at once he was nearly run down by two well-dressed riders galloping around the corner. He drew back with a shout of fright and indignation. One young fellow was tall and mirthful, mounted on a chestnut stallion; he cast back a look filled with curiosity, and reined his horse. The other, with wild hair and garments as handsome as the first, paused with a shout.

The tall youth dismounted, took several steps to confront Ader, admiring his tunic, running one graceful hand down the fabric. He spoke something that was obviously a question, tilting his head. The young man really was astonishingly beautiful, in a strikingly masculine way rather out of fashion at Center, if one ignored the likes of Magwareet.

The second man dismounted as well, pushed his companion to one side, said with a certain belligerence, "Alessandro di Mariano di Vanni Filipepi." Presumably a name. Aker nodded, gave his own. "Sandro," said the first youth in a chiding manner. He gestured at his friend, and said something that contained the words "Sandro Botticelli."

Michoo Ader felt his heart jolt. Was it possible? This was a name still known and revered in the early fifth millennium.

"An artist, a painter," the system told him. "This meeting cannot be a coincidence. There is a probability approaching unity that his associate is—"

And the inner voice overlapped with the spoken words "Leonardo di ser Piero da Vinci," as the tall man offered his hand. As he continued, the system rendered his words into Speech: "Evidently you are a stranger to Florence. I admire your garb, sir. Will you lunch with us and tell us your tales of travel?"

"Willingly, Leonardo," Akers said, and the words he spoke were modified into an approximation of the local language. The painter can't have done anything important, he told himself, pulse still thundering. Nor, as yet, can his friend Botticelli. I must keep our conversation from veering in that direction, he thought. Nothing about painting that might change history. I'll dazzle him with stories he'll take to be utterly imaginary. Flight to the stars. Dreadful war engines, the kind of thing I wouldn't dare speak of to an expert artificer in this period. Vessels to explore the depths of the ocean and capture realistic images of those denizens his century cannot even conceive.

Smiling, still limping a little, Aker was hoisted up behind da Vinci when that worthy took to his saddle.

"You have a curious accent, sir. Let us visit my master, Andrea del Verrocchio, the finest of all Florentine painters," said the translation system. "He will grumble that I am not about his work, but I vow he will listen eagerly to your travel tales, and he keeps a fine cellar." They trotted away at a fair speed, followed by the shrill and raucous cries of the children.

—— ∞ ——

## CHAPTER XXX

## 17th century: TIME SURGE Search for Wymarin

The record of Johann Friedrich Schweitzer, called Helvetius, distinguished physician and respected citizen of The Hague: "*The 27th of December, 1666, in the afternoon, came a stranger to my house...being a great lover of the Pyro-technian art (alchemy).... He gave me a crumb as big as a rape or turnip seed (of the Philosopher's Stone).... I cut half an ounce or six*

145

*drams of old lead, and put it into a crucible in the fire, which being melted, my wife put in the said Medicine (the Stone)... within a quarter of an hour all the mass of lead was totally transmuted into the best and finest gold....*

"*I...did run with this aurified lead (being yet hot) unto the goldsmith, who... judged it the most excellent gold in the whole world.*"

Magwareet carried off his unaccustomed garb with an air of distinction, but Red found it uncomfortable and awkward. They had managed to obtain samples of clothing and money while invisible, and after returning to the equally invisible ship had duplicated them. Properly equipped, they had set out. Now he fidgeted under the stern gaze of the landlord.

"So yuh meester Komm from Muscovy?" the fat man said. "An' yussef?"

"I've spent a long time there," said Red carefully. The landlord's knowledge of English was scanty enough, and his seventeenth-century accent—though unexpectedly close to some dialects of mid-twentieth-century American—added to the problem. "My master is a student of the philosophical art that men call alchemy."

"Dis gold—ist alchemic?" The landlord suspiciously rapped one of the thalers they had given him in payment for their accommodation. Red shook his head.

"No! Alchemical gold," he improvised, "is mystical and not to be used in trade."

The landlord looked relieved, but Red noticed that he put their payment in a separate bag from the rest of the money in his coffer. Turning back to them, he said, "An' yuh vant wat?"

"My master wishes to meet and speak of alchemic matters with the learned men of this city."

"Den go see Meester Porelius. Iss da assay-meester of da kinglich court. Ee'ull zendt my apprentist to guide."

He went out, and Red looked at Magwareet. "Are you getting what he says?" he asked.

Magwareet nodded. "What was the office of this man he wants to send us to, though?"

"Assay-master—if I heard him right. That means he's an inspector of currency, and probably an expert in the chemistry of metals. I think we've struck lucky first time."

He glanced down at himself ruefully. "I'm supposed to be used to this kind of costume, and I feel like an idiot. You're supposed to come from a barbarian country, and look much more at home in them."

There was a knock at the door, and a small boy put his head in. "This will be our guide," Red commented—they were talking Speech, chancing anyone meeting them who knew what Russian actually sounded like. "Shall we leave right away?"

"The less time we waste the better," said Magwareet, with a grave expression befitting an adept in the pyrotechnian art. "Lead the way, little one."

They followed the boy out into the narrow crowded streets they had already traversed on their way into the town. Two precious days had gone already, and they were only beginning their task.

As they passed men laden with goods, men selling fresh water from barrels, itinerant vendors of needles, distinguished citizens with attendants, rough artisans, slatternly women, they were predominantly conscious of one thing—a stink that was almost nauseating. Magwareet suffered even worse than Red. The reason was perfectly plain, of course—from upper story windows maidservants were casually tossing night slops into the streets, horses padded through the muddy pools leaving the inevitable reeking signs of their passage, and the inhabitants themselves were blithely and unselfconsciously unaware of the values of public sanitation. The most resplendently dressed people they met were scratching themselves for lice.

"This is a civilized country?" said Magwareet meaningfully as they paused to let a couple of packhorses precede them down a tiny alleyway, and Red shrugged.

"I see what you mean," he agreed. "Unpromising, isn't it?"

The house where the boy stopped was plainly that of a well-to-do citizen, but—like the majority of those in the town—owing to infirm foundations it was very slightly, but noticeably, askew. Their little guide, brushing his hair back with a quick gesture, stretched on tip-toe and banged the knocker.

A pretty young maidservant opened to them, and on hearing their errand, stood back smiling to let them enter. They hesitated on the threshold because of the state of their feet, but there were already muddy marks on the wood floor, and Red remembered that he had heard somewhere of a complaint by an Englishman of the Dutch custom of never wiping one's shoes.

They followed the maid into a large, well-furnished room, where she invited them to sit down. Red, after some difficulty—but he was getting used to Dutch by now—discovered that Meester Porelius was out at the moment on some mission, but was due back shortly.

He relayed this to Magwareet. "He's gone to see a goldsmith called Brechtel—as far as I can gather, about some alchemical business. So it seems we're really in luck."

They had not long to wait. Meester Porelius came in less than ten minutes later, with a companion, talking at the top of his voice. Red listened carefully, but caught no more than that something was fantastic and incredible.

Within a short while Porelius himself entered and, bowing to them, invited them to state their business.

"My master," said Red, pleased to find that Porelius spoke good English, "is a learned man of Muscovy, by name Andreev, and we desire to meet and discuss matters concerning the pyrotechnian art and mystery."

Porelius expanded like a flower in the sun, and called for wine to be brought. "Then you will be delighted and amazed to learn that in this very city at the moment is the most remarkable adept in that art who ever existed."

"Really?" said Red, glancing at Magwareet, who was preserving his dignity with difficulty.

"Yes, indeed." exclaimed Porelius. "I have myself been at the silversmith's this morning, submitting to the test of fire some alchemic gold that was transmitted by Meester Helvetius, physician to the Royal Court of Orange, using some of the Philosopher's Stone that was given to him as a token by a certain Meester Elias some few days ago."

"And the gold stood the test?"

"Most surely. More than that, I saw that it had itself some of the wonderful virtue of the Medicine used on it. For in my presence, gentlemen, I saw it transmute a full dram of silver into gold."

Porelius sat back with a self-satisfied air, and the maid poured wine and brought it to them. Red was so startled that at first he hardly noticed the girl waiting at his side.

"And this—Meester Elias who has the Stone?" he said at length. "What manner of man is he?"

"That I cannot fairly say," admitted Porelius, "for I myself have not seen him. But I have it from Meester Helvetius that he is a small man, beardless, with black hair, and that he is said to be a founder of brass who was taught the Art by an outlandish friend."

Red seized the chance with both hands. "This outlandish friend—perchance he came from Muscovy?"

"It is possible. Know you this Elias?"

"Not certainly. But a fellow adept of my master has traveled to this part of Europe before, and has recounted that he met one pupil especially apt to learn. Now that I bethink me of it, his name might full well have been Elias. If it is indeed the same, my master would much desire to have discourse with him."

Porelius chuckled, and held out his mug for more wine. "He is not alone. I too crave that, as does everyone who witnessed, the transformation that took place this morning. We have already criers out to find where he lodges, but no man knows him."

Red's heart sank, but he was puzzled beyond measure to know what sort of person this mysterious Elias might be. If he was indeed able to transmute metals, he would be an incredibly valuable contact.

There was the chance of trickery, naturally—Red had heard of the astute charlatans who duped whole groups of people with pretended transmutations—but Porelius struck him as a level-headed type, and certainly, if he was the equivalent of Master of the Mint, he could not be deceived in the testing of precious metal.

Fired by his new audience, Porelius continued to enlarge on what he had seen, and the idea in Red's mind grew to a certainty. Elias was their man.

But how to find him?

The best they could do was to extract a promise that Porelius would notify them if anyone found Elias; meantime, he promised to introduce them to such experimenters in the Art as there were at The Hague. With that, they departed.

Then began a dreary round of meetings with half-sensible, half-bemused mystics and serious but misguided experimenters. Helvetius himself they met, and heard his story—it convinced them completely that Elias was the person they were after. No one else had even the remotest chance of being useful to them. They simply lacked the necessary scientific discipline; their work was confused and muddled with so much esoteric jargon that both sides concluded that their new acquaintances were incompetent.

And still there was no sign of Elias.

Red began to doubt that such a person existed, but Magwareet, oddly enough, was perfectly ready to accept both his ability and his actual transmutation.

"It is entirely possible to transmute metals chemically," was the upsetting remark he made when Red taxed him. "I don't see why you're so distrustful."

"Well, then—*how*, for goodness' sake?"

"The nearest analogy is by saying it's a biological process," explained Magwareet frowning. "Certain atomic patterns have the property of reduplicating themselves by directed resonance under the right conditions, and it doesn't take the energy of a particle accelerator or one of those other early nuclear devices to force the reaction. But it required the combined resources of most of Center's computers to determine those conditions, and the one thing that does bother me is whether anyone would really have been silly enough to set them up by accident."

Slightly heartened, Red pursued his search. They had been there so long that they were almost used to the stench when, one morning, as they were setting off to meet yet another of these experimenters who might help them, they passed a small man in a dark fustian coat, who walked along the muddy road unattended and with downcast eyes. Magwareet looked at him, looked away, and then turned back with most undignified haste.

"Wymarin!" he shouted, and the little man halted and came back with all the self-possession in the world.

"Thank goodness you showed up," he said mildly. "I thought I was going to have to found nuclear and directed physics from the bottom up in order to get home." He looked at them inquiringly. "You don't seem very surprised to see me, I must say."

Red waited long enough to make sure he had his breath back, and then spoke equally mildly. "I suppose you're Elias," he said disgustedly.

"Of course. Where's the ship? I must get back. I've got something very important to tell Artesha."

—— ∞ ——

## CHAPTER XXXI

## 4070: Red and Chantal

*"Am I my brother's keeper?"*—Cain, the brother of Abel whom he slew....

" *No man is an island."*—John Donne, cleric, sensualist and master of the English language....

*One might think that Jung's simile comparing individual consciousness to islands poking up through the surface of a sea contradicted that dictum, but nonetheless the islands were indivisibly connected through the bed of the ocean.*

*And yet somewhere behind that antinomy, that paradoxical contradiction, was knowledge. Which of these was neighbor to him that fell among thieves?*

Chantal noted that Red still limped, automatically, in moments of stress as they entered the miraculous door leading to any part of Center's complex of ships. And it was a moment of stress, of awe. Their first meeting with Artesha had been no more than one in a long series of incredible happenings, most notably the extraordinary

151

formal dinner, and now they knew the nature of that—ex-woman. The phrase rang suspiciously true.

Yet there was nothing beyond the door except that same small room, warm and softly lit. In it, Chantal fancied she could sense *presence*.

There were chairs waiting. Magwareet took one immediately and spoke up. "Artesha!"

"I'm listening," said the detached voice. Artesha had never again manifested herself in an illusory body since that dinner; she was far too busy.

"I'll give you a brief run-down on exactly what we've done, first of all. Then Wymarin should be along. He went straight through to give the details of his last experiment to Burma. And Tesper brought up something in connection with one of the barbarians that I think is very important."

"Very well. Go ahead."

It took Magwareet less than five minutes to give a complete account of their trip, and at the end of it Artesha uttered a satisfied sound.

"We had a fantastic stroke of luck," Red ventured, "finding Wymarin the way we did."

"I wonder," said Artesha thoughtfully. "Wymarin doesn't think so."

"What?" The three of them—Red, Chantal and Magwareet—leaned forward as if she were in the room, seated before them.

"I'm monitoring his report to Burma. Wymarin believes that he succeeded in getting through to the Being, and although the reflex he stimulated tossed him into time the Being did its best to control the trajectory and make certain he survived. And then, perhaps, guided you to his general location."

They digested that in silence for a moment. Magwareet heaved a huge sigh. "Is it likely?" he asked.

"For the time being, I'll leave that to Burma to settle. I've told her that as soon as Wymarin has provided the information required, she must try to repeat the experiment with a little less force. I'm ordering out as many anchor teams as we can spare to help hold down the temporal surge if she stimulates one. Here comes Wymarin now."

The door slid aside and admitted not only the little dark-haired man whose alchemical achievements had amazed seventeenth-century Holland, but also Tesper. They greeted Artesha, and sat down.

"Well, Burma is going ahead," Wymarin informed them. "We can expect results in one form or another within a few hours."

"But how did you manage to provoke the Being?" Magwareet asked with more emotion than he usually displayed.

"Briefly, what I did was this. I've been struggling for more than ten years now to deduce by pure logic what an intelligent creature existing fully in four or perhaps more dimensions would recognize as a significant pattern. I had a great deal of help from Qepthin's team, but the one that seems to have been successful was entirely my own idea.

"So I set up a wave-pattern that was symmetrical in four dimensions, and then modulated it in accordance with a number system derived from the coordinates of the world lines of the major Solar System planets. We already knew that the Being was sensitive to high levels of radiant energy—witness the way it keeps a certain distance from the Sun and reacts convulsively to nuclear explosions. I fear, though, that what I did still affected the Being too powerfully. The shock actually pained it. But I am absolutely certain it recognized there was no malignity in what I did, and moreover knew that I, not the rest of my team, was responsible. So it looked after me during the surge." He sat back, looking pleased with himself.

"There's something fundamentally wrong with your analysis," said Red suddenly, astonished at his own temerity. Magwareet and Wymarin glanced at him, startled.

"Excellent," said Artesha. "Go on, Red—what makes you so sure?"

"Well…put it this way. I know how hard it is to get across even to another human being a meaningful statement, even in terms of a common language and culture. I found that back in my own time—I knew what I was trying to convey when I worked with metal and stone, but half the time people missed what I was trying to indicate."

He was warming to the thesis. "I just can't see what you could get across to a creature whose entire existence has nothing in common with ours, anything based on—I don't know, let's say number, which is a product of our idea of sequence in time or space. One precedes two, two precedes three, and so on."

"No, you're wrong there," Artesha broke in. "Wymarin's mathematics is purely non-sequential. But I think your basic point is perfectly valid.

"Wymarin," she continued, "we're beginning to break down the psychology of the specimen of the Enemy that we caught. Our only explanation of how it managed to penetrate our defenses is that the Being is actually used by them. It might even be a weapon they are only gradually starting to control. I want you to go down and see Qepthin and find out from him if the psychological pattern he is constructing agrees in any important features with the one you postulate for the Being. If it is—"

"If it is," said Magwareet flatly, "we've got to defeat both of them together, or we're beaten."

Looking thoroughly upset, Wymarin nodded and went out.

"How long do you think it'll take him to be doing useful work again after the break-up of his team?" asked Magwareet. "And have they recovered any more of the personnel?"

"No, they are still lost," said Artesha thoughtfully. "But I think he'll readapt quickly. He's collaborated with Qepthin before."

"What news of the fighting?"

"We're still pulling back. We took an Enemy fleet clear out of the sky—fifty-five ships—when they were pushing towards Tau Ceti. Your son was in that counterattack, Paulo."

Magwareet jolted upright. "Joaquin—"

"He is all right. Some slight burns. He fought very bravely and competently, I see a future for that young fellow."

He sagged, and color returned to his features.

"Thank you for the news, Artesha."

She said, "But I think we're going to have to evacuate that entire system."

"It's horribly close to home," said Wymarin slowly.

"Much *too* close, I've tried and tried, but I can't see a way out. We can't run, there's nowhere to run to—the Enemy controls space in all directions away from the Solar System. Every time we pull back, we have fewer resources to draw on, less space to maneuver—" Artesha, for one of the few times Magwareet could recall, sounded as completely human as she had been before she so nearly died.

"There are still possibilities we haven't studied," Wymarin pointed out, apparently trying to sound comforting. "Tesper, yours is very hopeful."

154

The ex-historian, who had been listening gravely to this exchange, leaned forward.

"Yes, it's this boy Vyko. You already know who he is, Artesha?"

"Staff magician to this Croceraunian war party you had to mop up. Yes, go on."

"Well, he holds the key not only to the problem of what made the Croceraunian Empire so phenomenally successful, but also to communication with the Being. If that's even possible. Here we have someone who genuinely possesses a sort of extended four-dimensional consciousness. I haven't been able to get details yet, because his language—though I speak it fluently—is very poorly suited to conveying the concepts. I'm having him given an intensive course of Speech at the moment."

"You'd better be careful none of the concepts he gets conflict with his ability," said Artesha.

"That's been attended to. Anyway, if there's a single person capable of identifying at all with the Being, he is the one."

"How does his extra-temporal perception work?"

"Well, we've established that it isn't extrapolation. Any reasonably good computer can be adapted to prophecy if required, and we do it all the time. No, his talent is under conscious control, although it extends more to emotions than actual events. He needs to know the people he makes prophecies about, or at any rate be associated with them, but details of their proposed course of action aren't needed. He can make forecasts completely without knowledge of the circumstances. He managed, for example, to forecast the probable fate of his war party when there had been no sign at all of an impending attack, though one was coming."

"How soon can we start making use of this talent?"

"He'll only have to get acquainted with Center and the general situation, that's all."

"I could figure out by pure deduction what it is necessary for him to know," Artesha remarked pensively. "But I shouldn't expend the time when we have two people who've been through much the same sort of thing. Red, Chantal—I have a job for you. I want you to take Vyko around Center—anywhere you like—and tell him what you wanted to know when you arrived here. Let him get the feel of things. You won't have to give him complex scientific or mathematical knowledge—he's educated, according to his standards. Maybe a brief summary of astronomical facts will be required. Do you think you can handle that?"

"Sure," said Red confidently. "Except that we'll have difficulty finding our own way around Center."

"You won't. Time is always valuable, and hence we designed Center so that its organization lets anyone find their way about after a minute's explanation. Magwareet will show you what I mean when we're through here."

—— ∞ ——

## CHAPTER XXXII

## 4070: Red and Chantal

*Take the Solar System, for example.*

*There was (or was there?) a certain moon of Saturn. "Themis." William Henry Pickering, its discoverer, was an experienced astronomer unlikely to be misled. He observed his find carefully enough to determine such things as its period of revolution. There was also the fact that it was many times brighter on one side than on the other—an easy aid to identification. Despite all this, people hunted for it afterwards in vain.*

*There was also, possibly, an intra-Mercurial planet, which was given the appropriate name of Vulcan. Urbain Jean Joseph Le Verrier and other distinguished men believed in it, believed also that it had been unmistakably observed. Nonetheless, only a few decades after, it was established that it wasn't there.*

*No reasonable person considered adding the qualification "any longer…".*

Tesper interrupted diffidently. "Artesha, there's one very important point we haven't seen to. Our ship brought back about forty other

Croceraunians besides Vyko, you know. I am concerned about deleterious effects we're having on history—and what we ought to do with them."

"We simply haven't got enough information to decide." Artesha seemed weary. "As I see it, we'll do least harm if we simply return them to the point at which the temporal surge first picked them up. But these surges have such complicated history we can't be sure we'd pinpoint their return address."

"Have they?" said Red sharply. "Are you certain their disappearance isn't already accounted for in the present?"

"Of course it is," snapped Artesha. "But *which* present?"

"What do you mean?"

"We obviously can't tell whether the temporal surges have changed anything or not—we live through their consequences. We can't tell whether the present that would have come into existence if you had not gone back in time chasing the Enemy raider, for instance, might not have been favorable to us. In using and interfering with the results of these surges we may be sewing our own shrouds. Before your crew entered that long surge, was the actual present different from what we now remember—different from the present that your actions caused? Somewhere in a five-dimensional continuum there may be someone the equivalent of you, Red, doing something totally different at what appears to be the same moment of time. Think it over—I wish you better luck with it than I've had. If we still slept, I'd get nightmares from it."

She broke off. "We must also investigate the possibility that the Enemy ship you chased and destroyed deliberately entered the surge in order to attack our past. Magwareet, I want you to see that attended to."

"Surely." Magwareet looked unhappy. "Very well. That'll be all for the time being."

Tesper went straight out, but Red and Chantal waited for Magwareet, who seemed to be making up his mind about something. At length he spoke.

"Artesha, let me tell you what's been bothering me. That Enemy raider we followed into the surge…. You warned us about it when we shifted twenty hours back in time. Why didn't you warn us when we passed that point earlier? Did you not know about it? If not, *why not?*"

157

"But I did," said Artesha. "There would have been no point in warning you before you shifted—"

"Listen! We were preparing to leave. Twenty hours before, this raider had entered the Solar System. Why was it not spotted and destroyed before it had a chance to enter the surge? Why didn't we know about it before we went back?"

"But—" Artesha hesitated. Then she spoke slowly, giving the words an air of puzzlement. "I—I remember the episode twice, Magwareet! Part of it is recorded in each of two mnemonic files. One time, I knew about it—that must have been the moment when we were passing that instant in normal duration. I could do nothing about it."

"Then there's your answer to the problem of the alteration of history. We do alter it. You couldn't have it destroyed immediately because, in the far past, it had already been destroyed, some thousands of years ago."

Red stared at him. In the creative space where he mapped and manipulated his art, lines of cause and effect twined themselves, complex yet vividly real.

"Analyze that, and you'll have the whole solution," Magwareet was saying. "You're the only person who can do it, Artesha. We've interfered with history to such an extent I'm seriously worried. Did you actually order that Enemy ship to be left alone?"

"I—I don't know. Magwareet, this is terrible. The human species is relying on my judgment, and I'm forgetting things—"

"There is no way you can forget things, Artesha. Except through algorithms in your own brain, and you have the tools to deal with those."

He stood for a moment, gazing at the featureless panels concealing Artesha's mind, and then turned and went out.


Pausing beyond the door, Red and Chantal saw that their companion's face was ashen with strain. He gave them a wan smile. "I'm sorry," he said. "I had to warn Artesha about that—she's the only person capable of psychoanalyzing herself, and although the majority of her mind is now composed of artificial units that can't go wrong, her actual brain-patterns—the human ones—are still fallible. Oh, but this tampering with time is risky."

He broke off, and showed them the way to get about Center's gigantic complex of individual ships. As Artesha had promised, it worked by such simple rules that only one brief summary was necessary. Then Magwareet took his leave.

As they headed towards the department where Vyko, unconscious again, was being taught Speech by the same direct brain-modifying method used on them, Red muttered, "What an extraordinary person Artesha must be, suffering an experience like hers and staying sane."

"I suspect Burma's love and patience had a lot to do with it," Chantal answered. "Imagine being her spouse."

"You know, something's changed since we've been away," Red said after a pause. "Do you—smell—tensions in the air?"

Chantal nodded. "People are certainly showing more signs of stress."

"It must be this news from Tau Ceti. Is that very close?"

"I suppose so—I don't know exactly. I'm so accustomed to googling that kind of factual detail, I'm lost without access to whatever the web has become. I'm sorry, I know that sounds like nonsensical babble to you, Red."

"I'm afraid it does. Ah—excuse me a moment, Chantal." Red turned aside into a washroom, and she waited in the corridor outside for a few moments.

Just as Red returned, a movement at the end of the passage caught her eye, and she gave a terrified gasp. "Look," she said faintly.

Red followed her pointing. At the far end of the corridor he managed to catch a glimpse of a man turning and going through a door marked with the resonance symbol. The only striking thing that he noticed was the other's hair; it was as red as his own.

"I don't see what—" he began, but Chantal cut him short. She put out a hand and touched his shoulder.

"Red—he was your exact double! Didn't you see the likeness?"

"I couldn't see his face, but I admit his hair was like mine. Well, what about it? Is red hair so very unusual?"

"Red, you don't understand," said Chantal desperately. "That other man was limping, exactly the way you do from sheer force of habit. He wasn't just like you, Red—he *was* you! *Is* you."

Chantal seemed completely unnerved by the shock, and Red put his hands on her shoulders. "Listen," he said urgently. "There are people from dozens of planets at Center—I expect lots of them have red hair. And what's so astonishing about a limp? Maybe the guy had a sprained ankle."

"But with the medical equipment people have now, sprains are easy to correct."

"Well, this is the medical section we're heading for, isn't it? Maybe he just sprained a muscle a few minutes ago and is going to have it fixed. Come on, that sounds reasonable, doesn't it?"

Chantal frowned. "I—I guess so," she agreed reluctantly.

"All right, then. We may very well find him in the room ahead of us. Let's go straight down and look."

Walking a trifle unsteadily, Chantal followed him the few remaining steps to their goal; he pushed open the panel and stepped inside, finding a small bare cubicle.

After a moment a plump woman in green came out to them from the room beyond. "Yes?" she said shortly.

Red explained their mission, and the woman nodded. "All right. I'm expecting to bring Vyko out of his coma in a few minutes now. If you'd just hang on, I'll call you in when I'm ready to waken him."

"Red," Chantal put in. "I'm going to ask Artesha if anyone like you is going around Center."

He turned to her in astonishment. "Chantal, for God's sake. We can't bother her with a figment of your imagination."

"Just a moment," Chantal called after the plump woman. "Is there any way I can get in touch with Artesha from here?"

The woman stopped dead in the doorway and stared at her. "Er—er, yes, there is. One moment, please." She stepped very briefly out of sight.

When she reappeared, there was a man with her who towered over her, more than two meters tall; his face was set in a menacing expression, and—most alarming of all—there was something in the woman's hand that they didn't recognize, but which looked purposeful. She kept it very steadily aligned on them.

"Get behind them, Duarak," she said softly. The man moved with the speed of a pouncing lion, and Red and Chantal found him with his hamlike hands poised above their shoulders. "All right, you two.

Explain yourselves. I should tell you this gun I'm holding will kill you before you can make a move, and it won't hurt Duarak either."

"Are you crazy?" said Red in utter disbelief.

"Not at all," the woman told him grimly. "The communicator system here is perfectly ordinary—standard pattern. Artesha is always available from anywhere in Center. I want to know why you asked that question." There was a hard note of stress in her voice.

Red felt Chantal relax with a shuddering sigh. He himself couldn't help smiling. "We don't know our way around Center yet," he explained. "The same thing happened to us as happened to this man Vyko you have here. We're both from the twentieth century. Well, the twenty-first in Chantal's case."

"Have you heard anything about this, Duarak?"

"Not a thing," the brawny man replied.

"All right. We'll have to check, then. Contact Artesha, will you?"

Without taking his eyes off them, Duarak reached for the wall behind and felt for a pattern on the icons below a communicator panel that they had not noticed.

"I apologize in advance if I've misjudged you," the woman in green said unsmilingly. "But since we discovered that the Enemy is oxygen-breathing, we can't take the smallest chance."

"What is it?" Artesha's familiar voice filled the air.

The woman summed up the situation, and Red and Chantal both showed relief when Artesha made a short and irritated answer. The gun was lowered at once.

"Sorry," the woman said without expression.

"Artesha," called Chantal suddenly, as if on making up her mind. "Chantal here. I want to tell you something."

"Chantal," said Red in annoyance.

"Let her go ahead," Artesha rebuked him. "Yes?"

"While Red and I were coming towards the section where we are now, I'm absolutely certain I saw someone at the end of the passage who looked exactly like him. Exactly—even down to his limp."

There was a brief pause. "Well, that doesn't surprise me—there are several million people in Center. But what you say about the limp is interesting. All right, I'll search my memory and check up for you. That all?"

"Yes." When the communicator went dead, Chantal looked trium-phantly at Red. "You see? She didn't think it was ridiculous, did she?"

Red muttered something inaudible. "We have a job to do," he said pointedly to the woman in green, and she nodded.

"All right, come along."

—— ∞ ——

## CHAPTER XXXIII

## 4070: Vyko

Such complete economy had been observed in the use of the space available within the ships of Center that even the medical clinic, where they now found themselves, was barely big enough for all four of them to stand around the couch on which Vyko lay. The tattoo marks on his arms and chest stood out vividly under daylight lamps. The woman in green went to a cabinet whose shelves were full of shiny sterile equipment; selecting an injector, she administered a quick shot of some straw-yellow fluid. Waiting for it to take effect, Red noticed the hypnotic equipment that had been used to teach Vyko Speech folded tidily away from the head of his couch.

The magician yawned and rubbed his eyes, exactly as if emerging from an ordinary night's sleep. After a moment, he looked up at them, blinking.

"I—I feel different," he said, puzzled.

"Are you all right?" Red inquired, and the boy nodded.

"Yes, I feel very well. And I—I seem to understand things better." Vyko frowned. "I know where I am, and I know that you've taught me your language by magic. Are you—" He checked himself, raised his body into a sitting position, and made a quick pass with both hands.

"Reman still for a moment, young man," said the woman in green. She checked his vital signs, and recorded them in the device attached to his couch. To Red she said, "He seems fine, physically.

Can you handle everything from here on? Duarak and I are wanted elsewhere."

"Yes, sure," Red said. "Vyko, we aren't magicians as you mean it. What you call magic, we call science, but it's...." He trailed off. "It works by rather different principles."

"I have been taught that word 'science' and what it means." Vyko swung his feet to the floor. "And I can't tell you how wonderful it is to be here. I expect you know all about me?"

"Well, not very much," Red admitted.

"You know that I am what we call a magician, I was taught all that the priests think about, but I used to wonder if the Old Days people understood the world better than we do. Now I have the chance to find out, and that's what I always wanted." He gave them an enormous, innocent smile, made disturbing by his sharply pointed teeth.

"What exactly did a magician do?" Red asked.

"Oh, he studies the old books, and services small arms, and makes the supplies of the Breath of Terror. I can do all those things," he added with pride. "But the most important thing about a magician, of course, is that we can look into the future. Priests can do everything else but not that."

Chantal muttered something in French, then said, "Presentiment, Red. This must be related to the time surges. Vyko, is this a gift, or a skill you learn?"

Vyko seemed to pay full attention to her for the first time. "It's just something you know how to do. You can't explain it. Many times my people tried to teach more people to see further in time, but it never worked. Yes, you're born with it or you're not. I was very lucky. And now, to be here!" His eyes gleamed.

Comparing Vyko's enthusiastic acceptance of what had happened to him with his own earlier overt hostility, Red felt a pang of shame. This was the right spirit, one of adventurous anticipation.

"Well," Chantal said, "we're going to show you around Center—that's this place where you are now. The same thing happened to us. We're from what you call the Old Days, before the wars that destroyed our countries. But the people of this time know far, far more than we ever did."

The young man ran his eyes curiously up and down her, noting her obviously feminine body under her coverall. "Are you not a woman?" he said after some moments' hesitation.

Chantal smiled broadly. "But yes, of course."

"Even though you also know about—science?"

"I am a medical doctor. We study a great deal of science."

Vyko stood up, shaking his head in a puzzled gesture.

"This is indeed a strange world I have come to. Among my people, women can be neither priests nor magicians—they have never been able to see into the future. Women's duties are domestic, like tanning hides and preparing food and liquor, and bearing children. Is that not so now?"

"Women have always borne children," Chantal replied, managing to keep her face quite straight this time. "But now machines do so many tasks that men and women alike can invest time learning about science and many other things."

"I see that it would be so," said Vyko, nodding. "And are these some of the machines?" He indicated the banked medical equipment. "Indeed it is very wonderful. I know that we are inside a metal boat that flies above the air. You call it a spaceship. But I do not understand what that means."

Red glanced wryly at Chantal. "Artesha said a lesson in the basics of astronomy might be necessary. I wonder where we can go to show him space, and explain about time war?"


They took Vyko to an observation mezzanine like a flattened bubble of glass overlooking the master control center. Below, men and women engaged with the plans hatched in Artesha's incredibly complex mind, translating them into terms of concrete action. This Vyko understood readily. Once he appreciated what the battleground represented—the vast empty reaches of space—he followed quite clearly the strategy of a struggle in four or more dimensions.

"How does he get a grasp of it so rapidly?" demanded the soft-spoken elderly officer who had explained what they were watching.

"He has rudimentary four-dimensional awareness," Chantal said. "We're hoping he can help us communicate with the Being."

"Damned sight more useful if he could tell us what the Enemy was likely to do at Tau Ceti," said the officer unhappily. "Can he?"

"Maybe he'll be able to after he's been shown all 'round the setup. Excuse us, we'll have to move on."

And they did so, throughout Center's manifold departments. They saved until last the most overwhelming experience of all, remembering how it had affected them—looking out into space at the magnified ball of the Earth.

Both had been noticing for some time, when they finally entered the ship orbiting closest to the planet, that Vyko kept casting curious glances at Red. Chantal hoped, though she felt unready to risk asking, that he was getting to be able to forecast things about them. Holding her breath, she waited as the wall display presented the brilliantly blue and white sphere that was their birthplace.

But Vyko took it without a qualm. He merely studied it for a few minutes in absolute silence. Then at last he gave a sigh.

"How wonderful to be able to *see* the truth, not guess at it," he said simply.

Red drew a deep breath. "Are you beginning to see into our future, now?" he asked.

"It's very peculiar," was Vyko's slow reply. "Yes, I am, but…. Red, I sense something strange about you."

"What's that?"

"It's like when you cross your eyes. You see two things that are the same but from slightly different angles. I find the same thing when I look into your future—only the two things I see are not just the same from different points. They are separate and distinct."

They thought over that amazing remark in silence. Before either of them had a chance to speak again, the wall communicator came to life. Artesha spoke from it.

"I was listening to that," she said. "Red, will you take Vyko down to the department where Qepthin is studying the Enemy? I want to know if he can make prophecies about another species."

"Right away," agreed Red, and shut out the view of space.

The fussy little alien biologist met them in person on their arrival, beaming all over his face. "We're making fabulous progress," he told them brightly. "Look."

He waved down at the big hall below the gallery where they were standing. Men and women, with every appearance of extreme concentration, were watching the five-limbed alien creature move in a slow rhythmic kind of dance.

"I don't see—" began Red.

"We're controlling it," Qepthin told him. "Its movements now are the direct result of our orders to it. It took us a lot of trouble, but we managed it. We can prepare coded molecules to make it perform more than twenty complex action patterns now. From the spacesuit the thing was wearing, we've discovered what bands they use for long-range communication. In another few hours we'll be *talking* to it, and it won't be able to lie when it answers. But by the stars around us, its communication technique is extraordinary."

"How?"

"It's an extension of the internal cell-to-cell contact. It's got a speech organ in which several billion different molecular patterns can be almost instantly compiled. If we can adapt that, by the way, we'll have a powerful new means of minting safe nanostructures—anyway, as I was saying, it amplifies the normal sub-molecular morphic resonance patterns of about sixty of the possible combinations, and uses them as syllables to construct phrases with specific meaning. It's astonishing, quite unlike DNA and RNA synthesis."

"Ask Vyko if he's getting anything, or thinks he'll be able to," Artesha requested over a wall speaker. Red realized she must be watching their progress continuously.

Vyko was staring in fascination at the Enemy. When Red repeated Artesha's question to him, he sighed and shook his head.

"I know I shall not be able to feel that creature," he said. "It is not possible even with animals on Earth. I am sorry."

"Oh, it's nobody's *fault*," said Chantal, touched by his obviously sincere regret at failing them, and he gave her a quick, warm smile. There was something extremely likable about this young barbarian.

"That's a pity," said Artesha thoughtfully. "Still, it was a very faint chance at best. Red, Burma is setting up the conditions for her next experiment on the Being right now. I'd like you to go over with Vyko and see if you have better luck in that respect."

"All right. Can we go out to an anchor team direct from Center?"

"No, I'm afraid not. I've ordered a ship to wait for you at the lock nearest to you now. You'll find spacesuits near the lock entrance, and I've told the pilot to come in and show you how to use them. Being in free space affects people different ways at first, but I think you should enjoy a little trip like this one."

"Okay," said Red, and beckoned for Vyko to follow him.

It was brief, their trip; the pilot used high acceleration. At first it was eerie being carried along between the unchanging stars on a skeleton of metal tubing to which their suits were merely clamped, but after a while they got their bearings and relaxed. The most frightening moment was not when they first felt the absence of gravity before the ship pulled away—the acceleration substituted for it soon enough—but their approach to the anchor team. Their pilot's skill (or perhaps it was his computer's, Red mused) was fantastic as the flimsy craft was juggled between the solid-hulled orbiting vessels.

Sweating, they scrambled through the airlock aboard the control ship of the anchor team and stripped off their suits.

A panel on the wall of the lock gave them directions, and they found their way without trouble to the big technical room. Here were seemingly endless banks of complex machinery; time maps glowed green from the walls, and many screens bore the red splotches indicating the existence of material bodies in the neighborhood.

Down among the time maps was Burma. As they entered, she was cursing aloud, and Red gathered that she had made the latest of several ridiculous mistakes. He called her name.

Burma looked up. Seeing them, she stopped what she was doing and came over to greet them, warmly. But there was something distracted in her manner.

"What's worrying you?" Red inquired in what he hoped was a neutral tone.

"You're right, I am worried—and it's such a peculiar thing, at that. It's quite put me off my work. Just a few minutes ago, as I was working at the far end of the room, I could have sworn I saw someone at this end who looked exactly like me."

—— ∞ ——

## CHAPTER XXXIV

# 4070: Red and Chantal

*Disappearances have never been confined to human beings, af-*
*ter all. Taking the proportions of habitable land and uninhab-*
*itable ice and wastes of ocean on Earth, one would expect to*
*find the latter yielding many more mysteries—but unknown,*
*because unobserved.*

In the silence with which he and Chantal greeted Burma's statement, Red found time to wonder exactly what was going on at that
moment. No one else in the technical room paid any attention; they
continued to work. A little distance away, Artesha went on attending
to the complex business of Center. Further out, the ships circling the
Solar System obeyed her commands, watched and waited and occasionally struck or were struck. All about and around them the Being
did whatever it did. (Or was its purpose confined to mere existence?)
Farther beyond that again, the Enemy plotted and planned, struck
and were struck.

But everywhere the universe followed its incomprehensible ways:
suns radiated, planets cooled, comets swung through their slow, age-
long orbits or drifted along vast hyperboles from sun to sun until
their substance was wasted by radiation pressure and they became
clouds of the ever-present interstellar dust.

The galaxies wheeled their slow way through time. New members
of their family formed from that same dust—taking an eon about it,
and yet not wasting time. Because time was not to be wasted. Time
was something—something very abstract—within which they simply
*were* as they were in the insubstantiality of empty space.

And this is our home, thought Red. Is anything—even seeing the
unknown close at hand—more amazing than this?

When he recovered from the moment of epiphany, he found himself looking questioningly at Vyko. The youthful magician was studying Burma in a puzzled manner.

"Red," he said hesitantly. "Red, do you have a—a twin?"

"Yes," said Chantal with sudden emphasis. "There's another man going round Center who's exactly like him."

Burma watched this exchange wonderingly, and Vyko turned to her, nodding. "That explains it," he said calmly.

"Explains what?"

"When I try to—feel your future, I get the same sensation that I do when I think of Red." Vyko repeated his analogy of seeing double. "And as you say you have a—a going-double—"

"Look, what is all this?" Burma demanded. Chantal gave a quick summary of her experience, and Red listened with mounting dismay.

"A going-double is a sign of disaster approaching," Vyko told them doubtfully. "And yet I do not read disaster in the future…. It is said among my people that to see oneself is a mark of death near at hand, and yet…." He shook his head as if giddy, and walked a few paces to be alone.

"Is this the result of our tampering with time?" Red asked apprehensively, and Burma looked worried. "Are we going to double back on ourselves from the future?"

"Physics says that's impossible. Of course physics has often proved too limited, and had to be altered to take account of new evidence. We'll get in touch with Artesha about it."

Artesha's synthesized voice sounded actually tired when they told her what had happened. "I'm afraid this is the beginning of something very big," she said. "And I can't spare the time to study it properly. We're getting reports of an Enemy attack massing—they've been at it for days, but up until a little while ago we thought it was aimed at Tau Ceti. It isn't. The Enemy is about to mount a full-scale offensive on the Solar System."

"Can we withstand an attack of that magnitude?"

"I don't know. I think so. We're rushing in extra resources as fast as possible, almost faster than we can handle them, and production of our most advanced ships is being stepped up to maximum. Have you had any results with Vyko?"

"We haven't asked him yet," said Red, and called the boy back. "Do you feel any special awareness of—presence?" he asked anxiously.

Vyko shook his head. "There is something," he began, and frowningly changed his mind. "But it is no more here than anywhere else. I have always known of a *sort* of presence."

"That fits," said Artesha. "The Being exists at least as far back as the furthest temporal surges. Have you been through the ship to find whether there actually is a double of Burma on board?"

"But there can't be," said Burma briefly. "How did she get through the airlock without—?"

"*Did* she get through the airlock?" said Artesha significantly. "Remember, that specimen of the Enemy found its way into the 129 Lyrae city."

She broke off, and when she spoke again was excited and dismayed. "Tesper has seen his going-double," she reported.

"This is too big," said Red abruptly, and Artesha agreed.

"I'll get Magwareet on to it right away. We'll have to turn Center and all the anchor teams inside out."

"Have you considered the possibility that we were deliberately allowed to capture that Enemy?" Chantal put in. "I mean—could the Being be signaling somehow?"

"That was a chance we had to take. But if, somehow, they are managing to get duplicates of existing human beings into our defenses, we're headed for *real* trouble."

"You had already thought of that," Red realized, recalling the behavior of the woman in the medical section.

"Of course. Magwareet will be over with some helpers to investigate as soon as he can arrange it."

Burma turned back to her team. "We've got to get this test set up quickly," she said with an edge in her voice. "How's it going?"

"It'll take another hour, ma'am," said one of the technicians. "Then we're all ready."

"Not bad," admitted Burma grudgingly. "I'm afraid you and Vyko will just have to stand ready for the time being. Maybe it'll give him a chance to get his bearings properly." Red and Chantal signified agreement.

Withdrawing to one side of the cabin, Chantal murmured, "I can't understand why they take all this so *calmly*."

"I guess they've just been schooled into concentrating on their own problems," Red answered softly. "Time's too valuable to spend worrying about questions you can't solve yourself."

The hour was almost half gone when Magwareet pushed his way into the room, still wearing his spacesuit. Frost was melting on the metal shell, and his helmet, thrown back on his shoulders, was misted inside and out. "Go through the ship," was his curt order to the men and women who followed him, and they dispersed with an air of grim intentness, weapons ready in their hands.

"Sorry to break in, Burma," the Coordinator said shortly, "but we have to check everywhere that a going-double has been notified. Won't disturb your equipment."

Burma nodded, and carried on working. When the members of Magwareet's party returned, they had nothing to report, and with a short word of thanks, Magwareet prepared to depart.

Red felt someone pluck at his sleeve, and glanced down to find Vyko staring at him worriedly. "That man—the one in the metal clothes," he said.

"What about him?"

"He too has a going-double! I don't know where, but I can sense it."

Red raised his voice and yelled after the departing coordinator. Magwareet turned back.

"Has your double been reported from anywhere?"

"No—not as far as I know," Magwareet answered, staring.

"Vyko says you've got one."

The young magician looked almost on the edge of tears. "It is beginning to seem as though everyone in this day and time has one!" he cried. "Some people's are very close to themselves, and hard to make out, like those of most of the people in this room. But Red's, and yours," Vyko nodded at Magwareet, "they are unmistakable."

Magwareet crossed the room with a bound despite the weight of his suit, and slammed open the communicator. "Triple emergency!" he said. "Anchor team"—he gave coordinates quickly—"Magwareet speaking, to all units, all anchor teams, all ships! Somewhere there is

171

a double of myself. Notify and capture if possible on sighting it. Any other doubles must be reported instantly."

"Wymarin," said Burma suddenly. "What are you doing here?"

They spun around, to see the familiar dark-haired man who had called himself Elias standing between the banks of instruments.

"You weren't quite ready to test," Wymarin answered. "I came over to see if you were doing exactly what I said."

"Where's he supposed to be?" Red asked a technician near him, whispering.

"Monitoring the test from another anchor-team's ships, just in case something goes wrong," was the answer.

Wymarin walked slowly towards them, eyes flickering over the massed dials and lights. "Not quite," he said at length. "Listen, Burma, I've been doing some figuring on a new tack. Suppose, instead of simply trying my original test on a smaller scale, you do this."

He went off into a language so full of technicalities they could no longer follow. Burma and her technicians, however, seemed to appreciate his reasoning.

Burma, in particular, was shaken when Wymarin had finished. "If I get you right, what you're proposing is to set up a *working vocabulary* based on a number code, that we can key to a machine translator and actually speak to the Being."

"Why not?"

"Hello, Burma," said a voice from the wall communicator. "Wymarin here. You should be almost set to go ahead now, shouldn't you?"

They wheeled together. In the instant when their eyes were all off him, Wymarin's going-double *went*.

Vyko whimpered. "This must be the end coming—for all of us. Never can there have been so many omens of ill-fortune. When every man and woman has a going-double—"

"Quiet," snapped Burma, and explained to Wymarin—the real one, speaking from the communicator—what had happened. "Of course, we don't dare automatically trust what he told us, though it seems logical enough. Still, I think we'll have to go ahead right away—if there's a chance of communication with the Being, we must grab it. Magwareet, pull your team out of here and get on with your own job. Red, Chantal, do you want to go with him? It's risky, staying here—"

Vyko turned mutely appealing eyes, and Red replied firmly that they would stay.

Hectic minutes of preparation passed; then everything was set for the great experiment.

Licking lips that had suddenly gone dry, Burma gave one final glance around her complex equipment, smiled forcedly at her anxious-looking team, and pressed the switch to initiate the signal.

Vyko gave a scream of pure terror and slid to the floor unconscious. A glass-encased indicator light burst and showered the opposite panel of dials with broken glass. The dials themselves wavered back and forth, and then stood still exactly like a human being torn between two courses of action.

This much Red took in before Burma indicated a livid green time map before her, and said, "This is it, my friends—we're headed for the beginning of Time."

—— ∞ ——

## CHAPTER XXXV

## 4070: Artesha

Extract from paper read to the British Science Society, Physical Division, September 28, 2031: "*It has now become abundantly clear—too clear, I regret to say, for some of the less flexible academic minds among us,*" (*mixed cries of "Shame!" and loud applause*) "*that we have for far too long been attempting to describe the universe in terms of petty-minded preconceptions as bad as the idealist tenets of the earliest Greek philosophers. In many ways we have never succeeded in freeing ourselves from bondage to Aristotle. We have spent as much time explaining away as we have explaining.*"

Charles Fort, the apostle of doubt, on the same subject many years earlier: "*A superstition is a hypothesis which has been discarded; a hypothesis is a superstition which has not yet been discarded.*"

The instant it happened, Artesha's fantastic mind began to balance her ledger. The reports that were streaming in did not make reassuring reading.

Net loss: hundreds of thousands of irreplaceable men and women—skilled technicians, scientists, experts in the fields most desperately needed by the human species; material by the millions of tons, including precious records inscribed in the memory files of Center (that was the first loss Artesha became aware of—it was as if she had lost part of her own memory); ships by the score, both civilian and military.

Net gain: one piece of information about the Being.

It was not enough.

The temporal surge had cut a swathe right through the defenses of the Solar System. A gap yawned towards Polaris that the already extended lines of patrolling vessels could never hope to fill. A few asteroids had gone along with the rest, and a gigantic volume of dust.

Magwareet was the first person to demand whether there would be any change in her previous directives in view of the disaster. She answered briefly that he was too involved with the problem of the going-doubles to back out now. What she was frantically trying to decide even as she spoke was how much, and on what topics, had gone from her memory; that could never be replaced, because the energies of the temporal surge would have wiped every trace clean away.

As big a void, but not so immediately important, had been left in her whole life, moreover: in that cartwheeling ship, headed this time for the Being alone knew where—and when—was Burma, whom she loved.

She contacted Wymarin for the newest data on the chaos boiling through the continuum, and the little scientist gave her a grim summary.

"We can't track this surge, Artesha. It goes beyond the furthest range of our instruments, and it's still gaining momentum when it disappears. We can't begin to guess where they'll wind up. Some of them may witness the formation of the Earth, or starve to death in a Carboniferous forest, or even be stripped to raw primordial zero-state energy in the Beginning of Everything.

"Even if they survive, I don't have any way to estimate whether the instruments they carry will enable them to find their way back into the surge after they are thrown out at the other end. I'd say it is highly unlikely. But I'm not the expert on temporal surges—only on the Being. And I can tell you nothing more than this about the effects of that experiment: we probably did succeed in getting through to it when we tried the test for the first time, and I got thrown back to the seventeenth century. But maybe we—*sensitized* it in that respect. At any rate, the violent result we got when we repeated it suggests something like that."

"Boil down your data—whatever you possess—and let me have it as soon as possible," Artesha said. "There may be something in it— anything—that will give us a clue."

*That* was a slender hope, she reflected sadly as she broke the circuit on Wymarin's acknowledgment. A hundred people were clamoring for her attention. Selecting one at random, she found it was Qepthin, the biologist supervising the study of the captured Enemy.

"I've got good news," he opened enthusiastically, and Artesha cut him short.

"Have you been affected by this temporal surge?" she asked brusquely. "If not, get out of circuit—there are people with troubles waiting."

Qepthin sounded blank. "What surge? I haven't been near a time map for days. I'm sorry if you're in a hurry, but what I have to say won't detain you long. We can communicate with the Enemy—talk to it. Red gave us the key clue."

Artesha's spirits rose a fraction. "What have you got out of it so far?"

"Oh, nothing yet. We're breaking its language by analyzing it from basics. But we can duplicate all its speech elements, and in just a little while we'll be able to talk to it fluently."

"Let me know when you do." Artesha cut off. She immediately regretted being so short with him—after all, he had brought her the first really constructive achievement in far too long—but she had no time for that.


Qepthin was turning away from the communicator, wondering with half his mind what could have put Artesha in such a panic, and worrying about it, and using the other half to review progress on a slightly-less-than-conscious level, when the doors of the hall opened and Magwareet's team, still cold from space, came in.

The Coordinator approached him and nodded a curt greeting. "Have you had any going-doubles show up in here?"

Qepthin shook his head. "I heard something about them a little while ago, but we've had no cases reported from here." He hesitated. "I don't suppose Red could have been a—No, surely not. What exactly *is* going on?"

Magwareet seemed to have his mind on something else, watching his team fan out discreetly and begin their thorough—if unobtrusive—sweep through the hall. He saw several of them stop and wait until one of the technicians came to a pause in his work, then ask a question.

"That fits," he mused half aloud. "If it is being directed from or by the Enemy, they'd try to draw attention away from the captive—I'm sorry," he added at proper conversational level. "I was far away." He gave the biologist a quick rundown on the appearance of the mysterious doubles.

Struck by a sudden thought at the end of it, he gave Qepthin a slow glance. "I don't suppose you've run into any creatures that have the power of—of disappearing, in your study of alien biology, have you?"

"What do you mean?"

"We've established that these going-doubles, as Vyko named them, can beyond doubt *disappear*. Without moving, without hiding. They don't do it when someone is watching them—but they're careful to appear only in places where they will not immediately be suspected. Many of them have been observed to go into rooms with only one exit, and never come back out; others have just melted into the air when the audience's back was turned. It's like quantum tunneling, but on a macroscopic scale."

Qepthin was startled. "No. Nothing like that has been heard of. I suppose you've ruled out the obvious—chameleony, proteanism, transparency, elongation and so on? Those are all fairly common protective devices."

Magwareet looked interested. "Elaborate."

"Well, chameleony explains itself, I think—instantaneous response to a background in terms of color match and surface texture. There's a creature called *Polyglossus toshii* that Hideko Toshi found on Tau Ceti II that can match virtually any color scheme in the infrared range in less than half a second. Proteanism is less common—I can only think of two or three animals bigger than a mouse that use it to any extent, and they're all slow-moving beasts from high-gravity worlds. Transparency—more strictly," he said pedantically, "forcing all the molecules in an object to match the transmission coefficient and refractive index of free air in the visible electromagnetic spectrum—is a permanent property of the body substance, and only slightly variable. *Pseudocynus ascopos* from 129 Lyrae exhibits the phenomenon quite markedly. But it's not something the creature can turn on and off—it just *is* transparent, and that's all. Elongation—again that's not known in any highly organized animals, but there are worms that can expand and contract up to five or six hundred per cent—far too thin to be visible when they're at full length."

Magwareet shook his head at the end of the long recital.

"Our checks would have revealed any tricks like that. No, I'm afraid it isn't just a protective device."

One of his team called to him across the hall in a sibilant whisper. He excused himself to Qepthin, and, giving one final glance at the five-limbed bulk of the Enemy about which the controlled busyness of the gathering revolved, led his party to their next destination.

He had been itching to get around to this one for some time, but he had been forced to wait while the data on the new temporal surge was evaluated. Now, at last, he was free to get at the man whose going-double had made the most spectacular exit of all: Wymarin.

The scientist greeted him absently when he arrived, stood abstractedly for some minutes while he waited for the team to begin their search, and then burst out, "For all the good I've done here, I might as well have stayed behind in seventeenth-century Holland."

"What do you mean?"

"Look at the result of our tests." Wymarin indicated the broad sweep of a time map that shone green from rim to rim. "We've caused the biggest disaster we've yet suffered, and got no profit out of it."

Magwareet waited for him to relax a little; with an effort, Wymarin achieved calmness. "I'm sorry," he went on. "But it's completely disheartening. What can I do for you?"

"What do you know about the appearance of your going-double?"

"I know hardly anything about it. It showed up aboard the main ship of Burma's anchor team, and I only got the barest details over the communicator." He summarized them. At the end, Magwareet remarked thoughtfully, "Did you ask for details of the change your going-double recommended in the projected experiment?"

"No! Why should I?" Wymarin asked, surprised. "I—oh, I see what you mean." His change of expression might have been comic under other circumstances. "You mean I took it for granted that the recommendations were hostile and designed to cause damage, which I shouldn't have."

"Exactly," said Magwareet, and there was a long pause.

"As it happens," Wymarin said eventually, "even careful planning couldn't have produced anything more damaging than what we actually did…. Is there a chance that this going-double of mine will turn up again, and perhaps give us the information?"

"I don't know. So far we haven't had any cases of a reappearance—these duplicates have just shown up, whether for a purpose or not, and never been seen again. I'm inclined to feel that Vyko's beliefs about them may have a grain of truth," he added pessimistically.

"What does he think?"

"According to the legends of his time, to see one's going-double is a sign of impending death."

"Have you *any* idea what they are?"

"Not yet. There is one very suggestive point about them, though. Did you hear that mine had been seen somewhere?" he put in parenthetically. "That is, that every one of the originals has been through time, either in a temporal surge or in one of our own ships making a hop."

"Very interesting," said Wymarin. "Anything else?"

"That they can disappear into thin air."

"Well—" Wymarin seemed to be fastening on a new string of ideas to get the memory of the crisis he had caused out of his head. "Well, that isn't unexpected, if they're a by-product of temporal co-existence.... Can you narrow it down still further—to people who *have* co-existed with themselves in a temporal surge or otherwise? It strikes me as feasible that on returning to one's own time after having been two ways through the same temporal surge, duplicates might emerge. Not from the future or past, the sort of thing we've become accustomed to, but from alternative nearby realities. Near-parallels from the multiverse. An unfashionable idea, but—"

"That's the sort of thing Burma is needed for," Magwareet said. "All right, I'll try to establish if that fits. All clues are helpful at the moment. But what has that to do with disappearing?"

"Look at it this way. Suppose that our interferences with the past have actually caused divergences in the main time-flow. That's to say, in a fifth-dimensional continuum there exist several parallel presents each dependent on a change effected in the past."

"Yes, as you say, the Many Worlds hypothesis. But isn't that—what did you say?—'unfashionable'...because it's been disproved?"

"No, you see, now we're working with new data. Old paradigms can be rebooted if fresh information supports them. But this would be a quite different variety of Everett's classic relative state model. Wait a minute—what year did Mr. Hawkins come from? Was it 1957?" His face showed shock.

Magwareet grimaced. "I believe so. And?"

"Just another loose thread," Wymarin said, looking pained. "That was the year Hugh Everett published his.... Oh, never mind, that has to be a chance coincidence. Let's get back to the going-doubles.

"Consider: if a great enough degree of correspondence existed between a place in one of those other presents, and our own present, it is possible that people might—unknowingly—turn in a direction that leads through the fifth dimension. Do you recall the old legend of Kasper Hauser? No? Oh well.

"Assume that the multiverse has a strong tendency to remain unified, at least in its adjacent bundles. Our original researches into four-dimensional existence suggested that likelihood. Then my going-double might have been firmly under the impression that he had remained in his own present and was giving information to the Burma of his own present. However, if that information had been acted upon, it would have ironed out one of the distinctions between the two time-streams. Follow me?"

"I do indeed," said Magwareet with rising enthusiasm. "You imply that all the appearances of going-doubles may be the result of this unificatory tendency?"

"Exactly. Now suppose you investigate the idea that a going-double, on vanishing, returns 'through' the barrier between parallel presents. We've got equipment that could detect the spacetime stresses I postulate as resulting from that."

"Give me details and I'll deal with it at once."

Artesha's familiar voice came to them. "Attention all units," she said. "Triple red—this is a major policy factor. I have had a report from Qepthin, head of the team studying the captured specimen of the Enemy. He reports that his technicians have succeeded in establishing communication with it. I have carefully examined his results, and agree with him that there is no reason to doubt our complete failure in attempting to understand the motives of the Enemy in their war with us.

"Their attacks on the human species are a purely secondary consideration. Their real and only objective is the final destruction of the Being."

—— ∞ ——

## CHAPTER XXXVI

## 1556: TIME SURGE Michoo

*A few of the people who walked into history were famous, and came to be notorious. Their names were Ambrose Bierce, Benjamin Bathurst, or—*

*And there were others, of course: no one remembered them except their acquaintances, and maybe the file clerk in the missing persons department of the local police force—if there was one.*

*There were people who seemed to have an odd knowledge of the future—that is to say, of what yet remained the future when they made statements about it. If a person who knew a little about history, but had forgotten most of the detail he had learnt in school, had to put down a complete record of the past, it would strangely resemble the prophecies of—for example—Nostradamus.*

Michoo Ader sat on the edge of his guest room bed, in despair, holding his head in his hands. There had been the authentic thrill of exploring Renaissance Florence, of seeing the early marvelous work of painters and sculptors whose names would survive apocalyptic wars, of telling Leonardo and Botticelli tall tales about impossible machines and hearing them laugh. He had not for a moment expected to walk down stairs to the studio and into the kitchen for breakfast and find his new friend scribbling excitedly: rough elegant sketches of flying machines, half bird, half helicopter, of submarines encased in steel, of military devices that could overturn all history if the Medicis and other autocrats got hold of them.

"I've changed history," he rebuked himself. Or at least made it possible for Leonardo to do so. What could he do? Seize the papers and burn them? But the young man had an excellent visual memory. *Kill* him? That would be an appalling blow to the future history of Italian art, even assuming he had the ability to perform such a crime. Double himself back in time and prevent the event in the first place? But even Burma lacked that skill.

Still, that had been true only until Ader's departure with his anchor crew. He sat up, buoyant with hope. The only sensible plan was to activate the time map and get catapulted back to his home locus in space and time. They could spend months, years, to contrive a way of interrupting his error and setting it right before it was made.

Ader drew forth the time map, held it firmly by its rounded ends. He heard a whoop of delight from Leonardo, coming into the guest room with a roll of paper.

"Michoo," the youth yelled happily, "I have a wonderful new—"

The green glow brightened as the time map came alive. Leonardo gaped, darted forward, dropping his notes. His hand passed through the edges of the field and he snatched it back, stung.

Ader stared, reeling in time shock. Leonardo was gone, Florence was gone. The 15th century was gone.


With a gulp of nausea, Ader found himself half squatting in a large room reeking of some evil disease. He stared at the date on the time map: 1556. He had jumped forward half a century, instead of to his home time and place. Dozens of men and women and squalling babies lay wretchedly on pallets or curled on the floor, gasping, breathing in stertorous, constricted gulps. He saw a fat rat chewing at the toes of a corpse. The system said inside his head, "Get out of here immediately. These people have the plague."

"No, no." Intolerable. Unacceptable. "After Burma's troubles," he told it, "all anchor team crews have been inoculated against the major bacterial and viral diseases of—"

"You are immunized against the cancers and many other infectious and metabolic disorders. Not, however, against *Yersinia pestis*, which has long been extinct."

Michoo Ader moaned, aghast. In terror and disbelief, he whispered: "The Black Death?"

"It slew one third of the population of Europe. Those who survived possessed a gene that built proteins inhibiting the plague DNA. Until the development of antibiotics, that gene was all that blocked recurrent outbreaks of *Y. pestis*. After the 20th century, genetic drift slowly removed that shield. In the fifth millennium, almost every human is again vulnerable."

"Am I going to die?" he said in terror.

"Many of those infected died within a day. Others lingered for a week or more. You have no protection."

Ader's eyes filled with tears.


"They are speaking a form of French," the system informed him. "I am adjusting your grammar settings and making the lexicon available."

Desolate babbling resolved into cries for help, for comfort, for release, for the aid of their deity. Filled with disgust and sorrow, Ader made for the light of the open door, doing his best to avoid brushing against the crowded sick. He seemed to feel fleas leaping at his legs above his ankles, and when he bent in horror to slap at them they seemed to leap to his hands and wrists and from there to his neck. Psychogenic phantasms, he told himself, and moved faster still. When he reached the open square beyond the emergency hospital, if that was what the horrid place was, he realized that he no longer held the time map. Somehow in his fear he had dropped it. Weeping, he turned back and forced his way into the mass of dying people.

A man in a horrifying costume stood four-square in the place where Ader had arrived. He wore a long black coat glistening with wax, heavy boots and leather gloves, and most fearful of all, beneath a leather hat, a bulging gray mask covering his entire head and neck, glass rounds set before his eyes, and a long birdlike beak. Ader's eyes adjusted again to the dim light. He pressed the empty time map harness against his mouth and nose. A sweet, sickening odor hung about the masked man, perhaps from a medicinal potpourri of spices and herbs secreted in the raptor beak. This figure of death had a green glow about his hands, from the time map he was examining.

"Give it to me," Ader said in what he assumed was French. "That is mine, you must return it to me, monsieur."

"Your amulet will not preserve you from the plague, sir. Still, here, take it. But you do not seem ill. Are you caring for a loved one? It is a hopeless exercise, I fear, and deadly. I must ask you to come outside at once with me. This is a place of pestilence. You must cleanse yourself immediately." The doctor unlocked a side door, let them both inside a room that was not remotely aseptic but at least was clean and free of rats. He removed his medical outfit with a sort of liturgical solemnity, and dressed in black. Together, they left via a back door, and the doctor locked it with the same large heavy key.

In the deserted square, the man introduced himself. "I hear from your accent that you are a foreigner, sir, but I cannot hazard from what port. I am Michel de Nostredame, sometimes named the Plague Doctor, although I confess I lack a formal degree. And you, monsieur?"

"Michoo Ader." Already his head was starting to ache. Could the disease be working so quickly to infect him? He sat down on the pavement, pulled off his boots and socks, peered at his feet and lower legs. Several of the filthy things were already there, feasting on his blood. He flicked them away, cold and ill. He had to go back to his own time. He could not; that would be to carry a plague that might kill far more of his fellow humans that either the invading Enemy or the Being's turbulence. Besides, where might he emerge next time? Next *time*, indeed. Here at least he had access to a medical man, however primitive and superstitious his training.

"Where am I," he asked, swaying. He pulled his footwear back on, sweating.

"Why, Salon-de-Provence."

"I have no resistance to this disease, you see, doctor. A bath would be welcome. You must keep the rats and their fleas away from yourself and your family, and if possible your patients. The fleas carry the plague."

"Hmm. An interesting opinion. Do you recall anything of how you came here? But I should not interrogate you in the street. Come with me, and I shall give you a clean bed in my home while we see if you can be saved. You are clearly an educated fellow, and I am loath to see learning extinguished by this filthy disorder."

"Thank you. Antibiotics, I need—" That way led nowhere useful. He touched his throat, which hurt abominably. Something the size of a small inflated blister was growing there. Already? I am truly, yet again, a dead man.

"There is no record of a Nostredame," the system told him. "If he is indeed a reputable physician, he might adopt a Latinized version, Dr. Nostradamus. But there is no record of that form either."

"What can I do to resist this bacterium?" he asked the system in the music of Speech. The doctor looked at him sidelong, but then smiled, perhaps taking it to be music, or a prayer.

"Your longevity modifications are working at maximum efficiency."

The doctor was saying, "If you can remain alive for the next two or three days, you will recover. You need clean bedding, healthy food and sterilized water, and as much sleep as possible. They were insufficient to spare my beloved Henriette, and my two sweet babies, but they are better than nothing. So far these precautions have saved me and my new wife, Anne."

Nostredame led him, stumbling, to a pleasant row house built directly on a narrow street. A man servant and a woman took charge, led him upstairs, bathed him, gave him a fresh nightshirt, put him to bed in a darkened room. They left his garments folded at the end of the bed atop a cabinet. He clutched the time map, masked in its harness, against his breast. He ached abominably. "You require suppressed mentation and awareness, to ease your pain," the system said. Somewhere, children ran and chattered. Was that Nostredame's voice? Pain ebbed, and with it his consciousness, although not entirely; Ader half-slept, and dreamed dreadful things.

"This magic device!" Astonishment in the voice. "Leave it to drop to the bed and it lingers aloft, as if held up like a kite on some current of air. Yet there is no breeze, and it is heavy as a brick."

Don't touch it, you fool, Ader tried to say. He could not move his head nor open his eyes. His lips moved.

"Sleep, lad, I spoke only to myself in my wonderment. But what can be the purpose of such a fabulous machine?"

"Time," Michoo Ader found himself saying, unable to prevent it. "To gain the future, where I live."

He sank deeper into inanition.

"It shows you the future? What kinds of marvels does it disclose? Quick, sir, I must have a glimpse. Astrology is my passion, after medicine, yet its premonitions are damnably vague and contradictory."

"We fly," Ader said, almost inaudibly. "As I told Leonardo."

"Ah, you have heard of the sage of Florence? It is said he planned to build a flying machine, and one for passage beneath the ocean waves."

"You are advised not to speak further," the system said. "It seems that your previous host has built upon your hints. That is not part of this system's historical record."

Ader's mind reeled. Nothing held still.

"Tell me the future," Nostredame said. "Will there be war?"

"Often. Always. Until world almost ended."

"Ah. How terrible! Who brings about the awful fate?"

The partial detritus of two thousand years, and more. The Plague Doctor would grasp little of it.

"Fire from the sky. The great city will burn. Wicked criminals seize power and would own the world. Nappaling. Napalm. Polyun." The words jumbled in his dry mouth. The doctor patted his lips with a damp cloth, lifted his head, poured a little water into his mouth. It was warm but soothing.

"Napauleone? That would be a Corsican name. Wait, let me jot this down." There was scratching, and a heavy sigh. "What other evil men? We must give warning to the world."

"Hist—Hitsler."

"The Hister? The river Danube, you mean, for that I believe was its ancient name?"

"A man of great evil. Death in clouds. Hit—Hit—Hitsta."

"The Beast of Revelation!" said Nostredame. "Your machine confirms the teaching of Sacred Scripture."

For two more days Ader lay in trance, his augmented metabolism slowly combating the bacteria swarming in his flesh and blood. The buboes subsided, as if by a miracle. He came back to his senses, and his muddled brain lost most of the recollection of his betrayal.

"The crisis has passed, Michoo," the doctor was telling him. "I call for some soup. You need your strength. Together we shall effect a mighty warning upon the evil-doers. I foresee a vast undertaking, mapping the unborn yet fated future. Quatrains, four lines of verse in each, you know, kept secure by anagrams and puns in Greek and Latin to deter the hounds of false righteousness. I shall have my new family kept whole and safe, and you, too, my friend. What do you say to a scheme of almanacs, calendars, and ten sets of one hundred verses each?"

Michoo Ader had stopped listening. It was recital of his crimes against the future. Fool, fool, even with the defense of illness. He reached beneath the bed, found the harness, strapped it across his chest. He found his tunic and boots, still piled atop the bedroom cabinet, dressed, and drew out the time map. It expanded in a green glow. He twisted the ends, activating it.

And was standing on cold grass, not back in his craft, not in the Center. He clenched his teeth. It would never end, because the power unit in the time map would outlive him even if he should drag himself through life for a thousand longevus years. He recalled a myth told him by Leonardo, in sunnier days. A man in the folklore of his faith, adrift in the river of eternity. What was his name, that fanciful wanderer? Not Ader, although it might as well have been. Ah, yes, that was it—the Wandering Jew. Ader opened the data panel. This year was 1654. The lighted place below the hill was Paris, the river must be the Seine. He shrank the time map and replaced it in its hiding place, conferring hopelessly with the system inside his aching head.

—— ∞ ——

## CHAPTER XXXVII

## Deep time: Burma

*An analysis of the opinions of the human species regarding that imponderable, Time, is illuminating.*

*It is not (which is interesting!) an innate item of experience. The Zunnis, so we are informed, have no concept of direction or length of time. Or hadn't, until contact with more elaborate world-pictures.*

*The most widespread image of Time is that of the river, bearing us, as driftwood, heading to the sea, past objects on the bank we recognize as events.*

*The dream of freedom from it finds expression in the ideas of Eternity, and Nirvana.*

*It obsesses scientists, philosophers and mystics alike. Dunne suggested that it might be possible to "remember" events which had "not yet" happened; Eddington, with his streak of mysticism blending into his scientific background, defined time as "an arrow which points the way in which entropy is proceeding."*

187

*It is of importance to note: (a) that entropy is the tendency of the cosmos to develop towards a state of ever greater randomness; and (b) that you, like all other living organisms—the term "organism" itself has that implication—are a localized reversal of that universal phenomenon, exporting disorder to shore up your own internal organization.*

"Somewhere out there," said Burma in a subtly amplified voice that carried through the room, as their craft tore backward through the manifold of time, "suns are being born, planets created…. Somewhere out there, if we could only watch and understand, we could find the answer to every question that has ever puzzled the human species."

Her words opened up in the imagination of her listeners a vista of incredible knowledge. It was as if their consciousness was suddenly no longer bounded by the walls of the hull; they could feel themselves on the verge of *seeing* the things she spoke of.

Like a cinema film run backwards, Red thought. The whole universe, tracking steadily and faithfully backwards towards its beginning—and they could not see it.

A little stiffly, Chantal went forward and bent to attend to Vyko, lying on the floor. The movement broke the spell, and the crew personnel turned to seek some task they might use to occupy their minds.

"What's happened?" Red inquired of Burma. She answered while studying the green-vivid time maps.

"Somehow, we hit the Being on a sore spot. This is a convulsion beside which the one that threw me back into your time was a mere twitch. Any sign of abatement?" she called out, and one of the technicians replied.

"If anything, the surge is building up."

"On Earth now," said Burma somberly, "early humans are eking out their existence in caves and shelters made of branches. In a little while, there will be only apes, and before that again the reptiles will rule the planet…."

A curious feeling of inversion came over Red as he heard that; somehow, the way Burma had used *will* in speaking of the past seemed significant, but he could not trap the elusive concept, and Chantal interrupted the train of thought.

"Burma, there's something I don't quite understand. Why are we experiencing normal time even though we're being thrown backwards? It makes it almost impossible to accept the fact."

"Are we?" Burma said pointedly. "Has it never struck you that if time *were* to go backwards, it would make no difference at all? At any given moment, you would still recall what you thought of as the past; your awareness would be identical in every single 'now,' no matter which way time was flowing. There is no instrument at all by which one can decide the answer." She broke off. "Is Vyko all right?"

"I think so. But you still haven't really answered my question."

"What we think happens is that the forces inside a temporal surge cause an encapsulation of the space surrounding the transferred object. The distortion of space around the capsule has an effect like the surface tension of a liquid; but we can detect its presence only by implication."

There was little they could do during the uncontrolled flight into the past. They monitored their instruments; at intervals they attended to Vyko, who seemed to have fallen into a deep coma. They could theorize about the cause of it, but his unusual consciousness was completely inaccessible.

They were, deep down below a protective illusion of normalcy, frightened beyond words.

Nearly a day had been measured by the clock displays on the walls when the first gap appeared in the greenness of the master time maps. Something crept into the air—a sense of destiny, a sense of survival.

"At least," Burma told them, studying the instrument readings, "we're going to emerge into the real universe. After that—"

"After that," said a technician, "the temporal energies will have overloaded our instruments until they are completely useless. What can we do about it?"

The helplessness of their situation was only too clear. Burma shut the technician up with a scowl, and leaned excitedly forward. "We're emerging," she said tensely. "I want you to watch those displays right up until the moment they stop registering altogether."

The instruments were not strictly suitable for studying a temporal surge, but they could be used. They were designed for investigating the fourth-dimensional extent of the Being. Probes revealed that this craft would be tossed up from the main peak, not a secondary one. The same could not be said of the rest of the team's ships, scattering already across alternative states of the manifold.

"And we possess no time-travel equipment either," Burma muttered. "At this stage of the universe's evolution, there are probably no planets where we could land and construct such equipment—had our ships been designed for landing on planets."

They broke free, then, in a dazing transition, and for better or worse their doom was sealed.


Burma recovered from the time shock first, tight-lipped, and walked briskly from the room. In a few moments she called back to them over the communicator, which was still functioning for some reason.

"Come out here," she said, voice filled with wonderment, and they obeyed without thinking. Red and Chantal were among the first to pass through the door into the only room in the ship from which there was a full-scale hologram view into space.

"This is a sight no human being has ever seen until now," said Burma into silence, and they stood transfixed.

At first it was incredible; eyes refused to take it in. Then logic supervened, and they began to be able to understand what they saw.

Beyond the port the sky was on fire. It shone so white it appeared almost cold. Nowhere was there blackness—nowhere at all.

"Why is there no black in the sky?" Chantal demanded, almost with a sob of terror.

"What we are looking at," said Burma softly, "is the universe when young. Those are all stars unlike those we are used to seeing scattered across millions of parsecs. They are gigantic, younger, simpler. Here they are so close some of them are only light-hours apart. Probably the accelerating dark energy expansion we know in our epoch has only just begun again, following the extraordinarily fast burst of the Big Bang itself. 'Only just,' of course, in terms of the universe's age.

"We have come billions of years."

Red was so obsessed by a discovery and a memory that he almost failed to hear her words. The discovery was that, once one's eyes were accustomed to the sight, one could tell that every star in the heavens was a different color. Most were white—diamond white—with subtle gradations, but some were blue, some yellow, and some few shaded all the way to the deepest imaginable crimson.

When he was a small boy, he had learned that jewels were dug from the ground, and he had pictured a jewel-mine, its walls sparkling, its floors sparkling, its roof sparkling—every inch in sight giving back multi-colored fire.

And here was the reality.

"The universe," said Burma, "is still so small that the light of the stars does not fade beyond visibility before it makes the complete circle. Beyond the near stars, out there, you can see the other side of the stars that are behind us as we stand now. This universe is like a gigantic hall of mirrors."

Something the scientist J.B.S. Haldane had written in one of his essays came back to Red. What was it? "I imagined myself in a—" What kind of space? *Riemannian,* that was it. "I was standing on a transparent plane. When I looked up, above me I could see the soles of my boots turned backwards...."

He had once tried to express that in visual terms in one of his sculptures, and failed. And now here was the blind force of Nature interpreting it for him on a scale he had never dared to imagine.

"Do—" He was surprised to find his throat so dry. "Do you think there might be life yet out there somewhere?"

"I doubt it," said Burma. "Almost certainly there are no planets. Those aren't the stars we know, of course. They are immense aggregations of dust and gas, barely beginning to radiate—in fact, much of their energy is probably still coming from gravitational contraction."

And this *is* the human species, Burma suddenly thought. The idea hit her in the pit of the stomach, leaving her limp with awe. Here am I, tossed into the very earliest days of the universe, and I can speak with certainty of things no living creature has ever witnessed.

"Perhaps, after all, time has neither meaning nor importance," she reflected aloud. She looked about her, to find that she was alone with Red and Chantal; everyone else had returned below.

"I don't know if you can understand this," she said after a pause. "But—well, think this over. Just half a million years ago, maybe even less than that, *time began.* Everything began. You can't say 'before that,' because there *wasn't* a 'before.' There was nothing. Nothing at all."

Chantal shivered, and her face showed that she was trying to control it; Burma saw, and put a comforting arm around her and drew her close.

"And here are we, a handful of human beings," Burma finished. "Standing on the very threshold of eternity."

"Red," said Chantal softly, "do you think this was worth it?"

"What do you mean?"

"I know exactly what Chantal means," Burma said flatly. "It seems unlikely that we shall get away from here, doesn't it? Was it worth it, do you think, for the sake of seeing this?"


Red had not begun to think about it like that; it took him a moment to utter the answer, though he never had a doubt of what it would be. "Yes. Yes, I do."

"So do I," said Chantal. "I never understood it before. But I suppose this is the feeling that was the reward for the first people to climb Everest, and Columbus, and Armstrong and Aldrin setting foot for the very first time on the Moon."

That gave Red a sudden shock, a sort of repetition of his astonishment, gazing up at Sputnik, the first artificial satellite. A man named Armstrong and…. The second name had not lingered in his overwhelmed mind. In Chantal's life, thousands of years before the time of these remarkable spacetime vehicles, men had already stepped from spaceships onto the face of the Moon. He felt tears spring to his eyes, and his heart accelerate. He took her hand blindly and clung to it. She gripped his hand, leaning toward him as he leaned toward her, just another orphan.

Burma looked at them and knew a feeling of envy. These two retained a sort of comradeship forged in their first displacement into an unknown future. For her, there was at this moment no equivalent—Artesha was apart from her now by uncounted billions of years.

Through their stillness cut a cry with the suddenness of a lightning bolt. "What was that?" Red demanded, turning swiftly, but Chantal had already drawn the correct conclusion.

"It sounded like Vyko," she said, and hastened out.

Other members of the ship's crew had already responded to that heart-tearing scream; when Burma and Red caught up with Chantal, they found her bending over Vyko with a tense expression. The boy's eyes were wide open, but they were unfocused, staring at nothing.

"Vyko! What is it?" asked Burma, and the boy moaned a little. Passing his tongue over his dry lips, he muttered a few words.

"What did he say?" demanded Red, and Chantal stood up.

"Something about everything coming to a stop," she said uncomprehendingly, and then, as the possible significance of the remark hit her, she put her hand over her mouth. "Burma! Do you suppose—he can see *backwards* in time, as well as forwards? To the very instant of the Big Bang, I mean? Maybe beyond it?"

"Possibly," Burma nodded. But this guess was immediately demolished by Vyko's next words.

"Nothing," he moaned. "Nothing at all. Only stars and stars going on forever."

"What do you mean?" Red leaned towards him. "Can't you tell us what isn't there?"

"*Something*. Something that's always been there before, in my time and yours. Something huge and friendly and safe. And now I'm alone."

"The Being," said Burma softly. "He can only mean the Being. But how did we escape from it, if the temporal surge threw us back here?"

"Inertia?" suggested Red. "You once told us the Being disliked the neighborhood of suns and high-energy concentrations. The whole *universe* is a high-energy concentration this early. Suppose the Being doesn't extend this far back? Then we might have been thrown past the end of the surge by the residual violence...." His voice tailed away.

"We *are* alone," said Chantal grayly. "Nobody in the universe but ourselves."

"Think how infinitely worse it is for this poor child," Burma reminded her. "He's lost something that's been a part of his very mind all his life. He's aware in four dimensions, and in one direction there's nothing to see, and in the other everything he knows is too far ahead."

193

"Look," said Chantal abruptly, and they glanced back at Vyko. He had relaxed on his couch with a smile of delight on his face.

"Ashtlik," said Burma. "Has anything happened in the last few moments?" One of the technicians stepped back into the instrument room. "Is it back, Vyko? Is it back?"

"Yes," whispered the boy in sheer delight.

"We just durated past the end of an important secondary peak," Ashtlik called out. "Burma, you know this means we've been wrong about the Being from the start. If these surges can extend past its limits, it needn't be a four-dimensional creature, let alone having extension in higher dimensions—"

"Time enough to worry about that later," said Burma. "Vyko, is everything all right now?"

The boy, his eyes closed, looked faintly puzzled. "No, it's too small. Somehow. But it is really there, I'm sure. I—I think it's trying to talk to me."

"And we wasted all that effort on devising an instrument to communicate with the Being," said Burma, bitterly aware of the consequences of their last disastrous attempt. "We had our instrument in the palm of our hands. Vyko, can you make it understand?"

"Yes, it understands. It's trying to explain to me what it really is. I—I think—" He got up, rather unsteadily, from his couch, and walked towards the observation room, brushing aside the hands that sought to restrain him.

The others followed in silence. Vyko paused before the massed glory of the suns, staring fixedly in one direction, for fully half a minute before he shook his head. "I see," he said, "but I do not understand."

Burma pushed her way forward and followed the boy's line of gaze. After a moment, she leaned forward as if that small reduction in the distance would help to clarify what she saw. Straining their eyes, the others made out nothing but several oddly-shaped blots of darkness on the shining sky. They had not been there until the moment of Vyko's recovery.

"Some time ago," said Burma after a while, and Red's awareness that the "ago" was really billions on billions of years in the future again brought shivers to his spine, "Artesha gave directions for certain of the ships in Center containing her memory servers to be heavily insulated against high-energy levels. I remember watching the work being carried out. I never got around to asking her why only those few ships were so armored, but I presumed they were repositories of vital information for use in case the Enemy ever did invade the Solar System.

"But the work that was carried out on them left them a different shape from any other ship in the sky. They *are* quite unmistakable."

It was a moment before anyone got the significance of that present tense. Red was the first to try and utter his conclusion.

"You mean—*those*—"

"Yes." It was Vyko, unexpectedly, who answered, in a clear and confident voice not his own. "Those ships over there are part of Artesha's memory. They are the only part of her that can stand the concentrated stress of space and time at this early stage of the universe's existence."

Dryly, the body and voice of Vyko added, "In case you have not yet realized, you are talking to the Being."

—— ∞ ——

## CHAPTER XXXVIII

### 4070: Magwareet

Qepthin to Artesha: *Herewith fullest possible vocabulary of the Enemy language, together with details of their communication bands.*

Artesha to all units, triple red: *Enemy mass attack being mounted from direction of Tau Ceti.*

Wymarin to Artesha: *Spacetime distortions detected in association with materialization and dematerialization of going-doubles bear strongest resemblance to manifestations already known to be connected with activity of Being. Details separately.*

Artesha to all units, triple red: *Investigate possibility that Being is non-hostile or actually friendly. Analysis of all its activities urgently reviewable in this light.*

Artesha to Magwareet, unofficial: *Magwareet, for pity's sake, help me!*

The desperate urgency of the plea brought Magwareet in panic and haste. But he concealed his emotions as far as he could from Artesha's view, although he was no longer certain if such dissembling was effective with the immense volume of knowledge she had at her command. He had to come into her presence, for it would not be wise to let the conversation he expected get to the ears of everyone.

"What is it?" he asked, as calmly as he could.

"Magwareet, you remember asking me why I didn't warn you of the Enemy raider that flew into the temporal surge you were using to go in search of Wymarin?"

"I do."

"I had the answer. I received a solution signal from the subsystems I had put to work on it just before Burma initiated her disastrous experiment. I'm certain of that, because the notification is recorded in one of the memory stores I still have.

"But the solution itself, and all the relevant data, were in the stores that have gone into the past."

Magwareet started to say something, but Artesha interrupted. "Let me finish. Do you recall that some while ago I had a group of my memory servers specially insulated?"

"Yes."

"It is that storage which has gone. *Only* those. But they also contained the reason why I had them insulated. I can do no more than guess at the reason why I did it—and all my guesses lead to one conclusion."

"Which is?" Magwareet waited attentively, feeling on the brink of a great revelation.

"That I have had knowledge of the future available to me—somehow—and I haven't made use of it. Magwareet, what *can* have happened to me?"

Magwareet knew that Artesha must have drawn the same—the only possible—conclusion. He steadied himself and voiced it with dispassionate lack of emphasis.

"Someone, or something, must have been tampering with your memory, your whole mind."

"And there is only one possibility, who it could be. The Enemy."

Magwareet waited a little longer, and then, realizing Artesha could not supply the missing explanation herself because of its very nature, finished for her. "I'm sorry, Artesha. You're wrong. There is a second possibility—and a much more likely one. The only person in the universe who could have tampered with your mind is *yourself.*"

If Artesha had possessed human lungs anymore, she would have drawn a long, shuddering sigh. "Yes, Magwareet. Do you suppose that I, like so many other people, have a going-double who is not quite the same as myself?"

The idea staggered Magwareet for a moment, he had a momentary impression that he had seen a vision of some all-embracing, transcendental truth, but it was gone, leaving him fumbling for the tail-ends of thought which in that instant had knit together in his mind.

Artesha went on, "But what is the reason for all this? Have the missing parts of my memory passed through that fifth-dimensional gap Wymarin suggested—to be going-doubles of another Artesha somewhere else? To unify the continuum? Why have none come to me? Is the unification of the continuum more important than the survival of the human species? And in *whose* opinion?"

"You're better qualified to answer questions like those than anyone else in history," said Magwareet soberly. "Why ask me?"

"How can I trust myself any longer?" said Artesha, and Magwareet, in a horrifying access of vivid imagination, pictured the breakdown of the entire structure of human effort, through the failure of the support it all relied on. He had to do something swiftly. What was still human of Artesha required comfort, friendship and reassurance like anyone else; Burma had long been accustomed to provide it, Magwareet knew, but Burma was *somewhen else* at the start of Time.

"There's one thing you can be certain of," he said in a matter-of-fact tone. "Which is, that all these putative Arteshas, like yourself, are working together like a vast quantum computation towards the survival of the human species. You can't assume anything else, can you?"

"No," Artesha agreed.

"Have you, since discovering that the Enemy is more interested in destroying the Being than ourselves, studied the possibility of combining with the foe to do that? After all, we'd be as glad as anyone to get the Being off our necks."

"We can't do that," said Artesha firmly.

"*Why?*'

"Because—" Artesha's first word was assured, but she stopped as if cut off with a switch. "Why, I know—I know there is a reason, but that must be in the missing memories, too."

"Where did you get your information from? Qepthin?" Artesha confirmed the fact. "All right, I'm going down to see him. That, at least, we can settle definitely." He started towards the door.

"Magwareet," Artesha called after him. "Do you think I should go on trying?"

"*Yes!*" said Magwareet forcefully, and went out.

Magwareet left Artesha's presence and went down to see

*Magwareet left the presence of Artesha and went down to*

Qepthin about the chance of a pact with the Enemy. However,

*the little biologist in his research hall. He found*

on his way, a general call from Artesha came to him over

*him excitedly analyzing the psychological implications of*

the communicators, and at her urgent command he returned the

*the Enemy signals that were now being intercepted. When*

way he had come as fast as he could.

*Magwareet broached his idea, however, Qepthin shook his head.*

Magwareet, of course, was completely unaware of what was happening, and Artesha's statement to him was a shock. "I'm *where?*" he said.

"According to my instruments, you are at present in the Enemy research hall, talking with Qepthin. Listen."

Artesha opened a communicator, and Magwareet, wondering, heard his own voice mingling with the biologist's in conversation:

"—you will see why the idea is impossible," Qepthin explained. "What it amounts to is this: the Enemy discovered the existence and possibly also the nature of the Being before we did. (How far it extends, I won't dare guess.) It was the first non-Enemy life form they had ever run across, and they've spread over numerous planetary systems—about twice as many as we have, I believe. Their background is likely one of extreme hostility between species, on their home world. They wouldn't keep pets, for instance. So when they discovered the Being localized in the area we inhabit, we automatically became a parallel object for attack. No, getting rid of the Being by joint effort is out of the question."

Artesha closed the link.

"Let's see what happens to this going-double when I call them up," said Artesha grimly. She threw in alarm circuits that shut off the research hall where Magwareet—Magwareet found it upsetting to think of himself in the third person—was, and alerted nearby personnel. Then she spoke. "Magwareet! Qepthin!"

"Magwareet's not here," said Qepthin blankly. "Why, what is it?"

"*Not there?*" Artesha consulted her instruments again.

"No. What's the alarm for?" Qepthin pursued. "You're interrupting our work, I'm afraid."

Artesha couldn't answer. She shut off the communicator and spoke blankly to Magwareet. "Didn't you hear for yourself? Magwareet, *how?*"

"Find out from Wymarin if there's been any activity from the Being over the past few moments," suggested Magwareet. Things were falling into place in his mind. There was a beautiful simplicity about their arrangement that was almost aesthetically satisfying; it made him certain that he was on the track of a right answer at long last.

"Yes," was Wymarin's report. "Very considerable activity. No temporal surges, but these associated side-effects which I told you were also found when a going-double appeared."

"What I hoped to hear," said Magwareet jubilantly. "Artesha, listen to this. Let's suppose that the Being does know we're not actively hostile, and the Enemy is. Let's furthermore postulate that it *really* exists in four dimensions, and is free to move through all of them as we are through three.

"Now suppose that *we* artificially move in time. Our actions create alternative presents. There must be hundreds resulting from our recent interference with the time-stream. But the Being's actions *don't* have this result. It would be a contradiction in terms. The Being, we can say, regards our alternative presents as identical, despite their possible superficial differences.

"It appears likely that the Being is responsible for the going-doubles, doesn't it? I think that what it is actually doing is attempting to assist us in our struggle with the Enemy. Witness, for example, the appearance of Wymarin's going-double with what Burma thought was a workable plan for communication with the Being, before she knew it was a going-double she was speaking to. I don't know in which alternative present that plan was hatched, but I suspect the Being approved of it."

"A hell of a lot of assistance it's given us," said Artesha. "It's stripped our defenses with its temporal surges and left us naked to the Enemy over billions of cubic kilometers of space. I hope you're wrong, Magwareet, because if the Being *is* taking a hand in our affairs, and we remain without a means of talking to it, how will we ever know what's going on?"

"Only the Being can know that, in all probability," Magwareet answered somberly. "But if my theory is right, it *does* know, because in all those parallel presents it is precisely the same. Our interference with the time-stream doesn't affect the Being in the slightest."

He broke off. "I wonder if the fact that my going-double appeared to Qepthin means that he doesn't have a duplicate—that he exists only in this time."

"He *must* have a duplicate," insisted Artesha. "He said that you hadn't been down there, didn't he? The other Magwareet must have been talking to another Qepthin—"

"And yet you noticed them," exclaimed Magwareet. "They must have been together in this time—either that, or you are breaking through the fifth-dimensional barrier."

"Then it is the Being who has been interfering with my mind," said Artesha stonily. "And the mess it has got us into—"

At approximately that same instant every communicator in Center awoke to life, as did everyone in the entire surviving defense fleet.

"Plan Red," said a crisp voice that didn't quite conceal a hint of panic. "Repeat, Plan Red. Enemy fleet approaching Solar System from direction Cetus. About one thousand nine hundred major warships, about fourteen thousand medium-class warships, twenty-six thousand raiders, and scouts upwards of a hundred thousand. Plan Red!"

"Well?" said Artesha. "At least they aren't coming towards the biggest gap in our defenses, but they'll find it soon enough. I think this is our last meeting, Magwareet, unless we eventually get a chance to pull off Plan Black. It's been nice knowing you."

"The human species has got itself out of some pretty tight corners before now," Magwareet reminded her, feeling the icy chill of resolve. His mouth was dry. "And, as you say, we may manage to pull off Plan Black. See you later."

On that note of false optimism, he hastened to take up the place prescribed for him in Plan Red.


Plan Red had been Artesha's greatest achievement. It was a means of mobilizing the entire defensive potential of the human species. Every man and woman in the Solar System, and every child old enough to be of use, had a part in it. At the last announcement, they had left inessential tasks and gone to essential ones.

Magwareet's, like the other top Coordinators', was in the master operations room. It was anticipated that the influx of data would swamp even Artesha's immense resources for computing. Therefore there were made available people who—like Magwareet—had a Coordinator's gift of snap decisions on the basis of incomplete information.

He was barely settling into place before the banked communicators, time maps and viewscreens that would be his ears and eyes for as long as the battle lasted, when Artesha came through. "Magwareet, handle Plan Black, will you? As soon as you've attended to it, cut back into Plan Red."

"Right," confirmed Magwareet, and studied the setup.

Plan Black was the last-ditch one. It was known that the Enemy's first move upon discovering humankind had been to englobe the colonial systems the human species inhabited, which was why no one knew where the Enemy actually came from. The creatures had been uncertain for a long time which was humanity's home world, but—inevitably—the slow withdrawals they had forced had led them to the correct conclusion. But they had never before assembled so large a fleet to reduce a single system.

It was suspected that from some of the outermost colonies small groups had broken away and penetrated the Enemy's space in search of planets beyond their influence. But it was not certain. Perhaps they had found safety and would ensure the species' survival. Perhaps not. In any case, it was probable that the victorious Enemy would hunt them down and mop them up after Earth was defeated.

Therefore—Plan Black.

Center was the nucleus of it. On the closing of one of many thousand switches, at the very last moment possible, all the ships composing Center—or rather, those that had survived—would immediately be thrown into faster-than-light drive. There was no way of reversing the process, short of mechanical failure or reduction of the available power below a certain minimum. Even at the emergency limit of the drive, it would be years before the crew of those ships saw starlight again.

Thus, like the bursting of a spore pod, the human species would erupt outwards among the stars. Some of the ships would be hunted down; some would emerge from the star-drive impossibly far from a G2-type sun; some few would collide with the worldlines of stars or planets and explode into energy.

But some fewer still might perhaps fall within reach of habitable planets thousands of light-years beyond the Enemy. It would be the greatest gamble in history—but it might spell survival.

There was only one person whose chance of enduring was negligible to the vanishing point, and that was Artesha. Her very mind was spread over so many ships that it was virtually inconceivable that she should live through Plan Black.

Like all other Coordinators, Magwareet had calculated the chances of survival from that plan so often that he knew its details by heart. It took him only minutes to carry out all that was necessary to prepare for it; to activate the switches Artesha, or one of her deputies, could throw. Then he turned his attention to the developing battle.

How is the Being going to like this? he wondered as he thought of the gigantic release of energies it would entail. The convulsive lashings in time and space—what a handicap to fight under!

Artesha was staging the defense fleet along the Enemy's line of attack; it was the only possible move. There was something enormously impressive about this sight of the concerted power of a whole species.

Until one looked at what it was opposing, that was. Magwareet felt his heart sink as he considered how badly humankind was outnumbered.

Seeing an opening to join battle, he did not await instructions from Artesha, but ordered up a squadron of heavies to take out the jutting wing of scouts closest to the ecliptic. It was over in moments, and scattered wreckage drifted in space. The first casualty report came in. "Forty-eight Enemy scouts destroyed," said an unemotional voice. "Our losses—one cruiser disabled, five damaged."

Heartened, Magwareet's companions bent to their controls. But before the next blow could be struck, a voice full of panic rang from the communicators.

"Unidentified fleet approaching from direction Ursa. Repeat, *unidentified!* And it looks like millions of ships. Ursa! Straight for the gap in the defenses!"

—— ∞ ——

## CHAPTER XXXIX

## Approaching the Big Bang

*Time is a river?*

*Time is an arrow? The movement of the hands, or the change of pixels, on a watch? Something an atom vibrates in? Is there an adequate answer to all these suggestions?*

*Time is an accidental by-product of the biological process.*

*Take something—a star, say. It moves: now it is here, now there, but one cannot say if it is moving or the other stars are moving. At one moment it is in one place—but it is equally correct to say it is in one moment at one place. Move it in space, move it in time.*

*Move it in time, to a moment when it already exists. It is the same star. Unless it is also moved in space, it is indistinguishable from its earlier self. But if it is in another place at the same moment—?*

*If you can move it in time at all, you can move it so that it occupies not two places at once, but one moment in two places. It can, after all, occupy one place at two moments—*

*The electrochemical process resulting in the localized reversal of entropy known as "life" might be insulated, so to speak—its reversal of entropy converted into an identification with the law of nature alluded to above.*

*A star, moved back in time, is itself at the earlier moment. An organism, aware of the fact that it has been moved, is not. In obedience to the special laws of biology, it will proceed to move "forwards in time" again at its habitual rate. Let it become aware of the co-existence of itself in the moments it occupies, and it is no longer one, but two, selves.*

*The discovery of time travel, in fact, is the first step only towards emancipation from the law of Time governing life-forms. But it is a step that brings them right up to the threshold of eternity.*

I t was the only time Red and Chantal had ever seen, or were ever to see, Burma at a loss for words. She sought clarity for fully a minute, before she made a completely incomprehensible remark to Vyko.

"Of course. *I* see why not. But why here? Why now?"

"Here is irrelevant," said the Being, through Vyko's mouth. "So is now. We are either at the very beginning of the universe, or the very end. That is to say, we are past a point at which the actions of an intelligent being—except myself—are of significance. But it was not until you had passed the point at which you entered this last temporal surge, as you count time, that you could be of service in exactly the way necessary."

So *that* was why Burma's use of "ago" in speaking of the far future was so oddly meaningful. Red felt astonished at his own intuition, but he had a complete vision of the universe as it must be in exactly the same way that he "felt" a sculpture before he commenced work on it—neither visualizing it, nor imagining its tactile qualities, but a non-separable combination of the two. He could not have drawn a view of one of the works he intended, for the flat projection of it would not have been the same thing. Only under his hands and eyes together could he capture the essential quality he was looking for.

But there was a question he had to ask. "You brought us here for a purpose," he said bluntly. "If you can communicate with us now, you could have done so at any time. All times are alike to you in four dimensions. What is that purpose?"

"It is exactly because all times are alike to me," said Vyko's voice, "that you, as you are, are here now. Burma, you are my interpreter. This boy Vyko is my mouth, because his is the only mind among you that is able to contain four-dimensional concepts naturally. For the others of you—all but two—I have certain small individual tasks that any-one else might have carried out."

Which other two? They looked at one another questioningly. Vyko continued to utter the Being's words.

"My purpose, since you ask it, is simple. To defeat the species that you call the Enemy, since they are intent on destroying me."

"But could they?" said Chantal wonderingly.

"Because I propose to destroy *them*, no."

And then, all of a sudden, a peculiar thing happened. Vyko's face for a moment went slack and relaxed. At the same instant, Burma's lit up with sudden delight, and she seemed to be listening to some-thing. Then the same thing happened to one of the members of the crew, and another, and another, in rapid sequence. Chantal's expres-sion changed in the same way.

These are the tasks the Being is choosing us for, thought Red. He wondered what his own could be. Then there was something in his head that was like a memory speaking, but was not one.

It said: *You are one of the two needed for a special task.*

It said: *You are a sculptor with a sculptor's mind and a sculptor's way of looking at space.*

It said: *There could be nothing greater for you than to create with pure space and pure time as well.*

205

It said: *You are to supply what is needful.*
It said: *You are to help in molding the universe itself.*


The human defenders, under Plan Red, had exactly enough time to become frightened after the panicky voice announced the oncoming unidentified fleet. Magwareet flinched rather than deliberately moved his head to look across his detector screens, and saw that the wild estimate of the number of ships—millions of them—must be very nearly correct. At least there were hundreds of thousands of them.

But it was another thing he noticed on the screens that really shook him. Forgetting that she would already know, he called to Artesha.

"Artesha. You've got your memory back."

"Yes, I have," said her calm, controlled voice, and he heard a sureness in it for which he had been hoping for an age. "Listen to this, please."

From the communicators throughout Center and throughout the ships of the defending fleet a voice, quiet and firm, spoke out. It was a contralto voice he recognized.

"I am placing my fleet of approximately one million vessels at the disposal of Center for the duration of the present operation. Please begin to compute with them in your attack plan."

*Burma's* voice!

Perhaps the Being might know from what unimaginable resource of time or space she had dredged up a million fighting craft. Time enough to worry about that later. Right now, there was a war to be won.

Another species allying with us? Where from?

What about—afterwards? They outnumber us hopelessly

And then Artesha put sixty thousand ships at his orders, which he immediately placed into action.


The formation of the Enemy was their standard one: a hemisphere, hollow face towards the Solar System, with a single line of heavy craft jutting from its center and two flat wings of scouts in the plane of the System's ecliptic. The nearest of the scouts had been half a light-year away when Magwareet had sent in his first attack. That distance had already dropped by a quarter, and the minor gap in the formation he caused had been filled.

The technique was simple and effective. The jutting spearhead was just out of range of the heaviest weapons carried by the ships at the rim of the semicircle—but only just. It was their business to transfix the oncoming ships like a butterfly on a pin. Whichever way the defenders tried to take evasive action, they would find themselves coming within range of the ships in the hemisphere, who could fire on them without endangering their companions.

By the time the engagement was properly joined, the hemisphere would have begun to contract into a sphere, enclosing their opponents and squeezing them like a ripe orange.

If, by some miscalculation, the fleet proved to be outnumbered, outgunned or outfought, the spearhead could accelerate just a little and close the front of the hemisphere, which would thereupon become the rear, concentrating the heaviest armaments on the pursuers.

Of course, the exact diameter of the fleet, its numbers and composition had been worked out in view of the Enemy's knowledge of the human ships' performance, to make certain they could not be encircled before they reached the Solar System. But, thought Magwareet with a savage and primitive joy, they weren't counting on this.

He had his ships, and an extent of space to marshal them in. Summing up the situation as it developed, he made his plans—with alternatives—submitted them to Artesha as fast as he could talk, received her approval, and waited.

The oncoming spearhead was within a quarter of a light-year when the original defending fleet struck home.

They had re-formed as a cone, point exactly aligned with the heart of the jutting Enemy spearhead. Their degree of stagger was precisely judged so that the rearward ships could distract the Enemy on the rim of the hemisphere while the main vanguard penetrated the middle.

Only this time, unlike many previous times, the head of the cone held its course.

It was like—like crushing together two candles against a red-hot stove. The tip of the cone melted away. So did that of the jutting spearhead. But as the cone grew shorter it grew wider, and soon the spearhead was dwindling the faster of the two.

This was allowed for, of course. The ships at the rear of the hemispherical bowl were there for just that reason. The closer the human defenders came, the more withering the fire they had to withstand.

If we'd been on our own—thought Magwareet somberly. There could have been only one end to that struggle. But they were not on their own.

The battle, as a unit, was now creeping towards the Solar System, from its original direction of Cetus, south of the ecliptic. Thus far, the original plan had been adhered to. The Enemy was making its inevitable progress. Now, soon, it would judge that enough of the defenses had been drawn from their regular beats, and send half one of its wings of scouts to try and carry the fight into the System. Probably, knowing humans were oxygen breathers, the Enemy would drive for Earth direct, for in the past they had often enough launched over-clocked missiles at it from far out in space. That was all right. It was only if they deduced—correctly—that Earth had been evacuated that they would turn their attention exclusively to Center.

Abruptly, Magwareet's battleground analysis proved right. The scouts went into maximum emergency drive and swung north towards the gap in the defenses facing Ursa Major. And stopped as if they had hit a wall.

For, awaiting them there, was a squadron of the newly arrived ships with drives cold, armaments switched off, and screens up in every conceivable electromagnetic and gravitic waveband. The scouts fought like hornets, but they were swamped.

The Enemy reacted quickly. They realized they had walked into an ambush, but assumed that where so heavy a concentration of ships had been made, another place must have been left thin. A ring of ships disappeared from the bowl of the hemisphere, and struck at about the orbit of the asteroids from the direction of Argo. This time, they were temporarily right, and Magwareet's heart sank, for this was the System's most vulnerable region.

The defending ships, lying in wait, took a few seconds to counter the blow. In that time, destruction had been sown, broadcast, and Magwareet was horrified to see that one of the last Enemy to be destroyed had vaporized ten of the outlying components of Center.

Artesha located an opening in higher spacetime, teased it into a torrent of duplications. Like twin packs, each containing a million or more cards, each card paired with another identical to itself, local reality split apart before her enhanced gaze. The million human ships in each parallel cosmos reverberated to their doubles, reinforced their presence and dominance over destruction, and then folded, converged, entered a single universe.

In her imaginary space, Artesha smiled the feral smile of a virtual carnivore defending her young.


Magwareet blinked, for the wrecked ships were instantly *back,* where they had been before. "Where—where did they come from?" he gasped, before he realized it was aloud.

"From the same place as the rest of the ships," said Artesha, with a hint of a chuckle. "You can stop worrying, Magwareet. We've won. It's only a matter of time."

Silently, beyond the limit of the Enemy's detector range, the friendly strangers had crept around the Solar System. Now some of them—most of them—dropped the pretense and made themselves known. The fleet of the Enemy melted like ice in hot sunlight.

Magwareet laughed aloud in sheer joy as he saw what was happening, and grew suddenly aware that someone had brought refreshments to him where he sat. Astonished, he noticed that the battle had been in progress nine hours.

The person who had brought his refreshments was a boy, no more than ten years old—one of those who had a place, an essential though minor one in Plan Red. Seeing Magwareet turn from his screen, he risked a question in high eager tones.

"How's it going, Coordinator?"

"Well," said Magwareet with a smile.

The tattered remnants of the Enemy were scrambling out of range as fast as they could, back the way they had come. Magwareet gave them enough time to feel secure, and then, only then, revealed what he had been quietly attending to all this time.

In those nine hours, sixty thousand ships had stolen with their screens up to the rear of the Enemy. When the remnants were already among them, they showed themselves. Outnumbering the Enemy as they now did, by three to one, they finished the job.

Completely.

Ten hours from the start of the battle, there was nothing left of the Enemy's proud armada—except dust and a heat haze of infrared light.

—— ∞ ——

## CHAPTER XL

## Outside Time

For the first long moment it seemed to Red that he was looking down on the universe as if it were a flat, broad road racing past beneath him. Then he remembered that this was not possible, and his mind rebelled. He found the presence of the Being in his head, supporting and strengthening him.

There was something about the touch—touch? It was nearer to that than anything. He felt it in exactly the same way he appreciated the form of a sculpture before he began to work on it. There was something *feminine* in it.

And then he understood.

"*Artesha!*"

"Yes, Red. I am the Being. That is knowledge I have had to conceal even from myself before I discovered what I was."

"How—?"

"By insulating certain memory servers, and filching them away when there was danger of my guessing correctly, in advance of the date when I actually *did* guess correctly."

"But—"

"I am no longer *in* time, Red. There's no paradox, for by becoming as I am I grew into four dimensions. After that—when there was never to be any more 'after' for me—why should I not control my earlier self? After all, I had already done so, as far as my earlier self was concerned."

"But then"—Red's mind leapt ahead with the swiftness of intuition—"then you have no more purpose in existing. You have nothing but the present."

"Exactly. But there is nothing *after* it, because there is no more 'after.' Look here, since you are puzzled, and I will show you." She did so, without words, and when it was over Red felt a little faint, but he understood.

"A present in which one is directing the universe is no small one," Artesha commented dryly. "Now, Red, this is what you have to do. You have a certain way of appreciating form, and space, and of effecting meaningful changes in it. I need that. Because I am completed, and cannot change again, I must borrow it from you."

A small area of the road that was the universe stilled within Red's comprehension, and he studied it. Somehow, it was blurred. He recalled Vyko's description of trying to look into the future of someone with a going-double.

Artesha focused it for him, and he realized it was the span of human history. "Why is it blurred?" he asked.

"Because of time travel, and temporal surges," Artesha told him. "There are several presents at this point of the universe—do you see? What we must do is to choose certain ones that are best for our purpose, mold them so that they are ideal. Then, at a certain point, we must bring them together, fold the several presents into one present, and—"

"And?"

"And that is all."

He studied the various parallel presents for a while, getting to know the subtleties that distinguished them. He could not quite work out how they were separated, because each and every one of them was *the* present. Something occurred to him, and he asked, "Why are there no presents in which humans lose our war to the Enemy?"

"Because the human species *wins* its war," was the answer, and it seemed sufficient.

"These," he said after another short while, as he might have selected a particular stone or piece of scrap metal torn from an accidental collision.

"They are yours, to do with as you like."

Then began for Red the sheerest ecstasy he could ever have imagined. The time-streams were like clay or metal under his hand, and yet the appreciation of them was not confined to his touch and sight. It was like creating an objective sculpture in his mind alone.

At first he was hesitant, but then he became absorbed in the joy of pure creation, and gave himself up to it.

It was necessary that certain actions occur at certain points. It was very necessary that an innovative sculptor called Red Hawkins and a skilled doctor named Chantal Vareze should be available at one point; that a Croceraunian war party should do certain things in a time not its own, and that a staff magician called Vyko should not die. These things gave basic form and balance to the creation, like the wire framework for a clay model.

But that was only the beginning. There were details, each tiny, each tending towards the perfection of the completed work. It was also necessary that certain people with an influence on scientific thought should be puzzled by the behavior of sub-atomic particles; that they should scratch their heads over the impossible appearance of a prehistoric monster in the twentieth century, so it was necessary that a certain spaceship should plunge from low orbit out of control with her structure burning, cast across a boiling sea in the dim dawn and then be hidden forever at the hot red evening of time. A prophet had to have a vision of angels, and thus certain primitive aircraft had to be lost in time to cause it.

It was necessary that the crew of another vessel should build themselves shanties of conifer wood on the shores of an ancient Paleocene swamp so that a single mutation might be spared extinction. Nobody but Red would ever know that time and natural processes erased the name they had carved on one of the shanties to give them an anchor to reality: *Mary Celeste.*

It was necessary that an army commanded by a king called Cambyses who had dreams of empire should march into a frigid snowstorm deep in the Antarctic. A man called Ambrose Bierce and another called Benjamin Bathurst had to do something related, and thousands upon thousands of others were moved in mysterious ways. For the luckier ones, it was an inexplicable mystery; for the less fortunate, it was hell, or insanity.

And on, and on, and on....

Until at last, there were five alternative presents, and each of them was designed to fit into the others like dovetails.

—— ∞ ——

## CHAPTER XLI

## 522 BCE: TIME SURGE Lost Legion of Cambyses

*It is highly improbable that the Persian King Cambyses II had heard of any atomic theory, even the Democritan one, when his army, with himself at its head, marched into the unknown vastness of history, and was never heard of again.*

Cambyses II, King of Kings, once chief priest of Marduk, bearing the Horus name Smayawy and Throne name Mesutire, ruler of all Persia like his father Cyrus the Great, rode across the trackless desert with his fifty thousand exhausted troops and their camp followers. His passion was conquest, like his father's and grandfather's before him. He had vowed to shame the Oracle of Amun at the Siwa oasis far to the southwest of the pyramids of Egypt. For all that, he rode in increasingly dingy glory as his gorgeously chased and painted regal garb and closed palanquin darkened and grew pitted in the ceaseless rushing sandstorms.

From his lap, as their palanquin moved in an undulant motion atop the double-humped back of an enormous gray camel from farthest Asia, his Principal Concubine Rhado raised her head and licked her glistening lips. He sighed, and with a nod gave her permission to speak. It galled him to do so; she was very beautiful, this

Egyptian courtesan, and remarkably gifted, but her attitude was sly and irritated him.

"Great King," she said, stroking his uncovered thigh, "are we there yet?"

It was moments like these that caused Cambyses to yearn for the company of his wife, Mahruyeh Shahbanu. But Mahruyeh would never tolerate such an arduous and dangerous expedition, and if she did the people of the Empire would be displeased with him.

"Rhado, we have many parasangs to go before we reach the Baharia Oasis, at least three more days. But never fear, my dove, we shall dismount within the hour and take an early dinner."

"I do not approve of these beasts you have introduced into Egypt," she said with a pout. "The brute hissed at me this morning, and spat."

"I shall have her beaten," Cambyses assured her, not meaning it for a moment. He would prefer to have Rhado beaten than to injure his wonderful Bactrian. No, that would not do, either. Her skin was soft and sweet, and he could not bear to have her marked.

"Good! Great Lord and Master, I am puzzled."

"Oh?"

"It is said that the King of Kings has with him fifty thousand troops."

"This is so. We shall storm the filthy gods-scorning heretics of the Siwa Oasis and trample this single god of theirs."

She ignored him with a wave of a perfumed hand. "And yet, my Master, when I looked out upon the plain of sand last night and saw the tents arrayed, it seemed to me that there might only be ten by ten by ten by ten?" She sent him another sly glance. "But then I have never been good with numbers, this was not taught to us concubines."

"Off my lap, you mischievous slut," roared the King of Kings, and slapped her naked rump. "So you know powers of ten, do you? Who taught you that arcana?"

He winked at his chief eunuch, sitting silent the while at the other end of the palanquin.

"I do not know this phrase, Great Lord," she said, cowering theatrically. "We girls are not taught numerical. But isn't it obvious? Why, if you count the number of tents pitched in a row, and then those in a column, which is ten times as long, and consider the number of men in each—"

"Yes, yes, very clever of you, baggage. Now get your shift over your sleek flesh and prepare for dismount. I've decided I am hungry."

Obedient and needing no direction, his eunuch turned and pushed his head through a double flap of heavy silk. His high light voice barely carried against the roaring wind. When he pulled his head back inside, his face was coated with sand, his eyes tightly shut, and his oiled hair disgracefully disheveled.

"As you ask, sire, it is done."


Despite the appalling buffeting of the sand-choked wind, his troops somehow managed to put up tents, losing only a couple of a percent of them to gusts able to knock down his hugest Nubians. Many thousands of camels were gathered and secured, their cries recalling to him the ambience of the souk. As the light of day swiftly ebbed, and the red and yellow glow of campfires sprang into existence, burning wood they had carried with them across the immense desert, he stood on a rise, wrapped in clean finery, beard combed and oiled, and surveyed his ranked companies.

For the moment, he was content. He had ruled more than half the world for more than seven years, and his greatest years of conquest lay ahead of him. A smudge at the horizon, or closer, troubled him. He rubbed his eyes absently, blinked, looked again at the farther tents. Blurred. Hell creatures! Were his eyes losing their acuity already, at his age? His physician claimed—

Sand rose like a wall, and assailed him. The tents tore up from the ground and flew in the sky. Fires began to spread. The camels were screaming in fright, and many of his troops as well. He flung up his bejeweled hands before his face, and then the cold, bitter cold, took him, and when he opened his eyes the blur was gone but so were the gales of abrasive sand. These pellets striking his check and hands were…ice. Or snow. He felt his sanity reeling. In Africa? Yes, it grew chill in the nights here, but not so cold as to be accompanied by snow. Underfoot the ground creaked. Ice, and more ice. And the dreadful, impossible cold.

"Gather to me, men," he cried in his deep powerful voice. "This is not the Afterlife! It is dark magic by the vile Siwan conjurers. I shall call upon Marduk, and we shall put the demons to flight."

Men in leather with snow in their beards came to him, clutching lamps alight with oil.

And a man stood in their midst, from nowhere. The brave warriors of the Achaemenid dynasty shrieked and cried out like women frightened by a shadow.

This man was taller than all but the Nubians, broad-shouldered yet beardless and with shortened red hair. He seemed to wince, hugged himself once and stared in what seemed astonishment at the falling snow, and uttered several words.

"Speak to me, ghost," the King of Kings said in his parade voice. "Who are you, what is your purpose here—and what is this bedamned place?"

Red had never been so cold, despite the immediate activation of his futuristic garment. It was intolerable, far worse than Korea. The air was not thin in the lungs, so not one of those high plateaus or mountain tops like Everest. No visible vegetation, no trees, no buildings. The Arctic, then? Antarctic? If so, what epoch? He was dazzled by light flung up from the whiteness all around. In the distance, it seemed a huge mountain loomed, white against white. A vast congregation of men in primitive military gear, animals bellowing. The outlines of what seemed to be sagging tents, already crusting with ice. Was that a *camel*? In one of the polar regions? And this haughty fellow, too, bellowing at him, like an outraged sergeant or general, more likely. An aristocrat in fancy costume and an implausible beard.

Something absurd snared the corner of his eye, hurtling toward him. He twisted, and the tasseled corner of a magnificent carpet struck him a blow across the shins and veered away on the wind. Dear god, he thought. A flying carpet! So that's how they got here? He found himself laughing helplessly, while the aristocrat general stared at him in growing choler.

"Sorry, pal," Red said, when he caught his breath. "Sometimes it all gets just a little bit too much." He pulled his fists from his pockets, thrust out his right hand. "As I said, I'm Red Hawkins. Pleased to meet you, and all your camels." He was at the verge of hysteria. "Is there a place we can get out of this goddamned sub-zero wind?"

But his hand had been slapped away by a burly fellow with a leather cap and padded leather buskin. Hefty knives pointed at him from a dozen soldiers in fancy dress. Hurriedly he dropped his own hand and stepped back, into the grip of another man with fingers of steel. Christ, he thought, I'm a dead man.

The general was giving a series of brusque orders to his lieutenants, who fanned out and passed along the word to their terrified subordinates. Freezing winds were lashing the tents men were trying to pitch in the metal-hard ice. Red raised his face to the sky and shouted, "Artesha, *do* something. We're going to *die* here."

The blast of bitter wind was gone, replaced by the uncanny doublings and trebling and pressures of the time storm. More screams and bellowing from men and animals. The Sun shone through feathery clouds, warming their traumatized bodies. Damp dripped from long braided hair into scowling faces. They stood in long grasses, trees scattered here and there. The immense mountain was still there, but now purple in its lower reaches with trees and bushes, rising to the north…. No, Red thought, checking the Sun again. The south, if this is still the Antarctic.

And the sky was full of ships.

—— ∞ ——

## CHAPTER XLII

### Unknown date: Lost Legion of Cambyses

Already, some of the yahoos had their bows cocked and arrows notched and were firing at the huge shining things overhead, crying aloud for their deities, perhaps, or just voicing their war chants and challenges. With a whoop, one of them saw his arrow pierce a flying machine, which tumbled and fell. Abruptly, Red felt his automatic estimates of size and distance jolt downward by orders of magnitude. These aerial craft were not bombers or fighter airplanes. They

217

were comparatively tiny, hardly larger than a hawk, maybe smaller still, and far closer to the ground. Men rushed to stare at the fallen foe, pounding their breasts with glee, not quite daring to touch it with their water-soaked boots. Others, emboldened, raised their bows and hurled shaft after volleying shaft at the silver talismans floating above them.

The rest of the small aircraft rose swiftly out of range of arrow flight and settled in place. Red had the sense that the machines were observing them, like a class of novice scientists staring through a magnifying glass at a pinned insect. Or like the experts at Center, he thought, peering at the great five-limbed alien creature they called the Enemy. Is that how we are regarded, he wondered. As enemy intruders in this unknown past or future? As he was regarded in Korea by the small men trying to kill him and his fellow troops?

Something happened inside his head, as if his brain was being churned.

This is what Teula did to Chantal and me, he thought in astonishment. Except that then we were asleep, drugged, narcotized against the change her machine wrought in us.

Another man appeared literally from nowhere in their midst, perhaps seventy years of age but with features ruined by hard sun, burning pipe clamped between his teeth. I'd like to render this man in rusted iron, Red thought. The soldiers stepped back, making superstitious gestures. Their leader bellowed at them, and they moved cautiously forward again but broke and ran when a third figure in dark early nineteenth century formal wear and a sort of black top hat materialized between Red and the second apparition, who seemed to be clad for a performance in a western movie set in Mexico.

"I say," said the top hat man, looking dazed. "What the devil is this? Some sort of bally raree show?"

Red stared, agog. The young man wore beautifully polished boots, a heavy frock coat, and at his neck an absurdly high white collar tucking under his clean-shaven chin, white silk ruffles surging down his breast. He appeared to have stepped out of a Jane Austen novel.

"You speak English," Red said.

"Of course I speak English, what else would I speak? You're an American, I take it?"

"You take it right. I believe this other gentleman is also American."

"Bierce," that man said. He was suddenly holding a pistol, but quickly tucked it back into his belt and stroked his thick sagging mustache. "I have the damnedest feeling I'm in the vicinity of Owl Creek Bridge, and we're all dead. Am I correct, sir?"

"We're not dead, although these guys seem ready to fix that lapse." His teeth were still chattering, and his feet and hands felt numb. "I'm Red Hawkins, I'm from the middle of the twentieth century. I know, you don't understand. We'll get to that if they don't kill us first. And you are—?"

The pale faced Englishman made a quick half bow. "Benjamin Bathhurst, gentlemen, diplomatic envoy to the court of the Emperor of Austria. Twentieth century? Whatever do you mean? I can assure you that it is no later than the 25$^{th}$ of November in the year of our Lord 1809. And this is not Berlin, even in winter."

"Hmm," said Ambrose Bierce, chewing on his smoldering pipe. "Guess I died partway between you two gents, in or around summer of 1913 on my way to Mexico to have a chat with Pancho Villa. I am a journalist, sometime soldier, divorced, two sons dead ahead of me, and a fulltime misanthrope. Who are these assembled gaping buffoons, and why are you covered in snow? I need a drink. Does the Devil serve whisky? Brandy will do in a pinch, although only a hero will drink it."

"Who are you devilish magicians?" demanded a fellow standing at the right hand of the general. He wore amulets and robes still dripping with melted snow and ice, but no weapons other than a large ceremonial dagger at his waist. "How dare you work your tricks upon The King of Kings, the great Cambyses, Master of Persia and the World?" He gestured the closest thugs nearer still. "Bind them, before they perform more wickedness."

What he had spoken was not English, and not Speech either, and yet certainly not whatever ancient tongue was familiar to these thousands of camel-riding warriors.

Bathurst, the diplomat, was outraged. "Unhand me, you wretches," he was shouting. "I am a proxy for His Britannic Majesty, King George the Third. I hold diplomatic immunity."

"Silence, dog of a dog!" One of Cambyses's men slapped Bathurst heavily in the center of his chest. He coughed, staggered, closed his mouth, and then opened it again in silence and shock.

Looking around, it was apparent to Red, and to Bierce and Bathurst and the general, that some instantaneous translation had been performed.

"This is the future," Red said in a low murmur. Acutely, Bierce met his eye, nodded. Bathurst recovered himself, self-esteem outraged, and started again to denounce his captors. Cambyses took a step forward, seized the diplomat's lower jaw in a powerful grip. Bathurst grunted, was silent. Cambyses ran his other warrior's hand down the man's finely woven coat. At his back, the army was sorting out the damaged tents, pitching them in the rich soil, starting fires with unpacked wood and fallen branches from nearby trees. Already a scent of roasting meat wafted on the warm air. A beautiful haughty woman observed them from a distance, wrapped in rich silks.

"You have an excellent tailor," the King of Kings told the diplomat in a deep voice with only the implication of menace in it. "I like your cloak. Give it to me."

"The better part of valor," Bierce muttered, head tilted. Bathurst nodded, grudgingly, removed his coat and handed it to a bejeweled fellow who surely had to be a court eunuch.

"Now, explain yourselves."


I am here for a purpose, Red Hawkins told himself. It will become clear in time, if one of these oafs doesn't hack off my head first.

A magnificent pavilion had been thrown up in double quick time. It was a marvel of portability, assembled from innumerable caskets carried by a team of camels that for now were being pastured on the rich grasses. Artisans had hammered wood into wood, looped and tightened rope, put down flooring of smooth cedar and covered it with incomparable rugs. More rugs hung luxuriantly on the walls of this tent-palace. The King of Kings sat now in a throne of some dark heavy timber, his staff coming and going with reports, offering dark looks at the three men squatting before their Master.

220

"Do either of you have any idea when these characters come from?" Red murmured without moving his lips.

"Skipped your homework lessons, did you, boy?" Bierce gave him a sardonic glance and also spoke from the side of his mouth. "This fellow here is Cambyses the Second, son of Cyrus. You've heard of them, I suppose?"

"Herodotus, was it not?" Bathurst spoke with difficulty, rubbing his jaw incessantly. "The Persian Empire. I have no clear idea when that was, I fear, rather before my time."

"In the vicinity of five hundred and twenty or thirty years before Christ," Bierce told them. "Wait a minute. Oh God." He started laughing, muffled it at a hard look from the King of Kings. "That's where these jokers were off to, when they took a wrong turn and ended up...well, where? The middle of the ice ages? And now this happy utopia, with its overhead shield of metal birds."

"What are you saying? *Where* were these jokers off to?"

"You've noticed them knocking piles of sand out of their baggage? You don't find that in the snow, I believe. No, these boys were en route to do some damage to a famous shrine, in an Oasis on the boundary of Libya. Siwa, as I recall. Headquarters of a cult of, uh, Amun-Ra."

The priest Gaumata was on them in a moment, striking Bierce with a switch. The old American seized it from his grip, flung it across the carpeted floor, then sat exactly as he had been. The priest capered, but backed away and prudently kept his distance.

"Great King," he shrieked, "they are conjurers of the vile demon god Amun, of Sawi! Kill them. They are snakes. They deny our gods."

Cambyses rose from his wide chair and stood frowning down at them, face darkened. "Is this so? Give an account of yourselves, or I shall have you whipped, then skinned, then cut into pieces."

"Do as you please, sir," Bierce told him, not budging. Bathurst seemed ready to faint. Red poised to leap, but his new leg seemed to cramp. "I have one message for you, Mr. Cambyses."

"And what is that, wizard?"

"Nothing matters," Bierce said with conviction. "All your brave triumphs, all your glorious sluts from the harems of the east, all the murders done to your tribe and by them, no, not your beloved wife and your children. None of that matters, finally."

"You dare speak thus to the King of the Achaemenids Empire that reaches from one side of the world to the other? Has your reason fled?"

"None of that matters, and I can prove it if you let me stand up."

The King waved his hand; the guards moved aside. Bierce reached to his waist, beneath his loose shirt, took out his pipe, looked at it sadly. He knocked the dottle out of the bowl, let it fall to the ground. "Don't suppose you have a cobful of 'baccy, Mr. Bathurst? No? Oh well, doesn't matter." He put away the pipe, but kept his hand beneath his shirt. "This loudmouth, your own priest and wizard, shall he and I contend to reveal just what matters, if anything?"

This was more to the priest's taste, Red decided. The man was puffed full of pride in his nation's gods.

"Okay, go over there away from the throne and bring down the wrath of your gods and demons upon me. Don't stint yourself, man, put your back and lungs into it."

Gaumata raised his voice in a shriek of divine invocation and anathema. For the first time the translation device broke down. Red felt the hair starting to lift at the back of his neck.

The babble ceased. On every side, soldiers were pale beneath their sunburn with terror, aghast at the forces their priest had unleashed so near the King of Kings. Cambyses had returned to his throne, affecting boredom, but Red saw that his large hands gripped the carved armrests.

"Fine," Bierce said. "Didn't even scratch me. Now, to prove just how little any of this matters—" and he drew his pistol out, cocked it, sighted at the enraged priest, and shot him dead.

A figure resembling a shroud of softly radiant gold appeared in the pavilion.

"Gentlemen." Was it a man's voice, or a woman's, or neither? "You have been brought here to seek insight into your condition. But first—Cambyses of Persia, do you wish to have your devoted servant Gaumata recalled from death? Decide swiftly, for his flesh is already cooling."

The King leaned forward in his throne, eyes bulging. A croaking came from his throat, and then a rasping. "No," he said. "Only the gods have that right. And you are not a god. Are you from Siwa?"

The glowing shroud made a movement of dissent. "We are not gods, neither are we the monotheistic god Amun-Ra whose myth shall spread from that place. There are no gods, as Mr. Bierce will explain to you, except those you invent and obey and for whom your species shall kill and kill and kill."

It paused. "But there is one tremendous gain—the consciousness, finally, that the world is one, or should be, and not divided. From Siwa will arise the wellsprings of science. And hence us. You could not be permitted to destroy that place and its future."

"You're not human?" Red blurted before he could stop himself. "What, are you machines?"

"Neither human nor machine, yet the children of both, and nothing is alien to us," the voice told him. "Convey our love to Artesha when you see her. We look forward with the keenest delight to the great merging."

Red said nothing. His heart felt swollen. He wished that Magwareet and Chantal and Burma could be here with him. He closed his eyes and felt tears leaking down his face.

"And for you, Mr. Bathurst—"

"Yes?" The young man sounded equally overcome, or perhaps he was just baffled by events far beyond his experience and imagination.

"You shall teach these people of Persia the skills and benefits of diplomacy and negotiating," the thing—the *person*—hidden in brightening light told him.

"Very well. Thank you."

"Your Majesty, gentlemen, ladies," for Rhado and her maid servant had crept in to crouch beside Cambyses' throne, "we must leave you to tend your future. Look after this place we give you. It is in your safekeeping. And now, Mr. Hawkins, I am charged to lead you again into the time storm. Do not lose heart."

The light filled Red's eyes, glorious, brilliant, but not burning like the Sun. Everything divided into pathways that diverged yet moved always toward becoming one. He was—

—— ∞ ——

## CHAPTER XLIII

# 4070: Red and Yeptverki

*Keen, poignant agonies seemed to shoot from his neck down-*
*ward through every fiber of his body and limbs. These pains*
*appeared to flash along well defined lines of ramification and*
*to beat with an inconceivably rapid periodicity. They seemed*
*like streams of pulsating fire heating him to an intolerable*
*temperature. As to his head, he was conscious of nothing but a*
*feeling of fullness—of congestion. These sensations were unac-*
*companied by thought. The intellectual part of his nature was*
*already effaced; he had power only to feel, and feeling was tor-*
*ment. He was conscious of motion. Encompassed in a luminous*
*cloud, of which he was now merely the fiery heart, without*
*material substance, he swung through unthinkable arcs of os-*
*cillation, like a vast pendulum.*

—Ambrose Bierce,
"An Occurrence at Owl's Creek Bridge"

Red viewed the torment of the five-limbed Enemy, of the Master Cleaner, of—give it the name it had chosen to accept from its peers—Yeptverki. He seemed to himself to be floating several feet above the seamless, transparent cage, yet he suffered no fear of falling. It was like a lucid dream. *Was* it no more than a lucid dream? Nothing so trivial. He felt like a ghost, or a spirit, the kind of luminous body they had taught him in Sunday school would grace the Saved, after the Resurrection. That made him smile. Had he become one of the golden glowing shroud people who came after humankind? He didn't feel especially saintly. In fact, he really needed a beer and good long walk with Ruth.

A sort of chilly tendril wrapped itself around his core organs.

Red sagged, slid through the interstices of the cage, and entered the yellow spiky integument of the Enemy. Of Yeptverki. How did he know that name? The immense molecular skein of their utterly different nervous systems merged without violence to either, slotted cell by cell and enzyme by enzyme, under the direction of Artesha the Being, merging for a moment into a sort of unnatural unity.

*We do not know each other,* he told the creature. Not creature: person. *Yet we might share a common understanding, if we make the effort, if we put aside the stupid limitations of our ancient genes.*

Yeptverki physically convulsed. *Get out. Get out. Get out, vile thing!*

Be direct, Red told himself. He tried to imagine how Benjamin Bathurst would approach this task, diplomat's training in hand. That made him snort, and the ripple of it ran through the two conjoined bodies. Bathurst would not be direct. Bierce, now. There was a man who spoke his mind without hesitation, even if his mind was too acerbic, too misanthropic, now, for Red.

*We have a job to do,* he said to the Enemy. *We have a task only the two of us in this whole damned universe are equipped to fulfill.* He hesitated. Then: *Why are you trying to kill us all?*

*You are the vermin of the Beast that is determined to destroy us and the True Teaching.*

The image was there, as if carved in steel. The Beast was the Being. And the Being was Artesha.

They knew nothing about Artesha, of course, or her origins, or her vast destiny within this universe.

Because they are so strong and unrestrained and incomprehensibly different from us, he thought, we could never have guessed that. Their enmity seemed, to most of us, born from some primal evil. And of course our resolve not to be slaughtered at their whim seemed entirely foundational and true and right to us. As it is, of course. As it must be. But what of their picture of us, and of the Being? It could be no accident that they stage the Being, Artesha, as a *Beast*. Not as a living mind at least as great as their own imagined deity. But then, he told himself, that is how we have perceived her also, most of the time.

*We have been prevented from speaking with each other because of our differences,* he told Yeptverki.

*We do not speak to wriggling vermin,* the large alien said. *We follow the True God and the True Way.*

*And yet here I am, and you cannot shut me up. Let us attempt to re-solve this problem. I tell you that we do not worship the one you call the Beast, who we have known as the Being. She lives beyond this universe, but she is not divine.*

*And so we shall slaughter her,* Yeptverki boasted, *and restore our hegemony!*

*Yes, we could make war on each other for a thousand cycles of a world about its Sun,* Red insisted, *and achieve nothing but mutual annihilation. Does your True God desire that?*

*Do not befoul Its name with your blasphemous intentions.*

Red sighed, and made ready to decouple from the prickly alien. Person. It was hard to keep that distinction in clear view.

*This discussion will continue, conducted by others. Strange as it might seem, Chief Cleaner Yeptverki, I wish you well.*

A soundless scream of fury. Red hung above the outside of the cage, not quite physical, certainly not an immortal golden shroud. And with a tremendous jolt, realized that the coding principles of the Enemy's communication were now held in an archive linked from his mind to the Being's memories. It was the key to negotiations conducted by others better suited to the role than he.

He saw the fragmentation of history that had just occurred. The two paths lay open before the universe. One raced straight toward apocalyptic interstellar violence. The other offered a kind of hope, with the golden people neither men nor machines at one point along its trajectory.

He had to prevent a tragedy of indeterminable consequence.

He turned and flung himself backward in time. As his own going-double, and now entirely conscious of what he was doing, he walked through Center along a corridor to the great laboratory where Qepthin's team of exobiologists and linguists was working with Yeptverki, and getting nowhere.

"Don't ask me how I know this, just trust me and work with this new information," he told the astonished scientist.

Red left the lab and returned to Artesha. The divided histories were now significantly more convergent. In the immediate future, though, he saw a choice that made him cold with dread. He flung himself futureward into the same laboratory. Qepthin stood with a massive firearm, pointed at the captured Enemy. An instant before he could activate its consuming fire, Red Hawkins stood directly in front of him.

—— ∞ ——

## CHAPTER XLIV

## Outside Time

Red tried to look ahead into the moment when his work would take its definitive form. He failed, because the effort of distinguishing between the five time-streams now was too great. "What have we done?" he said, conscious only of an all-embracing weariness that was the end product of having achieved something more than his greatest ambitions.

"You have given the human species a future, and a fleet to win its war with," said Artesha. "Watch."

Red did not understand how it was done, but the separate presents folded together and became one, and those objects which were important were in their proper place.

"So it was I who forced those temporal surges," he said. "And it was I who created the going-doubles." He remembered, but the memory was a poor shadow compared with the omnipotence he had briefly known.

Briefly? In a single *now*, like the *now* Artesha in her guise of the Being experienced. But she did not have to return from it to the tyranny of slow-seeping time. She had crossed the threshold of eternity. Almost, he found it in his heart to envy her.

"Listen," said Artesha, and he heard Burma's voice.

"I am placing my fleet of approximately one million vessels at the disposal of Center...."

The going-doubles had effected the final, incredibly delicate adjustments of the parallel presents. Finally, it was complete.

"And now I have something else to do," said Artesha. "I have to alter—very slightly—the whole pattern of the universe, because it is running, as one might say, at a small angle to the path it can most easily follow."

There was a brief pause. "After I have done so," Artesha went on, her tone seeming to change subtly, "I shall have achieved my purpose, and you will no longer know me. There is a little time—for you—in which you can ask questions if you wish."

Red cudgeled his tired brain. After omnipotence, omniscience....

"What is the eventual fate of the human species?" he said slowly, and knew as he asked what the answer must be.

"The same as that of the universe. To—keep going—and stop."

No, that direction was no good. There were too many questions to ask. He changed his mind. "Who was the other person with a special task?" he said. "What was it?"

"Chantal was the other person," said Artesha. "And her task—You know, I think."

"Burma," said Red with complete certainty.

"Of course. That is the one personal desire I have allowed myself in all this work. That is why I have something still to put right. Out of all the reshaping of history we have undertaken, I have left over one special person, who because of what she did to save my beloved wife was exactly the right person."

Some deep-sunk part of Red's mind flashed—like sunlight caught on a turning mirror—with a hint of jealousy. Chantal did not want a man, that delightful woman, she had made it plain enough, but if she had to fall in love must it be with Artesha's lover? Well, yes, she had been there to heal Burma when she fell into Red's century, and by that act to heal Red as well. And now his entire being was too suffused with the weariness of utter satisfaction for this sense of loss to rise to the surface.

"It was too much, and had been for too long, to ask Burma to love forever a ghost trapped in a machine the size of the Solar System," said Artesha, with her last hint of melancholy and pity.

"What will you do with me, Artesha?"

228

"You are part of the substrate, now, as I have been since the beginning. I shall have to do something with your body. Your family and others will be concerned by your disappearance."

"David, yes. Poor man. But he'll be expecting a brother with an aluminum leg."

"I can deal with that. You have fulfilled your purpose; now it is time for you to rest."

Red knew that his tiredness would overtake him and drown him in only a moment. Forcing himself to form the words, he asked, "And what is your purpose—the one you will now achieve?"

"I shall have created myself as I am," said Artesha, and took two planetary bodies away from the Solar System at precisely selected instants of time, flinging blazing Vulcan into the core of a primitive Earth four billion years past, creating from its terrible debris the Moon, and hurling the other, a far smaller moon of a ringed world, into a peninsula of the Earth 66 million years ago. The work was no longer perfect, for there was nothing imperfect to compare it to.

It was all there was.

— ∞ —

## CHAPTER XLV

## Neither the Beginning, nor the End

Artesha the Being gazed down upon the world without end, at the millions of people whose lives her first blind threshing had deformed and ruined, at those who all unknowing had turned history from one course into another. The mutilated artist turned from decorative triviality to profound beauty and significance. The marooned child who had spared a tiny scarlet life so insignificant that it never had a name, yet whose offspring would carry its genetic recipe into eons enriched by its presence. The lovely golden transhumans who blended machine and flesh into luminous unity, beyond her own humankind yet grown from the soil of that species' million years from Africa to the stars, a thousand millennia of strife, love, searching, joy. She looked into the depths of time and found those people who were her special companions at the crucial moment when she had awakened. What had become of them? Ah—

Magwareet stretched himself and rose to his feet. The defense of the Solar System was over. The power of the Enemy was broken, and in due course the still mighty fleet of Earth would search out humanity's opponents and finish the job. It was wonderful to anticipate walking under a blue sky, breathing air without accounting for it liter by liter.

His large body felt *alive*. Felt, to be honest, charged with sexual hunger. He had never gone short of bed companions, or indeed of love and devotion, in his long life, but right now he felt like a wild animal on the prowl. Magwareet activated a search program, sought that superbly competent engineer generalist, Tifara Cassiopeia. She showed herself in the display, weary but instant alive at his sight.

"Coordinator. This is a great day."

"I am Paulo, and you are Tifara," he told her. A jolt of excitement ran through him. From her eyes, the avid curve of her mouth, he knew that she saw it, appreciated it, returned it in kind. "Can we meet in Social 6 in, say, 30 minutes? I have to get cleaned up."

"Me, too, Paulo. Candidly, I stink like an animal."

He felt his eyes glisten, and his smile broadened.

"I sense that you're familiar with Burma's cruel, cruel limerick."

Cassiopeia sent him a quizzical look. "Burma Brahmasutra? Seriously? Our mighty commander writes limericks?"

"She doesn't write them, she composes them on the spot."

"Well, come on, sir, spit it out. I promise not to hold it against you."

"Don't say I didn't warn you." In a lighter tone, he recited:

" *'There's a fellow I'd like you to meet.*

" *'He's a roué, but frightfully sweet.'*"

He paused, and added in a slightly different tone:

" *'I hope you don't mean—'*"

Then back to the first tone:

" *'Yes, I do, He's quite clean*

" '*When he bothers to wash. Magwareet!*' "

Cassiopeia shrieked with laughter. "When you put it that way, my good coordinator, it makes me want to postpone the shower."

"Are you hungry, my dear engineer?"

"Hungry for everything," she said, stifling her laughter. "Burma? Really? See you in thirty." She vanished.

Magwareet, too, laughed loudly, in pure pleasure

Burma, still a little awed at the magnitude of the disaster that had overwhelmed the Enemy, completed the task of assessing her casualties—which were astonishingly few—and filed the report with Center. Turning away, she found herself looking at a young woman with light brown, color-splashed hair and an uptilted nose, and for the first time since Artesha's accident found herself wholly admiring another woman without guilt and with a surge of excitement.

Wymarin stared at his instruments, hoping to find a hint of how a fleet whose members almost precisely duplicated the ships already in space in the Solar System had penetrated what he still thought of as the fifth dimension.

Qepthin heard the news of the Enemy's defeat, took a shot of issue alcohol, and went to the research hall where the captured specimen waited dumbly in the confinement they had imposed on him at the beginning of Plan Red. "You poor bastard," the biologist said softly, and wondered in the same instant whether pity was not wasted on the creature.

But there was no further need of the specimen now, and on a sudden impulse he brought a heavy weapon from a nearby arms rack, aimed it.

*aimed it,*

An instant before he could activate its consuming fire,

*and ended the Enemy's life.*

Red Hawkins stood in front of him, shouting "No! Qepthin! Wrong choice."

*Qepthin replaced the weapon in its rack.*

Qepthin dropped the unused weapon with an echoing clang.

Time changed tracks, but the biologist had no way of knowing that. Within a few days he would find himself deeply thankful that Red had thwarted his burst of vengeful pity, and profoundly ashamed of himself for nearly giving way to it.

Vyko awoke from some sort of a deep trance, wondering how it could be that the going-doubles of the people about him no longer affected his visions of the future, discovered that half a day had elapsed, and went to ask someone what had happened. He found time to ask himself how Khasnik, his former captain, would have reacted to the news that his staff magician would wind up planning the actions of a fleet of spacecraft mopping up among the Enemy in the distant stars.

Artesha the Being watched, finally, herself: Artesha in the year 4070, taking in the battle casualty reports with part of her mind; with the rest, she was engaged in analyzing the fantastic facts stored in the data caches of the section of her memory that had been restored to her at the outset of the battle. It would be a long job, but there was a promise of *something* at the end of it....

In time, that first Artesha would begin to discover what she had hidden from herself about herself. In so doing, she began to create herself.

Except that she already *was*, and had been since the beginning and would be until almost the end of Time. Even the Being, she knew, required the universe in which to *be*.

This was neither the beginning, nor the end, for there is, was and will be, nothing but everything, which is the universe.

— ∞ —

# EPILOGUE

Los Angeles *Herald,* October 5, 1957:

SCULPTOR DIES IN FREAK ACCIDENT.
Lightning claims well-known victim.
Three Waters, October 5.

A victim of a freak lightning strike was sculptor Lawrence Hawkins, at his home last night. A bolt struck the artificial leg he wore as the result of an amputation following a mortar attack near the Korean DMZ in February 1951. His faithful dog Ruth drew the attention of a passerby to the body, and was later taken in care by the brother, Mr. David Hawkins. Dr. Meade J. Galloway, who carried out the autopsy, said death was instantaneous.

The Weather Bureau reported no thunderstorms in the area on the night in question. Chief Meteorologist Jack Ellis commented: "It may have been due to static electricity building up in a pocket of dry air. Weather does funny things sometimes."

Hawkins's death will be regretted in California art-loving circles. Not yet thirty, he was held to have great promise. He was unmarried.

— ∞ —

# ACKNOWLEDGMENTS

I greatly appreciate the kindness of Mrs. Liyi Brunner, the late John Brunner's widow, and Ms. Jane Judd, Mr. Brunner's agent, for allowing me to undertake this intriguing and rather challenging experiment in science fictional collaboration across some sixty years.

As often, much thanks for careful reading and suggestions from Gary W. Livick, engineer, robotics hobbyist and Certified Wilderness First Responder. Thanks also for useful critiques from Lezli Robyn and Denise Little.

—— ∞ ——

CPSIA information can be obtained
at www.ICGtesting.com
Printed in the USA
LVOW11s1635291217
561233LV00002B/225/P